THE

SOLICITOR

To Annette
ewg friend
st Arts A
st Anger!

~ 2017

other books by Sean Keefer

The Trust

THE
SOLICITOR

A NOAH PARKS NOVEL

BY
SEAN KEEFER

The Solicitor

Printed in the United States of America.

ISBN 10 – 0-9989835-0-0
ISBN 13 – 978-0-9989835-0-9
LCCN – 2017941675

Four Hounds Publishing, LLC
www.FourHoundsPublishing.com

DEDICATION

for Wendy Keefer

Grá agus go raibh maith agat

ACKNOWLEDGEMENTS

The book you hold in your hands is the culmination of the efforts of a great many people, all of whom I owe a great deal of thanks.

Thanks to Wendy Keefer in immeasurable ways.

Thanks to Bradley Keefer, Peggy Keefer, Bob and Liz Johnson, Jim Keefer, Dolly Garfield, Kinn Elliott, Michael and Shawn Barfield, Ed Thomas, and all of my family and friends.

Thanks to the Four Hounds for their assistance and guidance.

Thanks to my editor and friend Carl Lennertz who was appropriately critical, brutally honest, infinitely patient and the epitome of encouraging. I look forward to working with you on many future books.

Thanks to Drew Kellum of Sandcastle-Creative for an amazing cover.

Thanks to Pete Paulatos for his incredible photography.

Thanks to Brendan Clark of Village Books.

Thanks to Oona Sherman for her expertise in getting The Solicitor ready for publication.

For all of their assistance, guidance, support and encouragement - thanks to Melissa Storm, Rachel Thompson, Terri Giuliano Long, Kristin Hackler, Andrew Fischer, Liz Stringer, Jeanine Edmondson, Noel Blaha, the Charleston River Dogs, Carol and Bill Killough, Richard Bethel (aka Xavier Cross), Ida McCaskill, Jack Bannon, Cyndi Williams-Barnier, Diann Shaddox, Andra Watkins, Karen Snyder, Julie Shay, Victoria Boneberg, Miller's Book Binding, Independent Publishers, Beach Book Festival, Sunset River Market Place, Loris Library, the Loris Literary and Music Club, Old Line Publishing, and all who helped make The Trust such a great experience and provided me the encouragement to keep writing.

Thanks to all of the IndieGoGo supporters.

Finally, I want to thank Litchfield Books in Pawleys Island, South Carolina for their amazing support. Though he is no longer with us, I want to express my tremendous thanks to Tom Warner for everything he did in support of my first book and in making me a better writer. He will be missed but never forgotten.

A good act does not wash out the bad, nor a bad act the good.
Each should have its own reward.

— George R. R. Martin, A Clash of Kings

PART ONE

PROLOGUE

The sun's arrival just as it cleared the horizon had always marked my favorite time of day. It wasn't unusual to find me at dawn on the Carolina shore gazing to the east in anticipation, the ocean breeze softly brushing my face. The fleeting moments when the first rays of sunlight painted an explosion of color were more than enough to leave me knowing I was fortunate having witnessed it. Those, those were my favorite mornings and anything that followed was a bit less complicated, easier to handle.

I found myself in desperate need of such a morning.

But today there would be only cold concrete.

For the past five days, my sunrise had been a sliver of light crawling across the floor of my jail cell.

At first, I'd looked forward to it, but on the third day I realized I'd need a lot more to get me through the day, otherwise, that mere slice of sun would soon be pushing me into the icy grip of depression.

I'd quickly learned jail had a way of ushering in melancholy, even for the most optimistic. Most everyone inside, even the guards, were simply miserable.

My bail hearing had been a waste of everyone's time. Accused murders don't get bail with their first request, sometimes not on the second, if at all. The fact I'm a lawyer wasn't helping. The last thing a judge wants to do is give the impression that a lawyer, particularly a criminal attorney like me, is entitled to special treatment.

Things change fast. Days earlier, my life, while not perfect, had been good.

I'd taken my girlfriend to the airport to catch a late-night flight to Chicago. She'd recently relocated to Charleston, but was wrapping up her ties to Chicago.

After returning from the airport, I turned on ESPN, eager to hear what the talking heads had to say about the South Carolina Gamecock's next football game. As was the case for most Gamecock fans, their football season sanity ebbed or flowed with the team's weekly performance.

It was a cool fall night and the windows were open as I watched TV from bed, my dog at my feet. Both he and I looked up as we heard a car outside—odd for that time of night in our quiet neighborhood.

The sound of the doorbell was even more unexpected, so much so I didn't immediately get up. Rarely did anyone just drop by, especially near midnight. The second ring was immediately followed by a knock. I got out of bed, pulled on jeans and a T-shirt and went down the stairs. Austin, my Australian Shepherd, was barking and jumping beside me as I unlocked the door. He sat on my command.

I opened the door to the sight of a tall black man in plainclothes with a Charleston Police Department badge on his belt. Three uniformed Charleston County deputy sheriffs flanked him. Three police cars occupied my drive. An unmarked cruiser in the cul-de-sac completed the scene. Thankfully none had their lights on. I shifted my gaze back to the officers. Not a smile among them.

This couldn't be good, I remember thinking.

"Noah, how about I come in?" Emmett Gabriel said. He looked me straight in the eyes. We were the same height, just under six feet tall, but the lack of a smile, his badge, and the deputies that flanked him made him feel bigger and much stronger than me.

I'd heard his voice many times before. At the police station, in his backyard, over a meal, on my back deck, other times through the years but never near midnight with other police officers standing on my front porch.

"Since when have you ever asked permission to come in the house? What's wrong?"

"Noah, let's talk inside?"

I just stood in the doorway. Silent and motionless.

One of the officers behind him coughed, jarring me back to reality.

I stepped to the side. "Sorry, certainly, come in."

"Wait outside," Gabriel said to the deputies.

We walked down the short hallway into my living room in silence.

"Where's Anna Beth?"

A feeling of panic ran through me as he asked about my girlfriend.

"Is she okay?"

"As far as I know. She not here?"

"No. Chicago trip."

The feeling of panic faded to one of wonder, wondering why at midnight a detective I knew was standing, unannounced, in my living room while three other anxious officers were staged on my front porch. I asked why he was here. Wonder quickly faded with the next words I heard.

"The officers outside have a warrant for your arrest."

Having never been one to miss the obvious, I remember uttering my insightful reply, "A warrant?"

"Yes, for the murder of Andrew Stephens.

ONE

After a rather uneventful day at the office, I walked into my house and was surprised by the silence that greeted me. I lived with my girlfriend and my dog. Though it wasn't always the case that both were there waiting on me, I was generally greeted by at least one of them. Today though, there was only the faint whir of the refrigerator.

"Anyone home?"

No answer.

I climbed the stairs to the second floor and walked into the bedroom.

Empty.

I changed from my button-down shirt and khakis into shorts and T-shirt. I loved wearing shorts deep into the Southern fall. Even better, the shorts were a little loose on me. I was down under two hundred pounds for the first time since college.

I headed back downstairs.

Nothing. The house was still quiet.

It'd been a long day. Two hearings and several client meetings, but the most interesting part of it had been an unexpected morning call from a friend and fellow attorney.

I walked through the kitchen and opened the refrigerator reaching for a beer, but thought better, remembering my last visit to the scales, and grabbed a bottle of water instead and carried it to the back deck. The yard was empty.

My house was a rarity for the city. With almost an acre of land, there was plenty of room for the dog and me. He was one of the reasons I'd bought the place, to make sure that he had enough room to run around. More than one eyebrow was raised when people found out I was serious when I said I bought the place because the dog liked it. Even with the addition of my girlfriend, we still had plenty of room.

It was a pleasant early fall evening. The smell of fresh-cut grass mixed with the aroma of steak on a nearby grill. This divine scent traveled on the breeze on the signature nose of what the locals called pluff mud. Something really only to be encountered near the coastal marshes of the lowcountry. Some would literally turn their noses up wash of aromas, but me, I called it home.

I had news, and wanted to talk about it with Anna Beth. Not too long ago, I'd have been deciding things on my own, but now that she had moved in, it was something I was starting to enjoy, making decisions together.

We met when I was handling her deceased father's estate. What should have been a simple case turned out to be a tangled process that neither one of us expected, but that's a story for another day. Though when the dust cleared, Anna Beth Cross and I decided that having endured and emerged unscathed from such a dramatic beginning, we might well have the foundation for a relationship.

As far as I knew, neither of us had been disappointed.

Anna Beth had grown up very wealthy in Chicago. Her two siblings had taken their station in life for granted and neither had what one would call a productive track record. Anna Beth, on the other hand, had looked at her resources as a foundation for opportunity to build upon what her father had started. She'd been focused and worked hard, and, despite family money, she paid for her education all the way through a year of law school before she married. Her marriage hadn't worked out, but she even used this as a learning experience to become more confident in her ability to make it on her own. Once I had teased her I was a rebound relationship because she needed a man in her life. I learned quickly that was not something that I joked about with her. She valued her independence and was guarded about who she let in.

When we met, neither of us had been looking for a relationship, but neither seemed upset that one happened. We were two independent people, but we were learning that collective independence was fun.

#

My thoughts were broken when I heard a familiar bark. My solitude was broken by the hurried sound of Australian Shepherd paws on the hardwood floor. Austin came flying onto the deck, jumping to greet me. To say the red dog was excited didn't even get into the arena.

"Hey boy, I missed you too. What have you guys been up to?" I turned to see Anna Beth. In jogging clothes: garnet top, running leggings, hair pulled back, and slightly out of breath.

"I got invited on a run." She rubbed Austin's ears and then tousled my hair. "You need a haircut."

"Was wondering where you guys were," Austin was clearly bothered I'd distracted the attention of the person who'd been scratching his ears.

Anna Beth was tall, slender, and attractive, and didn't seem to mind putting up with an attorney and his demanding dog. She reached and took the bottle of water from my hand and turned it to her lips.

"What's the news?"

"News?"

"You left a message."

"Right, yes. Andrew stopped by today."

Andrew Stephens was a local attorney and close friend who was a candidate for the position of head prosecutor for our local judicial district.

"What is it you call the DAs down here? Solicitors?"

"Yes, our prosecutors are called solicitors."

"Well I'm guessing his stopping by isn't the news."

"Andrew wants me to help him with his campaign. And, well...he also asked me to be his chief deputy if he wins."

"That's pretty big. Did you say 'yes'?"

"I didn't say anything. I was flattered. That's a pretty big thing, going to work in a new solicitor's office. With the right people, it can be great, with the wrong ones, awful. And I told him I had to talk to you first."

"You wanted to talk to me?"

"Why wouldn't I?"

"You do know how to make a girl feel special, but I don't think something that big is a simple 'yes' or 'no' or 'whatever you think is best.' From what I've seen the solicitor position isn't just another job, it's a completely different way of thinking; different hours, different responsibilities. It sounds like a lot comes with it, good and bad."

I smiled. Something about an attractive and wise woman.

"That's spot on. I don't have to give him an answer right away. In fact, I told him an offer like this one deserved some contemplation and he seemed okay with that."

"Then we need to talk more about it."

I watched her as she disappeared back inside. She smiled back. Austin pawed at me and I looked to him. He gave a single bark.

"What?"

Austin stared back and wagged his tail.

TWO

Whoever said it was darkest just before the dawn had never seen a Charleston sunrise. This was also the reason that I preferred early morning runs. The sun had not yet risen, but the neighborhood was illuminated in the glow of the pre-dawn half-light. From the end of my drive I could hear the distant hum of traffic on Highway 17. I looked up and could still see the moon hanging low in the sky. A breeze caused the moss in the oaks to sway gently, I heard a car door in the distance, and a dog barked in response.

Otherwise, it was quiet. And the morning was mine.

I headed down the still-dark greenway, though my eyes soon adjusted. As I cleared the wooded pathway, I entered a long stretch of marsh. I had timed it perfectly to witness the sunrise. As I ran I could feel the morning light start to surround me. My morning runs were almost without equal in their ability to invigorate as I settled into a rhythm and cadence.

Afterwards, I returned to my house for a shower. My efforts to wake Anna Beth were futile. I was quickly coming to the realization she was a classic late sleeper; while ambitious, a morning person she was not. I kissed her and was off to the office.

My office on the peninsula, as downtown Charleston is known, was an easy drive from home. While work awaited, I thought of Anna Beth. It was clear for me she was more than just a girlfriend.

From time to time I'd contemplated a serious talk with her. I thought about letting her know that all too often my thoughts were taken over by her, how often I wanted to drop what I was doing and call her, hear her voice, see her, taste her. But I didn't want to upset the balance we had. That, and maybe I was still not sure her feelings were the same. Maybe they were, maybe they weren't. For now, while I felt good about a future with her, I was more interested in today and tomorrow.

I'd actually talked more with Gabriel about my relationship with Anna Beth than with her.

Emmett Gabriel and I met our first year at the University of South Carolina. We'd grown up in the same city, but it took a university computer randomly assigning us to the same dorm room freshman year for us to meet. Gabriel, as he allowed (requested) his close friends to call him, was a driven soul, even at the age of eighteen. Since he was in grade school he'd wanted to play basketball for the Gamecocks. Despite being told time and time again he couldn't complete at the collegiate level, he channeled rejection into drive and determination and ended up walking onto the team.

From the time I met him, he told me his career goal was to be a Charleston police detective. His motivation was a motivator to me. With him around it was hard for me not to be focused. To this day, I credit him with helping me to get into and finish law school.

Now the skinny kid with two first names I'd met on a humid August afternoon my freshman year of college was the new captain of detectives with the Charleston P. D.

I drove past my office, traveled two blocks further, turned onto a side street and pulled into the small parking lot of Andrew Stephens' office. As was standard with Charleston law offices, Andrew's had the main entrance on Broad Street where the office fronted. However, it was quite common to have a rear entrance just off of the main reception area where the staff could come and go without the clientele seeing. I used the back door. There was a corridor that paralleled Andrew's reception area. Just a few steps into his office was a door that opened into the reception area. While I had no problem coming in the back door, I always liked to let someone know I was there. I knocked lightly on the interior door and opened it to an empty lobby, well, empty except for the just over five feet of green-eyed redhead who turned to greet me.

"Mr. Parks, good morning."

"Morning, and Rebecca, please call me Noah. He busy?"

"Okay, Noah, I'll work on that. He's just finishing something up. I'll tell him you're here. Give me just a minute."

"Thanks."

Rebecca disappeared down the hall toward Andrew's office. Andrew had a practice of hiring College of Charleston students, attractive female ones, to greet clients and help around the office. In the past, he'd rotated them like clockwork, a new one each semester. However, Rebecca was an exception, or perhaps an expansion, of this. She clearly had the attractive part down, but she contributed a great deal through her management of Andrew's schedule and calendar.

She was very loyal, perhaps even a little overprotective. The result was she had been around longer than most.

On Rebecca's desk was a copy of today's *Post and Courier*, the local paper. A front-page headline on the upcoming election caught my eye.

"Solicitor's Race Likely to Go to the Wire."

Andrew Stephens vs. Samuel Bartholomew Michaels, S. Bart for short. No matter who said his name, it always came out Sbart. The thought made me roll my eyes.

I scanned the article. Nothing new. S. Bart had been thought the sure winner following the announcement of the special election with the former solicitor's unexpected retirement. Michaels' father had been solicitor and a great-grandfather had even been governor. However, when Andrew announced his candidacy, the race suddenly became interesting. With less than two weeks until the election, it was anyone's call.

Rebecca reappeared.

"Mr. Par.., I mean, Noah, go on back."

"Thanks Rebecca."

I walked into Andrew's office and found it empty. Empty as in no Andrew. Otherwise, it was quite full. The office teemed with very expensive and comfortable furniture, loads of photographs, antiques, and a wall covered with photos and awards.

Walking across an oriental rug, I sat on a roomy leather couch. A door behind the large hand-crafted desk opened and Andrew appeared, wiping his hands on a monogrammed towel. He was fit, with a youthful appearance and a way of making those around him feel at ease. We'd met in law school and had remained friends since. Although he had blond hair versus my brown, it wasn't unusual for people to think us related, if not brothers.

Through our legal careers, we'd always practiced within walking distance of each other, even sharing office space for a time. Frequently we pitched in and helped with the other's cases.

While we both had gone on to have successful and similar practices, Andrew had always viewed the law as his calling and built his life around his work. He was always on. This meant bigger cases and, not surprisingly, bigger fees, but it also meant less time away from work. My path had been a bit different. I had no shortage of clients (not all with deep pockets), but I worked to have time to myself away from the law. Though in the end, I knew him well enough that and he I could look at each other and know the other was happy with each other's success, though I did wonder why he had never married or settled down.

Through it all, I was in Andrew's debt. If not for him I likely wouldn't have a law practice, let alone a law license, thanks to his help when I first met Anna Beth. Her case became so consuming I essentially had to have Andrew take on my entire practice to devote all my efforts to Anna Beth. He had done so without a word. I only hoped that one day I'd be able to repay this debt.

"How long's she been here now?"

"Rebecca?"

"Someone else standing guard at the front door?"

"I think I hired her about two years ago."

"And how old is she? Twenty-two. Twenty-three?"

"Twenty-one."

I didn't say anything, just looked at him.

"What?" Andrew said.

"Nothing, I was just curious."

"Did you think my offer over?"

"I did. Talked it over with Anna Beth last night."

"Here to accept?"

"No, but I'm not here to turn you down either. I need to think about it some more."

"What you're really saying is you want me to win before you accept, right?"

"No, not at all. I'm just not sure I'm the best person for the job."

"You are. Wouldn't have asked if you weren't. So, when can I expect an answer?"

I stood to go. "Soon. Listen, seriously, I owe you. More than you know, but I want this to work out best for you."

"Good. When you accept it'll be best for both of us."

Something was off. Andrew wasn't the pushy type, not with me anyway. I'd known him long enough to realize something was on his mind.

"Don't wait too long. Might offer it to someone else." He didn't smile.

"Don't worry, an answer's coming. You okay? You don't seem yourself."

"I'm fine. The election's got me preoccupied. You know how it is."

"No, but I can imagine."

When I saw that he wasn't going to say anything more, I was pretty sure that I had him on a bad day. But there was another way to find out what was on his mind.

I'd ask Rebecca.

As I approached the reception desk, her back to me as she worked at the keyboard, I saw her reflection in her computer screen. She was smiling. At least someone in the office was happy. She turned to look at me and made no effort to hide that she was looking at a Caribbean travel site.

"Someone going on a trip?" I was nothing if not observant.

"I hope so." Her smile beamed even more.

"It's hard to go wrong in the Caribbean. And see if you can't cheer him up."

"Cheer him up? How so, did he say something? Did he see me looking at travel sites?"

Now that was odd.

"No, nothing, he just seems a little on edge."

"Oh. Then it's just the election."

I waited for her to say something else. After several moments of silence, I realized there wouldn't be anything else.

"Well, have a great day."

She smiled as I walked out into the morning sun.

Little did I know it would be the last time I'd see Rebecca smile.

THREE

Downtown Charleston is the definition of pedestrian friendly. In the last twenty years, Charleston has gone from a hidden gem to a Southern travel and business destination. *Conde Nast* had fallen in love with the city and the net result was a huge uptick in visitors. A Southern cuisine revival, a craft cocktail explosion and inclusion on numerous travel lists has made Charleston the place to be.

Locals call it the Holy City because of a history of religious tolerance, but today the Holy City is gaining a reputation as a hip and vibrant place to live, work, eat, drink, and play, while retaining the character and tradition that holds together the foundation of the city. Yet with its newfound spotlight, the city remains relaxed and serene, a hallmark of the lowcounty

As I stepped from the car in my own parking lot, there was a pleasant early fall breeze coming off the harbor that surrounded the peninsula. The fronds on the palmettos lining Broad Street quietly rustled.

I noticed two tourists standing just off the street alternately looking at a large map and then pointing down Broad Street. "Good Morning." I wanted to make sure to do my part to help Charleston retain its reputation for Southern hospitality.

There wasn't much waiting for me at my office, which was nice for a Friday. My paralegal, Mrs. Laye, was out, so I had the office to myself. In the past, I'd taken a page from Andrew's playbook and hired younger, less experienced assistants. That hadn't always worked out that well for me. My past luck, or lack of it, had changed with Mrs. Laye. She had quickly become indispensable.

I sat at my desk and called Anna Beth to tell her about my meeting with Andrew, but she didn't answer her phone. That likely meant that she was occupied with handling the start-up of her foundation. She'd received a sizeable inheritance from her late father who had been a Charleston resident for a number of years. It was still in the fledgling stages, but it was clear she was determined to make an impact for the better in Charleston to help foster the memory of her father. The last thing she wanted, and I admired her for it, was to just sit around and spend an inheritance. And I'd be lying if I said I wasn't happy that she was looking to make Charleston her home.

I continued to roll around Andrew's offer. It would be fun working with him and he'd be a great solicitor. That in and of itself made his offer attractive. There were few solicitors who met that qualification and fewer chances still to work with one of them.

The people of Charleston County would be the real losers if S. Bart were elected. He'd load up the office with friends, friends of his wife, children of friends, and friends of friends. He'd walk the ethical line on cutting deals with his cronies in the defense bar. If you were a well-heeled criminal, a great plea deal was only a retainer fee away.

For the rest of the defendants who couldn't afford the right attorney, well, S. Bart would use those as his high-profile cases to show he was a tough prosecutor making sure criminals paid the price for their crimes.

#

I switched gears and put on the lawyer hat. I read my mail, drafted several pleadings, answered emails and returned phone calls. I found myself staring out of my window and decided Anna Beth and I could do with a night out. I also decided to take the rest of the day off. Sure, it was early but I'd practiced enough law for one week. Before I left, I called a friend who owned The Old Post Office, a restaurant near Edisto Island. Charleston may have been a travel destination for the rest of the country, but in Charleston, when we decided to get away, Edisto was near the top of the list.

The Old Post Office had a reputation for great Southern comfort food with a gourmet flare in a timeless atmosphere. It was also terribly popular and that meant you either needed reservations weeks in advance or the owner's cell number. Fortunately, I had the latter. I booked a late table and had them chill Anna Beth's favorite white.

I left a message for her to be ready at seven p.m.

#

As was usual for my return home, an eager canine greeted me. I'd adopted Austin five years before and couldn't imagine not having him around. Sure, I received my fair share of eye rolls and questions from people when they realized he was considered a full family member, but that didn't concern me at all. He was loaded with personality and he and Anna Beth had instantly become fast friends. I walked with him through the house and opened the back door. He rushed across the deck, down the stairs, and into the yard to chase a squirrel. Watching him from the deck, I didn't hear Anna Beth come up behind me.

"You're home early, Noah Parks. Trying to surprise me?"

I started to speak, but just smiled, opting to enjoy the moment with her behind me, arms draped over my shoulders.

Austin stopped in the yard and looked up towards us, giving a single bark before he returned his attention to his search for squirrels.

"What would you like to do tonight?"

"Depends on how you're dressed. How 'bout this? I'll turn around and decide if it's Taco Bell or deserving of something a bit more upscale."

"Not a very good deal. What if I've come up behind you wearing nothing but underwear?"

"Then I don't think Mrs. Hardee over there would be smiling and waving like that."

"Smart ass." She waved back to our neighbor.

I turned and saw Taco Bell was out. Khakis and a white button down. Long hair pulled back and a great smile. Her eyes glowed.

"You look beautiful. And no Taco Bell. Let me go change and we'll be off."

#

As you head south on Highway 17 you start to realize Charleston's beauty could never be contained by a city limit sign. Its grace, charm, and elegance flow far beyond the geographic trappings of a few zip codes. The reality is that the South Carolina lowcountry is one of the most inspiring, beautiful places you'll find.

And just an hour to the south is Edisto Island. Edisto is a rural island/beach community full of rustic charm all its own, but the drive there is a visual treat itself. Back roads that alternate between canopies of oaks, tidal creeks, and vast open tidelands where the marsh grass native to the lowcountry sways in the wind. Today, the sun, hanging low in the sky, cast a golden aura on everything it touched.

Anna Beth crossed her legs in her seat and turned to face me as we drove; Austin was on the floorboard.

We chatted about South Carolina Gamecock football. Her being from out of state, I had to explain that, despite what appeared to be several options, there was only one choice for college football allegiances in South Carolina. That was the Gamecocks.

Early in our relationship she had, in a very serious tone, asked if I had an aversion to the color orange.

As a fan of the South Carolina Gamecocks, and the football team specifically, it was near mandatory that you dislike the school colors of the Clemson Tigers, the Gamecock's cross-state rivals. Hence orange was taboo. Ditto for several other SEC schools - Tennessee, Florida and Auburn.

Now, as we passed under the canopy of live oaks draping Highway 174, my thoughts returned to Andrew's offer. I reached over and took Anna Beth's hand.

"If I end up an assistant solicitor, you'll have to make sure to mind you P's and Q's."

"Funny you should mention that, I've been thinking about Andrew's offer. For you to work in his office. And I always mind my P's and Q's, yours's too."

"Yes, you do, so care to share your thoughts?"

"I had a lawyer friend in Chicago. She was a prosecutor after school. Briefly. She talked about highs and lows, stress and burn out. She made it sound love/hate."

"I've thought about that. I like being my own boss, not being beholden to anyone."

"That's the other thing. What would it be like working for Andrew? You and he are so close. Wouldn't it be a risk to put your friendship in the balance?"

"I've thought about that too. I'd hope it wouldn't be a problem, but mostly I think I'm flattered that Andrew thinks enough of me to ask, but all that aside, at the end of the day, I'm not sure if I'm the most qualified."

I started to slow down. We were approaching the Old Post Office.

"Don't sell yourself short. You know you're qualified and you have a relationship with him that not too many others do. That could be invaluable. You should talk to him about that and--"

"Did you see that?" I said.

"What?"

I looked into my rearview mirror at a brown sedan heading in the other direction, back towards Charleston.

"I think that was Andrew, but that's not his car. And he had someone with him. I think a woman."

"Really? Who's he dating?"

"I don't think he is. Odd, I saw him this morning and he didn't mention anything about coming down here."

"Maybe we just stumbled onto a secret campaign meeting."

"Maybe, of course maybe I just don't need to be involved in politics."

FOUR

The weekend was a blur. There was the always-amazing dinner at the Old Post Office: white wine, shrimp pate, crab cakes, seared local grouper, and a sinful dessert of the Old Post Office original, Charleston chewy cake with Chantilly whipped cream. Austin spent our meal at the owner's house behind the restaurant, playing with his labs.

Thoughts of Andrew's job offer faded and the weekend was only Anna Beth and me.

About halfway through dinner, plans of a return to Charleston changed. With a quick call, I extended the surprise for Anna Beth when I confirmed a college friend was out of town and his island house vacant for the weekend. I let my friend at the Old Post Office know that next time my friend's meal was on me.

After dinner, we collected Austin and headed toward the interior of the island.

The house was in an area of Edisto called "The Neck." Despite the development that peppered the beachfront, Edisto was still a heavily wooded, rural place and in the Neck, in the battle against the night, nature won. Even on moonlit evenings, the abundance of oaks and their interwoven canopies kept most of the light out. The result was pitch-black, save the headlights that pierced the darkness and the small circles of light projected by the random streetlight.

Austin curled up on a couch and Anna Beth and I made ourselves at home in the loft bedroom. The house was oriented on the lot so that the skylights escaped the coverage of the oaks and showed the sky, and tonight, the moon above.

We took our time falling asleep in the soft moon glow.

We welcomed morning by sleeping in. Austin had joined us on the bed sometime during the night. It was an unseasonably cool Saturday morning late in October, and it seemed the thing to do was absolutely nothing. Fortunately, I had commandeered a stocked house so we were up to the challenge.

We let the morning linger with the windows open and the sound of rain on the house's tin roof. Normally we would've spent the day watching South Carolina football, but it was a bye week. Instead we watched the tidal creek, a couple of deer (Austin was quite happy with this), and marked the hours with the sun's jaunt across the sky, punctuated by the rhythmic sound of rain on the tin roof.

It was a weekend without agenda or concern. With each passing moment, thoughts of the election, Andrew's offer or much else besides Anna Beth retreated to the recesses of my mind.

The morning became the afternoon that rolled to the evening and night. We didn't leave the house until Sunday came around. We took our time getting up and out and the three of us headed back to Charleston.

#

Several times through the weekend I thought of having a serious talk with Anna Beth about our relationship, but each time I stopped. Maybe it was the demons of my past. Maybe a fear of tipping the balance on something I hadn't enjoyed in a long while. Maybe it was my fear of pushing Anna Beth to move faster than she wanted.

I was beginning to realize perhaps my reluctance to give Andrew an answer was because I was beginning to realize the real decision in my life was not whether I would be a solicitor in his office, but rather what my future looked like on a more personal level.

Maybe I could have one and enjoy the other. Maybe I needed to pick one and go all in. So, there wasn't a serious talk over the weekend but as it wound to an end, I knew I'd made a decision.

Now I just had to figure out how to tell them both about what I had decided.

Thing was I had no idea how challenging this all would become.

#

After my Monday morning run, I detoured on the way to the office to stop at Gabriel's. One of the perks of being a captain of detectives was schedule flexibility. Gabriel liked to come in a little later on Monday mornings, so I knew he he'd be at home.

He lived in an older area of downtown Charleston beyond the historic district in a neighborhood you wouldn't find in any tour book. The neighborhood had been settled originally more than a century and a half ago as a freeman's village for former slaves.

Gabriel's house started as a two-room dirt floor shack his great-great-grandfather built on land he'd been given with his freedom. Through the years, the home and accompanying property had grown substantially. Though the small cabin was gone, there was a very nice home on more than an acre of land; which, in Charleston, qualified as an estate.

The years had seen Gabriel's neighborhood undergo a transition from freeman's village to a bleak urban landscape with gangs and drug activity, but with the work of some of the area's long-time residents, Gabriel included, the area had undergone a rebirth and was now one of the up-and-coming areas in Charleston.

Gabriel projected an intimidating persona, one that made him very successful as a police officer. Back in his uniformed days, the mere sight of him was intimidating for criminals and even some of his friends. Since he'd become a detective however, his image had been refined and while he could still muster the intimidation when needed, he was able to turn it on and off at will. He generally checked the edge when he left work.

His home bore a closer resemblance to a bed-and-breakfast than the enclave of a career police officer and bachelor. Most visitors expected guns, weights, and frozen dinners. What people found instead was a gourmet kitchen and a backyard bonsai garden that could have been featured on the cover of *Garden & Gun*. I'd had many a conversation with Gabriel in his garden under the watchful eye of his beagle, Rudy.

I parked in his drive behind his unmarked cruiser, got out and walked onto his porch. I knew immediately Gabriel wasn't in the house. His home alarm system, Rudy, didn't go off. I walked back down the steps and followed a path to the fence that surrounded his lot. To the naked eye, the fence would have appeared a solid wall of ivy, but, knowing where the latch was hidden, I opened the gate and entered the backyard, after which a small blur came towards me. Rudy stopped just short of my feet and sat as Gabriel had trained him to do. I reached down and rubbed him on his head.

"Go get your ball."

He was off toward the back porch. After shutting the gate, I set out across the yard towards the bamboo archway that marked the entrance to Gabriel's bonsai sanctuary. Through the arch was a crushed white pebble path circling the garden. Several sections of oak trunks, bench height, had been placed beyond the perimeter of the path for seats and several large boulders with uneven surfaces housed a number of small bonsai trees. Within the interior of the pebble path was a Zen garden of sand and stone, the entire garden was surrounded by a bamboo fence. In the center of the interior Zen garden was a single larger bonsai tree.

I found him sitting, staring at the small trees. I walked in and sat on a tree trunk to his right.

We sat in silence.

"Morning," he finally said. "There's coffee on in the house if you want."

"No, just thought I'd stop by."

"Hear you were down in Edisto over the weekend."

"And how did you hear that?"

"Have a good time?"

"Anna Beth, she says hi by the way. We stayed in the Neck."

"So, the answer is 'yes,'" he said as he studied one of the small trees.

"We did."

"I also hear someone asked you to be his deputy once he wins an election."

"Andrew's been running his mouth again I see."

"He asked me what I thought about it, you being his deputy."

"And you said what?"

"I told him you'd been playing cop out of jealousy ever since I joined the force and maybe if you got to lock a few people up, you'd get the bug out of your system and finally be a decent attorney."

"Thanks for the vote of confidence."

He was silent for several moments as he shifted his seat to look at the same miniature tree from a different angle.

"What did you say to his offer?"

"Nothing yet. Don't want to appear too eager."

"You'd make a good solicitor, Parks, but you could have called me to talk about that and I know you're not here for the trees."

I looked over my shoulder and saw Rudy waiting patiently by the archway. He wasn't allowed to come into the garden, so I walked over, bent to retrieve his ball and threw it across the yard. He raced off after it.

"He does like it when you visit. You and Anna Beth should come for dinner soon. Bring Austin too."

"We'll do that. But I do have something I want to ask you about."

"Shoot."

"Anna Beth."

"You know how I feel about her, Parks. You and her kinda got started off in a way that makes people either really dislike each other or get really close really fast."

"You could say that."

Gabriel's hand rose to his head where it stopped on a scar, a scar he got in the process of saving Anna Beth's life.

"What are you getting at?" he said.

"I've been thinking about Anna Beth and me a good bit lately, our future."

"Just be careful you don't lose her because I'd hate to see how far you'd fall. Anna Beth is a good person and the best thing to happen to you since Claire. Maybe the best thing period."

Claire. My last serious relationship. I hadn't heard Gabriel say her name since the day he told me that she was dead.

"No, I agree with you completely. Who knows? Maybe we end up getting married."

"Wow, married, really?"

"I, well, I didn't think it was that much of a stretch."

"Jesus, Parks, take half a step back and watch you don't land in the sarcasm. Anyone that knows you finds out your thinking marriage and Anna Beth in the same thought is going to say, 'About time.'"

"She still has a few things to finish up in Chicago. I don't know, I think there's something holding her back."

He looked at me a moment, smiled and then shook his head.

"Parks, Parks, Parks. Ever think the something holding her back is you?"

"Me? How? You know how I feel about her."

"I do. Does she? You can be a closed book sometimes and, who knows, maybe those things in Chicago are really her way of telling you she wants a home here. But what do I know?"

FIVE

The sound of the phone broke the still of the night. I sat straight up in bed.

"Ouch," Anna Beth said. She had been asleep with her head on my shoulder. The chain of events startled Austin who went to the window, looked out and gave a low growl and a single bark.

"Sorry. Hello." Silence. "Hello."

"Noah? Andrew here."

"You say that like you didn't know you called me. You realize it's four thirty in the morning?"

"Yes. Noah . . . "

"Andrew, I haven't decided yet."

"Decided what? No. Noah, this isn't about that, something else has come up. Can you meet me at the office in thirty minutes?"

"Who is it?" Anna Beth said, rolling the other way.

"Andrew"

I hung up the phone.

"Awful early for him to be calling."

"Yes, and he sounded, well, really odd."

I got out of bed, went into the bathroom and took a quick shower. After throwing on khakis and a button-down, I saw Anna Beth was sitting up in our bed.

"I'm going to go see what's bothering him."

"Just let me know how I can help."

I kissed her and headed to his office, not at all sure what to expect.

#

Charleston at five a.m. is void of any activity. Houses were dark; street lights and traffic signals and store fronts provided the little light there was. I felt as if I had the city to myself. I pulled into Andrew's empty parking lot behind his office. I got out and tried the back door.

Locked.

I knocked. No answer.

I had absolutely no idea what Andrew wanted or why it was so important I meet him at this ungodly hour. But like I've said, I owe him, so if he calls, I'm there.

I walked around front and tried the front door. No lights.

Locked. No answer when I knocked.

I tried his cell and office phone with no answer at either.

I texted him. Then followed with an email.

At five forty-five a.m. I started to feel like I'd been stood up on a date. At six a.m., I realized I was already past perturbed. Even with Andrew, near an hour of waiting was more than generous, particularly when the wait started before the sun was up. I jotted a note on the back of a business card and left it on the back door.

"Waited for an hour. Going for coffee. Call if you want me to pick up two."

One of my favorite coffee shops was a short walk from my office. I decided if I was going to wait downtown, I could do it from my office.

#

Before Anna Beth, my office had always been one of my favorite early morning places. It dates back to the eighteenth century and had seen all sorts of different uses prior to becoming my base of legal operations. Something about all the history made me feel more like a lawyer.

From time to time I still liked to start my day spending a couple of hours in the office with no interruptions. It gave me an opportunity to see what the day or week to come held. If I was going to be stood up for a meeting at least I could salvage something of my day.

What seemed like an eternity later, I heard the backdoor open. Glancing at the wall clock, I saw it was only about fifteen minutes after eight o'clock in the morning. That would be Ms. Laye.

Andrew appeared in my doorway. Dressed in full business attire, sans tie.

"Well, good morning to you. You're running a little late."

"I wanted to apologize for calling you this morning."

"No, that's not necessary, but another call would have been nice when you decided that only one of us needed to be at your office before dawn. Sit."

I motioned to a chair.

"No, I need to get going."

"If you can call me before dawn and drag me out of bed, you can sit and talk for a bit."

He stepped in and took a seat.

"What was so important this morning?"

"I was wondering if you had a chance to think about anyone else that might be a good fit in the office."

I waited to see if he would say anything more.

Nothing.

"No, I can't say as I have. I'm still at the point of deciding if I'll be one of the names on your new letterhead once you're in office. I'm happy to give it some thought, but a question for you."

"Sure."

"What's going on? We haven't talked about other people for the office before and I'm certain that's not really fodder for a pre-dawn call."

I knew him well enough to know something else was bothering him, but also knew that if he didn't want to tell me, I wouldn't be able to pry it out of him. Andrew wasn't always a sharer when it came to personal issues. Even with a close friend.

"Nothing much. I mean I guess I'm getting a little stressed with the election coming up."

"You forget, I've known you a while and when I hear you say, "nothing much," I hear that something's really bothering you."

"Honestly, the election's got me stressed and yes, there is something else, but I'm not quite ready to talk about it. Thought I was, but maybe later."

Some progress.

"Fair enough, but how about being sure next time you call on the other side of sunrise."

"I am sorry for that. Tell Anna Beth I'm sorry for bothering. I do need to be going though."

"We can talk later."

"When I can focus on it, you'll be the first to know. We should all go to the Old Post Office for a break in the campaign."

"You know how I love the Old Post Office. We should do that."

I started to say something about having seen him as he left the last weekend, but I held my tongue.

I watched him leave, passing Mrs. Laye as she came in.

"Good morning, Andrew," I heard her say.

She stopped at my office door.

"What's wrong with him?"

"Hopefully just pre-election jitters."

"Hum. If I was running against that S. Bart, I mean, what is it he likes to be called, S. Bart? Just knowing I was being a pain in his rear end would make me happy."

"Yes, you would think."

SIX

Soon after Andrew left, Mrs. Laye brought in the local newspaper. There was a story, replete with photos, on S. Bart having attended two fundraisers the prior day. One event was sponsored by a group of retired police officers and the other by a wealthy local businessman, Billy Litman. Litman had a fresh-out-of-law school son, Dave-- in need of a job, so it was easy to see the motive there. Trouble was, junior had a reputation as a hothead and someone that wasn't likely to make a good attorney, much less an assistant solicitor.

I started to suspect what was behind Andrew's behavior. I could have been overanalyzing things, but it made sense. It was well known Litman was no fan of S. Bart. But it wasn't enough he just didn't like S. Bart; Litman knew his money could make a difference in the election and there would be a price for his support. For Andrew, the price would be a job for Litman's son. Andrew wasn't one to take well to that kind of pressure and wouldn't be too quick to share that kind of dilemma.

\#

When I arrived home for the evening, I learned that the pressure on Andrew was only going to increase.

The local evening news was on and one of the local anchors was discussing the race.

"The solicitor's race heated up today with the debut of a new television spot from Samuel Bartholomew Michaels. The ad, which does not mention S. Bart's opponent--local attorney Andrew Stephens--by name, is being viewed by some as raising the question of Mr. Stephens' sexuality. We go to Morgan York reporting from the newsroom. Morgan."

"Thank you, Ben. An interest group supporting local attorney S. Bart, candidate for Ninth Circuit solicitor, today debuted a television ad blanketing the local markets. This ad, from the group, Values United, is being viewed as raising the question of Andrew Stephen's sexual preference. The ad, forty-five seconds in length, features longtime state senator, Berlin Rawlman. In the ad, Rawlman praises S. Bart as a model father, husband, and family man. Rawlman goes on to say how tough S. Bart will be on crime and how the voters can't go wrong with him as solicitor. At no point in the ad does Rawlman mention S. Bart's opponent, Andrew Stephens; however, he does say, and I quote, 'S. Bart is tough on crime. His every action is guided by the finest moral compass I have ever seen. With him you won't have to worry about your solicitor being soft on those of questionable upbringing or supporting what I understand people are calling gay marriage.' S. Bart, when contacted concerning the ad, issued a statement wherein he thanked Rawlman for his support and his assistance in the campaign."

"We contacted Mr. Stephens, who has never been married and while he had no comment, he did issue this statement."

The screen was replaced by a graphic of a letter from Andrew on his letterhead. It read:

"I am deeply disappointed that negative campaigning is being condoned in this race. This is something I refuse to do. It is important the voters look beyond the implication of the negative and cast their vote for the most qualified candidate, the candidate with the best solutions to the issues that are important to each and every voter. The candidate that is most qualified for the job."

"Thank you, Morgan. Has there been any indication as to the impact this ad will have on the election?"

"Ben, the election is just more than a week away and before this ad, the race was neck and neck according to a News2 poll. Given how tight the race is, it is likely this ad could have an impact but it's anyone's guess as to which candidate will see the benefit."

"Thank you, Morgan."

"Is Andrew gay?" Anna Beth said, putting the TV on mute.

"He's not. Wouldn't matter if he was, but what that ad didn't say is S. Bart's an asshole."

"So you've said. I'm glad Andrew didn't dignify it with a denial."

"S. Bart may be an ass, but he's an intelligent ass with money to spend. Whoever he's hired to run his campaign is good. Not that it should matter, but if Andrew admits or denies anything, then that becomes the issue and everything else Andrew is trying to accomplish becomes lost in allegation."

"I can't believe that S. Bart let that ad run. You have to think that the voters will be smart enough to see through that."

"Careful there, Mayor Daley."

"Things weren't perfect in Chicago, but that was a long time ago. You're sure he's not gay?"

"Positive. I've known him for years and he's heterosexual. And even more, he's one of the most open-minded, tolerant people I know. What people do is fine by Andrew, as long as they don't hurt anyone else doing it.

"Alright, Andrew needs focus. What are we going to do to help him?"

"Not sure."

I picked up the phone and called Andrew. No surprise. Voicemail.

"Noah, I noticed something that might explain how Andrew has been acting."

"Noticed what?"

"The letter that Andrew sent in response to that ad, I saw the date. It was dated yesterday. That means he sent it before he called you this morning."

"You're right. Then the question is why didn't he tell me about it?"

"I'm only guessing, but I'm pretty sure that he's telling you he could use some help. Who's running his campaign?"

"He is."

"Then be his friend."

SEVEN

It was well into the twentieth century before travel across the Charleston Harbor to and from Mount Pleasant was possible by way of a bridge. Prior to this, harbor crossings had been accomplished by a number of ferries. However, in the 1920s, a two-lane, two-mile bridge was built spanning the harbor, joined in the 1950s by a larger, separate bridge that added three more lanes. The ferries disappeared.

And bridges continued to evolve.

Less than ten years ago, the old bridges, as they were collectively known, slowly disassembled and a new eight-lane bridge grew to take their place.

We decided to go over to Andrew's house to check on him. And offer our help. Anna Beth's talent was grassroots fundraising for nonprofits, which translated to her being great at getting people excited. She figured it wasn't a stretch to do the same thing for Andrew as he headed into the election.

We crossed the bridge into Mount Pleasant and made our way to the Old Village to Andrew's house. It was older than many of the homes in historic downtown Charleston, on a large lot with a clear and commanding view of the bridge and downtown Charleston.

As we approached his house, a familiar looking brown sedan drove by. I watched in the rearview and as the car disappeared from view, it came to me. It was the same car I'd seen leaving the Old Post Office on Edisto.

I parked in his drive. As was the historic norm, when the home was first built, the present garage had been the kitchen. As colonial kitchens were the frequent starting point for fires, the cooking house was generally separate as it was easier to rebuild a kitchen as opposed to the rest of the house. The result was many Charleston area homes with a separate structure that was a guest house, or in Andrew's case, a garage. I peered into the garage and saw both of his cars.

A wide set of steps led to the double front door of the three-story weathered brick house.

Anna Beth knocked. Nothing. I tried his cell again. Nothing. We walked around to the rear of the house. Several scattered palmettos formed the boundaries of a path to a large oak near the water. In the shade beneath the oak there was a bench overlooking the harbor.

Gabriel had his bonsai garden, Andrew his backyard.

"Sorry I didn't come to the door."

I almost jumped out of my skin.

Andrew stood in the doorway of his back porch.

"Christ, a little warning next time. I've been on edge worrying about you."

"What's to worry about? I mean isn't everyone's sex life the topic of the five o'clock news?"

"Well, I for one have always been curious."

"Cheap politics. Makes me feel like I'm still at home in Chicago."

"I knew it would be an eye-opener, running for solicitor, but I never thought being single would be a campaign issue."

"I'm not sure is should be, but that's the thing about South Carolina, there's a political current running under pretty much everything. But since you know how S. Bart is going to play the race, it should make it a bit easier to plot out your approach. At least I would think it should."

"Your timings good, there is something--well, someone--I want to talk about."

"Dave Litman?" Anna Beth said.

"Perceptive. Maybe I offered her your job."

"That's flattering. Maybe I could use you at my foundation."

"I can see why you like her."

I didn't say anything, but I saw Andrew smile. That was a good sign, even if it had been fleeting.

"We saw the article in the paper on the fund-raiser he did for S. Bart and guessed he would be coming your way, offering support for a job for his son."

"You hit that nail on the head."

"From what Noah tells me no one really wants Litman's son working for him," Anna Beth said.

"That's likely the long and short of it, but Litman's endorsement unfortunately carries some weight. Probably not enough to win or lose the election alone, but with him onboard, I'll pick up other support and without him, well, you get the picture."

"And let me guess," Anna Beth said. "If you don't have him, S. Bart will offer his son a job just for revenge."

"She's good."

Andrew walked back inside his house, waving us in as well. He had notes spread all over his kitchen table. I noticed a bottle of diet Coke on the counter with a bottle of water beside it. Andrew nonchalantly picked them up and deposited them in the trash without saying a word. Andrew didn't drink soda, diet or otherwise.

"What are you going to do about young Mr. Litman? Or should I say his daddy Billy."

"I've told his father that if I'm elected I would gladly consider his son for a job on my staff."

"And let me guess. That wasn't good enough for the senior Mr. Litman."

"Billy wants a senior deputy spot guaranteed for him. God, I hate politics."

"Said the politician." Andrew ignored my comment.

"The Litman thing will work out, but since you're here, want to play sounding board?"

We sat down and started going over some notes Andrew had made. As I suspected, he wasn't going to make any statement about S. Bart' ad though he was frustrated as to how to handle it.

"I have an idea," Anna Beth said as she reached for a legal pad and started writing. She turned it so we could read it. "Something we did back on some of the campaigns I worked on in Chicago."

"Andrew Stephens. Tough on Crime."

"That's what Rawlman said in the ad," Andrew said.

"Doesn't matter that he said it, what matters is that he tied that to what makes a successful solicitor," Anna Beth said. "Now you can hammer it down S. Bart's throat. And best of all, you don't have to mention the ad."

I smiled.

"It's brilliant," Andrew said.

"Thank you. We call that the 'Chicago Way.' Take their words and use them against them. If they brought them up, they can't really argue with them."

EIGHT

I didn't see Andrew for much of the next two weeks leading up to the election. What I did see was Anna Beth rising to the occasion-- organizing and managing his volunteers in a grass roots style that any politician would envy. His "Tough on Crime" campaign was working. By all accounts, it had S. Bart scrambling.

As election day approached, S. Bart turned up--as best he could--the charm offensive. You couldn't turn on the television or pick up the paper without seeing his face.

He became a fixture at high school football games. I never realized how many restaurants opened in Charleston, but S. Bart was at near every one. Cameras were there when he spoke at a banquet for the Charleston Junior League. His wife, Tamara Michaels, was a longtime member and in charge of social programs. The Charleston Exchange Club made a donation to the Charleston School of Law, and S. Bart, the president of the Club, together with his wife, were there to hand over the donation. No one bothered to mention the Exchange Club held monthly fundraisers for the law school's pro bono program or that the checks were normally delivered via the good 'ole postal service. I'm pretty sure if he had given a prayer at his church he would have had someone trying to get the press in.

Andrew took a more calculated approach. Flyers, campaign signs, and banners were everywhere. Anna Beth had his people going door-to-door. He joined in everyday and made a personal connection when he asked what he could do to make voters feel safer in Charleston County.

Finally, election day arrived. I closed the office and joined Anna Beth and the rest of the campaign in handing out fliers as close as we were allowed to the local polling places.

I stopped at home to change before we went to the election party. I looked up to see Anna Beth standing in the doorway to the bedroom.

"You look stunning," I said.

"Thank you, Noah."

She walked a few steps to the bed and sat down.

"I trust Charleston."

"Sorry?"

"I've met a lot of people in the last few weeks helping Andrew and I've gotten to know him even better. Chicago was different. You expected politicians to be corrupt and the vote to have been bought and paid for. Here, it's different. The people care and Andrew's the better candidate. They'll do the right thing."

I smiled.

"I couldn't agree with you more."

#

There was already a small crowd at Andrew's house when we arrived, hopeful it would be a "Victory Party." I parked on the oak-lined street and walked up the drive. Andrew spotted us as soon as we walked in.

"Noah, Anna Beth," he said as he worked his way to us, beer in hand. "I was wondering when you two were going to show up. Beer's on the porch, wine on the counter, and, just for you Noah, scotch in the liquor cabinet. Help yourself. Oh, Anna Beth. Your help these last two weeks, words don't do enough to express my thanks."

"Well, Andrew, hopefully soon, Mr. Solicitor, you are most very welcome."

"Well damn, pardon me a minute."

I shook my head. Andrew knew I steered clear of scotch. He headed off towards Billy Litman who was walking in the front door with his son, Dave Litman, and his son's rather buxom blonde girlfriend. God, she looked like barely out of high school. Odd, given Andrew's thoughts about Litman, I was surprised to see Litman here.

Then the elder Litman planted a kiss full on the mouth of his son's girlfriend and I realized I likely had been a bit hasty putting her with the younger Litman. I remembered Billy had married what was likely his fourth or fifth wife a few years back, but either he was auditioning a new one or he had already negotiated the trade-in. With another shake of my head, I grabbed a beer and then wandered into the living room to check on the returns. Still too close to call, or so said the anchor on the screen.

"Look what I found."

I looked and saw Anna Beth standing with Gabriel.

"I didn't expect to see you here," I said as I shook his hand.

"That makes two of us. I was surprised to have been invited, well I say invited, Andrew called me yesterday and told me to stop by."

The numbers stayed even, prompting the local newscasters to begin contemplating when an election had ever been this close. Through the evening, the count never shifted more than one hundred votes in either candidate's favor.

Billy Litman was turning the evening into the shadow Andrew show, leaving the new wife to babysit the younger Litman.

Andrew walked over to us, leaving Billy Litman standing alone.

"Noah, did I tell you how happy I am you're here?" He looked around the room and turned back to me. "I only know about half these people. I guess that's politics for you. Oh, Detective. Thank you for coming."

"You're welcome. Happy to be here."

For the first time in several weeks, Andrew seemed in a good mood though I was betting that was alcohol.

I'm not sure how it happened, but as Andrew moved by me, his shoulder hit my arm in just a way to cause me to stumble and drop my beer. As I reached for it, off balance, I rammed the end table, knocking a statue from the table to the floor.

In a throwback to our roughhousing fraternity days, I went chest to chest with Andrew.

"You better watch your ass. No telling what I might do."

"Bring it on, buddy, bring it on," Andrew said.

At the exact same moment, we both realized a hush had fallen over the party as the focus shifted in our direction. We froze for a moment.

Andrew put his arm around my shoulder, and pointed me toward the kitchen. Just as quickly as the crowd had silenced, the normal party chatter returned.

I glanced back at Anna Beth who was smiling, shaking her head.

"Come join us for a drink," Andrew said looking to Anna Beth and Gabriel.

"I'm fine," Gabriel said. "Thanks."

"You've got a nice turnout here. Lots of people supporting you. Though I see, or should I say, don't see Rebecca," I said as Andrew lead Anna Beth and me into the kitchen.

"If I'm not mistaken, Billy Litman seems quite interested in us," Anna Beth said.

I followed her gaze to see Billy Litman standing alone across the room. He was staring at me as if I'd stolen his prom date. I locked eyes with him and held his stare until interrupted by Andrew giving me a beer.

"Your friend Billy over there seems to be a little put out."

"Oh, Litman, screw him. He wants to make sure I don't forget his kid needs a job."

"You mean the one out there hitting on daddy's wife?" Anna Beth said.

The three off us looked out to the back porch to see Dave Litman sitting a bit too close to his father's wife, her leg draped across his lap. We looked back and Billy Litman had intensified his stare toward the kitchen and the three of us.

"Maybe someone should tell daddy he should worry more about what's happening at home rather than trying to get junior a job." I raised my beer to him.

At about that same time Dave Litman stood and took the woman's hand in his, pulling her to him. They paused, then separated and moved toward the steps leading into Andrew's very dark backyard.

"I think someone might be figuring out that something's amiss. Look," Anna Beth said.

Billy Litman realized we were no longer looking at him. He'd followed our gaze and was now heading through the door from the house to the porch just as his son and wife were heading to the backyard. He moved with a sense of urgency.

"This should be interesting," I said.

Billy Litman reached for his wife's arm. She pulled away from the senior Litman, looked to the younger then moved away from father and son. She rushed through the backdoor, into the house, past us and out the front door. I noticed that Gabriel was watching from the edge of the living room. Ever the police officer.

Dave Litman started to say something to his father, but stopped when his father put his finger up to his son's face.

Billy Litman took his son by the arm, led him off the porch, into the house and over to the kitchen once again nearly running into Gabriel in the process. The Litmans stopped before Andrew, Anna Beth, and me.

"Andrew, Andrew. I want to thank you for having us over tonight. It seems that my bride isn't feeling well, so we'll be going now. I'll look forward to hearing from you after your election's certified."

Andrew took a long pull from his fresh beer.

"You okay there Billy? Looks like there might be a few things going on at home you need to check into. I'll give Davie there his props, he's ambitious. Goes after what he wants. And he really seems to like his stepmom. Where'd they meet? Middle school?"

Anna Beth suppressed a laugh. I didn't. The younger Litman glared at Andrew and pulled his arm away from his father's grip.

"I'm what? You know shit, asshole."

"Speaks his mind too."

"I ought to…," Dave Litman took a step closer to us then his father grabbed his shoulder and pulled him back.

"Keep your mouth shut," the senior Litman said.

Dad's finger was back in his son's face where he held it a moment as the two locked eyes before the senior Litman turned his attention back to Andrew.

"Authority problem there with little Davie?" Andrew said.

"Andrew. We can talk about this later. My son's had a few drinks and doesn't know what he's saying. Please forgive him."

"Of course, how could anyone have a concern with him. Besides, he's probably ready to make sure his step-mommy gets home."

Dave Litman twisted from his father's grasp and lunged toward Andrew. His father held him tight.

"Thank you, Andrew. I knew we saw eye to eye."

"I think we both see what's going on here. Have Davie give me a call after he gets his attitude worked out and he can apologize. Noah, would you show the Litmans out?"

"After ... What are you talking about?" But Andrew had turned and walked away leaving us with Billy and his visibly upset son.

"I take it you don't need to have me show you the door?"

"No. Though do tell Andrew I'll be willing to overlook this. Tell him I still expect certain things."

"You'll probably want to tell him that yourself."

"You listen closely. You'll not be his deputy. That position belongs to my son and the sooner you and Mr. Stephens appreciate it, the better. And just remember that if Andrew's not elected..." He apparently loved to put a finger in the face of his ire.

"What?"

"Just keep that in mind. And remember you'll do best to stay out of our way."

I said nothing as Billy Litman turned, pulling his son behind him.

We watched them go out the front door.

NINE

Andrew and S. Bart were still neck and neck, separated by a scant seventy-six votes. The polls were closed and the news anchors had just interrupted programming to inform everyone watching that the election commission would not declare a winner that night.

A groan went up from the room.

The evening wore on and Andrew's guests started to depart. Like Andrew, I realized that I didn't know even half of them. Finally, it was only Andrew, Anna Beth and I remaining in the midst of a sea empty bottles.

Andrew moved into the living room. Drunk would be a fair description for him. Anna Beth was dozing on the couch, her head in my lap.

"Your campaign manager apparently needed a rest."

"So how'm I doing?"

"Last count, you were up by seventy-six votes."

"Hardly a landslide."

Andrew got up from the couch and walked back into the kitchen. He came back with two more beers. I hadn't even seen him finish the prior one.

"You plan on starting your first day as solicitor hungover?"

"Why not? All I'll have to do is smile for a few pictures. Hey, I got an idea, why don't you and Anna Beth crash here tonight then in the morning I can call a press conference and we can all show up on my front porch together. Straight outta bed. Maybe I could get upgraded to bisexual or maybe even questioning."

"That ad bothering you? And you know, you'll probably be okay without a label."

Anna Beth shifted on the couch.

"It's been on my mind. I ran a clean, fair campaign. S. Bart, rich, old money, gets a little heat from a nobody and first thing he does is get in the mud."

"You didn't and you're the better man for it."

"Better man, but that doesn't mean I'll be solicitor. You decided yet?"

"On being your number two?"

"Yes."

He reached in his back pocket, pulled out a folded sheet of paper and handed it to me. I opened it and saw a list of typed names with titles beside them. At the top, beside the words, "Chief Deputy Solicitor" was "Noah Parks." Young Mr. Litman's name was nowhere to be found.

"Andrew, you know I'm flattered, but I have to say no."

I pulled out my Mont Blanc and crossed my name off the list. I wrote in the name of one of the senior solicitors currently working in Charleston. I handed the paper back to him. He looked at it a moment before he folded it and put it back in his pants pocket.

"You know he'll make a better deputy than I ever would. You'll need someone around there who knows what they're doing, who knows the politics."

"Maybe, but I'd still rather have you. How about I get Rebecca from my office to be your assistant?"

"Nice try. Say I didn't see her tonight."

"She had something tonight. I do want to thank you for your help in the last few weeks. It's made things a lot easier, but I was hoping we could be a team."

"You know I'm flattered, but answer this for me."

"What?"

"Something other than the election's on your mind. What?"

"You know me too well, but I'm too drunk to talk about it. I promise we'll talk tomorrow."

He picked up his beer and finished it in with one long pull.

The news anchor broke into our conversation to report all the votes had been counted, and as a result of the narrow margin in the initial counts, a mandatory recount was necessary. The recount would be done immediately, but it would be eight a.m. before there would be any new information.

"Looks like that's it for the night."

"Election night, election morning. Doesn't matter as long as you win."

"True. You want to stay over?"

"Thanks, but I've got to get home and take care of the hound, but we'll talk tomorrow?"

"Sure thing. Thanks again for coming."

I gently shook Anna Beth who quickly sat up. She stretched and rubbed her eyes.

"You okay?" I said as I was helping her to the car.

"I think so. I'm feeling really out of it," she said as she leaned on me as we walked to the street.

I fished the keys out of my pocket and clicked the door unlocked, opening it for Anna Beth. She was asleep by the time I walked around to the driver's side door. Strange she was so groggy, she hadn't had that much to drink. Andrew was still on the porch. He returned my wave and walked back into his house.

Had I known this would be the last time I was to see him alive, I'd have had a bit more to say.

TEN

"Anything on the election?"

I'd just emerged from a pleasant night's sleep to find Anna Beth had the local news on to watch the returns in the living room.

"Same as last night, they're still doing a recount it looks like." She rubbed her eyes then stretched her arms over her head.

"You feel okay?"

"I'm not sure what it is. I feel a little foggy headed this morning. And I only had two glasses of wine."

"Lightweight," I said just before a pillow from the couch hit my head.

The voter turnout set a record for a Charleston election, but we were still without a new solicitor more than twelve hours after the polls had closed. A news conference was scheduled for later in the morning.

I picked up the phone and dialed Andrew's home number. Answering machine. I hung up and called his cell. Voicemail. I left a message asking him to call me, thinking he'd probably like some company as the returns were announced.

I hadn't heard back from him as the news conference was starting.

Edward Peterson, the Charleston County Election Commissioner appeared behind a podium covered with a haphazard mix of microphones and digital recorders before a room full of reporters beyond. Peterson was a short, stocky man in his sixties or perhaps in his fifties with a decade of stress-related aging. A pair of reading glasses perched on the top of a head that was otherwise occupied by but a few wisps of gray hair. He wore a rumpled sports coat and his shirt collar was unbuttoned, his tie appeared hastily straightened and even as he was beginning to speak, his hand went to his neck for a tug at his collar. He shuffled through a stack of papers and raised his eyes to the camera. With a slight wheeze, he took a deep breath and looked into the cameras.

"Good morning. We've been up all night counting the ballots and have an update. As I'm sure ya'll know from the returns last night, the initial count was extremely close. This new count's even closer. I do want to thank all of the commission staff who were up all night working on this. Now, by way of review. On the initial count, Andrew Stephens, out of 92,352 votes cast received 46,214 votes. Samuel Bartholomew Michaels received 46,138 votes. Making, as I am sure most have heard, a difference of seventy-six votes. Based upon this, as state law requires a recount in any election where there is less than a two percent margin in the vote, we automatically initiated the required recounted. The results of this second recount are as follows. The initial total vote count, 92,352 was verified as accurate. Andrew Stephens received 46,232. Samuel Bartholomew Michaels received 46,120.

Based upon this, Andrew Stephens is declared the winner with .5001 percent of the vote."

A reporter behind one of the cameras spoke up, breaking the brief silence.

"Mr. Peterson, are these results official?"

"Yes, as of 8:55 a.m., these election returns are certified."

"Have the candidates been notified?" another reporter said.

"No, but calls are being placed to their individual contact numbers. But it's been my experience that when we reach the candidates, it's pretty much old news to them."

"Mr. Peterson, will there be another recount?"

"At this point, without further order or direction, this election is certified final."

I looked away from the screen to Anna Beth.

"Well my dear, it looks like you may just have a future as a campaign manager. You're one and zero."

"And thank you. I'm so happy for Andrew and if you'd have said yes to him, looks like you'd have a new job."

The live broadcast from the election commission had returned to the newsroom and the anchor was recapping high points, though it all boiled down to one thing: Andrew had won. Despite the negative campaigning, despite his refusal to use the same negative tactics as his opponent, despite his lack of resources and despite the lack of a family name. He'd won. I always knew that he'd make a great solicitor and now he'd get the chance to prove it.

Anna Beth's cell rang. She looked at the number.

"The Election Commission," she silently mouthed. "Hello. Yes. This is Anna Beth Cross. Yes, Mr. Stephens' campaign manager."

She had stood and was saying, "Yes," and "I see."

I was proud of her and proud of Andrew. From whatever reason, knowing Andrew had won, I felt a weight lifted from my shoulders. Austin and I went out to the backyard. I watched him while I called the office and let Mrs. Laye know I'd be in late. I heard a door and Austin stormed back into the house and launched himself on the couch beside Anna Beth.

"That's interesting."

"What's interesting?" I said looking over to see Anna Beth was off the phone.

"The election commission was calling me. Andrew had me listed as the second contact number for the campaign."

"That's flattering that he would list you. Show's he really valued what you did. Not that there was a question about that."

"No, I mean he told me he was giving them my number, but it's interesting because they said they couldn't get him at any of his numbers. It's odd he wouldn't be by the phone."

"He's probably busy taking congratulatory calls. Which I think I'll do myself."

It went straight to voicemail.

"You might want to check this out."

The anchor was still talking about the election, but had apparently just introduced a caller on the election issue. A banner came across the screen that read: *SAMUEL*

BARTHOLOMEW MICHAELS, NINTH CIRCUIT SOLICITOR CANDIDATE. S. Bart began to speak.

"Thank you, thank you. I wanted to call in and make an announcement in regard to the election results."

"Yes, Mr. Michaels," the news anchor said. "We want to thank you for calling us to concede victory to Mr.--"

S. Bart cut her off.

"Don't get ahead of yourself there, this is not a concession call, quite the opposite. I've just received information concerning the results, information concerning what appears to be the invalidity of certain votes. It's come to my attention that certain individuals were allowed to vote though they were not in line at their individual precincts by the seven p.m. deadline. I have already filed a formal challenge with the election commission and hope to have a special hearing in the coming days seeking to have the votes in question thrown out, allowing the election to be certified for the proper winner."

"Mr. Michaels, how did this information come to your attention?"

"My campaign workers were following the election and the returns, obviously, very closely. As well, many individuals in the community have given a great deal of attention to the mechanics of this process. Several very civic-minded individuals have called with this appalling information that bears consideration. Whatever it is, the people deserve to have their voice heard. I wanted the voters of Charleston County to know that I will be contesting these results. That's the story."

I slammed my hand against the wall. The sound caused both Anna Beth and Austin to jump.

"Well, fuck. Now what?"

"Noah. Calm down. Getting angry won't change a thing. And certainly won't help Andrew. Now's not the time for emotion. We need to find out what is going on."

I took a deep breath, walked to the kitchen and took a long drink from a bottle of water.

"Alright, what would they do in Chicago?"

ELEVEN

"You're his lawyer and his friend. He seems to have a bit of a legal problem developing. This may be a bit too obvious, but call him and get moving on it. I know the Election Commission will talk to me, so I'll call them. I'll keep trying Andrew too"

"Yes, ma'am. I'm on it."

Anna Beth went off to find out what precincts were in question and I started making mental notes on what Andrew and I needed to discuss.

There was only one problem. I couldn't find him. His voicemail was full. Emails went unanswered, texts weren't returned and Rebecca had no idea where he was. He might actually be in a worst state than I first thought.

I heard nothing from Andrew through the day. The radio silence extended into the night.

I tried to get some work done at the office, but the phones wouldn't stop ringing and emails and texts were all about Andrew. When I got home that evening Anna Beth had an update.

"You're not alone. No one has heard from Andrew."

"No one meaning who?"

"Meaning no one. All the news stations have been trying to call him, the Election Commission has reached out several times. No one has heard from him. S. Bart is getting his challenge filed and then there will be a hearing. And, I guess, this means you haven't heard from him either?"

"Nothing.

I tried again. No answer. I had no explanation for his silence. I wouldn't have expected him to act this way even if he had lost, but he hadn't lost, he'd won and now all he had to do was stand up and claim his victory. Trouble was, he didn't seem to be interested in that process.

I didn't know what to think. Then I realized I wasn't upset, I was starting to get worried. I didn't like the feeling because until I heard from Andrew, there was nothing I could do to fix it.

#

The next morning I was in the office just before nine a.m. when I heard the door, but it was Ms. Laye.

I wasn't quite sure what to do. Pretty soon the phone calls would start about Andrew and I didn't have a good idea as to what I was going to tell people. I needed to check with Rebecca and see if she had heard from him. As I was reaching for my office phone, the text alert sounded on my phone.

"911 Anna Beth"

That couldn't be good. As I reached for the cell, it rang with Anna Beth's number.

"Oh, thank God, Noah. Did you hear from Andrew?"

"No, why, what's going on?"

"We have to get down to the Election Commission."

"Slow down. Slow down. What's going on?"

"I've been talking to one of the clerks there. We hit it off for whatever reason. Anyway, she called me just a few minutes ago and said that S. Bart had been able to get an expedited review hearing set because of the alleged violations. Anyway, they delivered notice to Andrew's house. The clerk said that all that needed be done was to leave it at the residence. Long and short of it is that the hearing starts in thirty minutes. If Andrew hasn't called you or me, well, I'm worried he doesn't know."

"Get in the car and meet me at the Election Commission."

I grabbed my keys and rushed out and was in the Jeep headed to North Charleston. Of course, traffic was not the least bit cooperative.

Thanks to road construction and a fender bender Anna Beth beat me.

She was waiting just outside of the commission door. As I hurried towards her, the door opened and S. Bart walked out.

"S. Bart, I don't know what you're playing at here, but this whole thing just doesn't feel right."

"Mr. Parks. Hope you're having a good day. Oh, by the way, that's Solicitor to you."

He flashed a politician's grin and turned to walk away with two attorneys in tow.

"Tell me you know what that was all about," I said to Anna Beth.

"Unfortunately, I do. You just saw our new solicitor."

"You have to be kidding me. What happened?"

"Turns out the news I learned was almost correct. The hearing was starting as I got the call. When I showed up and went in they were into the hearing. I tried to interrupt, but S. Bart objected and the Election Commission, well, they were very nice, but they told me that regardless of my being his campaign manager, only the candidate or his attorney was allowed to participate in the hearing. I asked them to wait for you, but S. Bart objected to that and the commissioners said they have no option but to proceed. And, well, since Andrew wasn't here they threw out the votes that S. Bart had questioned and it looks like he's the solicitor. Just like that."

Now I was really worried. And I had no idea how to salvage this election.

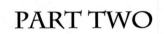

PART TWO

TWELVE

It wasn't like Andrew to just turn his back on something into which he'd invested so much. I'd told Ms. Laye to stay at the office in case he came by or called. Anna Beth was headed home to do the same. In a matter of moments after I left the office I was standing outside of the law offices of Andrew Stephens. I took a deep breath and opened the door.

Rebecca wasn't behind her desk. Rather she sat in the middle of a long couch in the lobby. She sat with her shoulders hunched, hands in her lap. She slowly raised her head.

"Noah, I'm worried."

"No need to be worried. He's probably just decided to lay low and let this blow over. He…"

"Don't try to make me feel like something's not wrong. This election was important to him, since I've known him he hasn't wanted anything more. He's not just lying low."

What could I say? She was completely right.

"I'm sorry. There has to be a simple answer to where he is. But you're right he wouldn't just stay away like this, not without a good reason. When's the last time you saw him?"

"Two days ago, at the office before his party. You?"

"Late election night. Has anyone you've talked to seen him since the election? Has he talked to anyone about it?"

"No one's said."

"I guess you've called him, or at least tried?"

"Home, cells, even here after hours. More times than I can count."

"And I take it he's had a lot of calls here?"

"Lots of them and everyone's asking the same thing."

The phone rang. She looked to me, then walked over to her desk.

"Law offices of Andrew Stephens. Yes. No, no sir, he's not here. I know, I have your message right here and I'll give it to him as soon as I see him. No sir, he's not avoiding you. No sir, I'm not lying to you. No sir, you can believe whatever you want, but as much as I'd love to let you talk to him, you can't because he's not here."

She was good, but if anyone knew where he was, I had a feeling it was Rebecca.

"Okay Rebecca. Where is he? Think. Where would he go?"

"I, I don't know. He's either here or home or in between. That's what he does."

I believed her.

"Just before the election, there was something on his mind, something that was bothering him. Any idea what it was? Maybe he decided to deal with that."

She looked at me and started to say something, but stopped.

"He, he, why is he not calling us back?"

That was a question I couldn't answer.

"Here's what we're going to do. You stay here, keep normal hours and keep doing what you are doing with the callers. Tell them Andrew's out, tell them he's busy and isn't taking calls. Think about anything he said or anything he had going on that may help. I'm going to drive over to his house. We both keep calling him. If one of us gets him, as soon as we do, call the other. Give me your number."

I handed her my cell phone and she dialed in her number. Then I called her so she'd have mine.

"His house, that's a good idea, I was thinking of that myself, but Noah, if we don't hear from him, then what?"

"We're going to hear from him."

"Thank you for coming."

I was surprised when she hugged me.

#

I pulled into Andrew's drive. In every window a closed plantation shutter. I tried calling again, but as had become the norm, no answer. I got out of the car and stood with my hands on my hips for a moment, then walked across to and looked in his garage. Cars both still there.

The small front porch was empty except for three days of newspapers. One for each day since the election. I walked around the side of the house to the backyard that not surprisingly, was also empty. Remembering my last visit, I looked to the back porch, only to find it empty. I could see into the house. With the big back windows and open floor plan I could see part of the kitchen and into the den.

Odd, there were still signs of the election night party. It looked like someone had started to clean up, but then stopped. The deck and porch were clean, but inside I could see empty glasses and cups scattered on the counter.

I walked out into the middle of the backyard again and looked up at the house. More plantation shutters. I heard a car door in the distance. Somewhere a dog barked. A dragonfly darted past, but otherwise, I stood in complete silence. I turned to face the house, studying the windows, curious if perhaps Andrew was watching me, but the shutters stood still.

"Damn it, Andrew, let me in."

But there was nothing in return.

THIRTEEN

For a moment, I was out of sorts. It was if I had been pulled from a dream, but as I awoke, I felt the memory of the dream slipping from my grasp. What it had been about eluded me. As my head cleared, I remembered the trip to Andrew's and his absence. That had been just, my God, yesterday.

Perhaps that had been the dream? However, I knew I couldn't be that lucky.

I checked my phone, but it hadn't rung all night. Not sure it that was good or bad news. I turned on the news just as the anchor was reporting Andrew was still MIA and S. Bart would enter office the following Monday. Andrew had won and we end up with S. Bart. Something had to be done and I'd need some assistance. I dialed the phone. Two rings and I heard Gabriel's voice.

"Little early to be calling on a Saturday morning, Parks."

"I know, but I need some help. Andrew's disappeared."

"Sure he's not just keeping to himself?"

"Disappeared, gone, no one knows where he is. Pick one. After the election, I'd give him a day or two and I certainly don't talk to him every day, but no one can find him. Hell, maybe vanished is a better word. Last anyone saw him was the night of the election."

"Okay, okay, I get your point. You called anyone else?"

"By anyone, you mean any other police?"

"Yes."

"No, no one."

"When's the last time you talked to him?"

"Election night, with you. Anna Beth and I were the last ones to leave the party."

"Okay, I'll come over and we'll decide how we hit this."

"See you in a few."

#

I heard Gabriel's voice downstairs.

Austin greeted him at the front door. "Hey boy," I heard in Gabriel's rich voice.

"Thanks for coming." We shook hands and I lead him to the kitchen. Anna Beth turned and smiled.

"Coffee?"

"Please and thank you."

She poured a cup and he took it from her with a smile. He blew on the surface of the liquid, causing steam to rise up before his face, pulled out a bar stool and perched under Austin's watchful eye.

"So, where is he?"

"I've got no idea," I said.

"Anna Beth, how often were you talking to him during the days up to the election?"

"Every day. Several times a day actually."

"And when you say you haven't heard from him since the election, is that a straight up haven't heard from him. No texts, calls, voicemails, missed calls, emails, heck, even carrier pigeons?"

"Nothing," Anna Beth and I said in unison. "No sign he's even been to his office."

"He call his office or has anyone there heard from him?"

"No. He has a college student who works there. She's been coming in to work like usual. He's had lots of calls, but she hasn't seen or heard from him."

"And he didn't show up at his hearing on Thursday either, the one on the contested votes," Anna Beth said.

"Unless he has someplace he would go to get away, I agree it's odd behavior in light of what's been going on. You don't put in the time he did and just disappear. But then again, he's a grown man and if he wants to disappear, he can. He have a vacation house or anything?"

"No."

"Then I agree, it is odd."

"I want to go over to his house and look around inside."

"You mean you want to go break in Andrew's and give the new solicitor his first case."

"Yeah, not your best idea," Anna Beth said.

I picked up my cell phone and dialed Rebecca.

"Hey. No, haven't heard anything. Listen, I have a friend here, a detective with the police department. Does

Andrew keep a spare key to his house at his office? We want to go over and take a look around his house. Good. Even better. Can you meet me at his office in twenty minutes? Great."

"Parks, what was that?"

"Yes. Who was that?"

"That was Rebecca, the college student who works for Andrew. She says there's a spare key and she has the code to his alarm. Can't have a break-in if you have a key and the code, can you? She's meeting us at his office. Let's go."

"I guess I need to make this coffee to go."

#

After a quick stop for the key, we arrived at Andrew's house. It looked the same as the day before and the countless other times I'd visited.

I walked to the road and looked up and down the street. Not sure what I was expecting to see or find, but it seemed like the logical thing to do. Gabriel was slowly walking around Andrew's garage.

"It rained the day after the election. There is still ground splatter on the garage door. This door hasn't been opened since then."

We stood a moment more then I took a step toward the front porch. I felt a hand on my shoulder.

"Wait a minute there. Let's have a look around, but let's do it the right way. If we see anything unusual, we call the Mount Pleasant Police. Remember you're worried about your friend. I am too, but if something's happened, I don't want to compromise a crime scene. You hear me?"

"Crime scene?"

"I hope not, but till we know different, we treat it like it is."

I was already up the steps to the door.

"Yes, I hear you."

"Then wait a minute."

He walked to his car, opened the trunk and returned with two pairs of latex gloves.

"Put these on."

I reached out and took them from Gabriel's hand. Surreal doesn't come close to describing how I felt putting on gloves as I was going into my friend's house.

FOURTEEN

On the front porch, I looked down to see things as they had been last time I was over, only with the addition of one more newspaper. The key was smooth as silk in the lock. The door swung inward and I stepped over the papers in the doorway. Gabriel followed, closing the door behind him.

I took a step toward the alarm system and reached out a hand towards the keypad.

"Wait a minute Parks. Listen."

"For what?"

"Just listen."

Then I realized it. "The alarm panel. It's not beeping."

The display screen read, 'Ready to arm."

"System wasn't armed. He normally leave without turning it on?"

"I wouldn't think so. He got it after some kids in the neighborhood started breaking into homes."

We stood in silence for a few moments. I could hear the ticking of the antique grandfather clock in Andrew's study echoing each second. From the kitchen, I heard the ice machine drop new cubes. Despite the cool outside, I heard the air conditioner come on. But other than these normal sounds, the house was silent.

"Okay, you look around upstairs, I'll look down here. Don't touch anything."

I nodded and headed up the stairs. I looked in the three bedrooms, the bathroom, Andrew's large media room, and upstairs office. Nothing. Just to be complete, I looked in them all again on the way down, even under the beds. Everything looked perfectly normal, nothing out of place. All of the beds were even made.

"Parks, down here."

I hurried downstairs and found Gabriel in the den standing over the coffee table pointing at a piece of paper.

"What's this?" I reached out for it and he caught my hand.

"Don't touch it."

I crouched and studied it.

"It's the list of people he was considering for his deputies. But it's not the one he had Tuesday night."

"What do you mean?"

I pointed to the document, "You see where my name's crossed off? He showed me a list on Tuesday night with my name on it here where it says, 'Chief Deputy,' but I crossed it off and wrote in another name. This list just has my name crossed off with no name written in and it's been crossed off with a red sharpie. I used my pen. And this one isn't folded. Andrew folded the one I gave him and put it in his pocket."

"You sure?"

"Positive."

"Okay, I'm starting to get a bad feeling on this. You notice anything out of place?"

"No, everything was normal upstairs and…"

There was the sound of a sharp snap.

Gabriel and I looked at each other, then our eyes looked to the floor. Gabriel had stepped on a fragment of glass and broken it. We looked across the floor. Beyond the fragment Gabriel had stepped on, there were more leading to the largest fragment, the base of a broken glass on the hearth of the fireplace.

"Okay, we're leaving and calling Mount Pleasant PD. Come on."

I turned to go, but stopped as my gaze crossed to the kitchen.

"Hang on."

"Come on, Parks."

I walked into the kitchen and looked down. The sky outside had become overcast as was common for late lowcountry summers. Clouds would roll in and make a sunny day instantly seem like twilight. If you were indoors, rooms could quickly grow dim even in the middle of the day. When we'd first come in Andrew's house it had been such a sunny day, but the clouds instantly made the kitchen dark. Otherwise I wouldn't have noticed the light on the floor. It was but a narrow sliver, but just enough to catch my eye. I followed it to the pantry, the door just slightly ajar. I walked over to the door and opened it with my foot.

"Damn," Gabriel said from behind me.

I'd found Andrew and it didn't take much to see that more than his political days were over.

FIFTEEN

I stood out in Andrew's backyard looking out to the harbor and Charleston beyond. If a time traveler from a century back had joined me, the view would've still seemed familiar. Some things in Charleston were slow to change, but that isn't the case when it involves the unexpected death of a close friend. I couldn't begin to get my head around the fact Andrew was gone.

I was left with an image of Andrew hanging in his pantry, an overturned stool beneath his feet. That was going to follow me a while. I knew what was going to be said and I refused to believe he'd killed himself over an election.

"Hey."

I looked around and saw Gabriel coming toward me. I didn't speak.

"They got him out and went through the house. Doesn't look like anything was taken, though they were a little interested in why we decided to drop by today."

"And you told them what?"

"Don't worry, I should've said 'interested at first.' They hadn't realized you were as close to the election as you were. They're going to have their crime scene techs go over the place and then they'll talk to the neighbors, but it looks like a pretty clear-cut case of suicide at this point."

"Bullshit. There's no way Andrew killed himself. Not over an election."

"Parks, I know Andrew was your friend, but think about it. You said he'd been acting odd. Maybe he wouldn't do this over an election, but would someone really do a murder in a county solicitor's race? Was the election the only thing going on with his life? I mean, can you say that for sure?"

"He didn't kill himself."

"Let'em work. There'll be an autopsy and hopefully some answers, but for now, let's go."

"Give me a few minutes, okay. I'll meet you out front."

"Sure thing. Take your time."

I watched him walk back toward the house. A man I didn't recognize met him at the back porch. He had gloves and was holding an iPad. No uniform, just a sports coat and a tie. Probably a detective. He and Gabriel walked back into the house.

I looked at the panoramic view that was downtown Charleston and the serenity that was the harbor. I reached into my pocket and pulled out my cell phone. Rebecca. Three missed calls. I held my thumb over her number then decided it would be better to tell her in person. I looked out over the water one more time, then turned and walked back around the side of the house to Gabriel's car where he joined me. As we were driving down the street away from Andrew's home, a county deputy sheriff passed us, lights on, headed towards Andrew's house.

"What's that all about?" I said.

"What?"

"The deputy sheriff."

"Mount Pleasant got a call from our new solicitor. He wants the county to look into things, just to keep him posted."

"At least he seems to be taking his job seriously."

The rest of the way we rode in silence.

I replayed my last conversation with Andrew over and over in my head.

"I promise we'll talk tomorrow."

That was what Andrew had said to me just before I left his house the night of the election. Not that I would expect him to say, "Don't worry you're right, something is bad wrong, but it will be okay, I'm just going to kill myself tonight," but people were predictable. If he'd been planning to do himself harm, no way he would have said that. And that was all I needed to know to confirm he didn't take his own life.

"You want me to come up?" Gabriel said as we pulled in my drive.

"No, thanks though."

"Call me if you need anything."

"Thanks, Gabriel. You're a saint to put up with me."

"Believe me, I know."

"I'll call you soon. I've got to give a few people some bad news."

SIXTEEN

Glancing at my watch as I walked to the front door, I saw I'd been gone almost five hours. Austin came walking out of the living room, yawning, tail wagging. Anna Beth was sitting at the dining room table just off of the living room with her computer open and papers spread out before her.

"Hey. I was getting worried about you. I got wrapped up in all of this and didn't realize till just a bit ago how long you've been gone. I think that there is something off with the reports of improper ballots, and," she looked at me and paused. "Noah, what's wrong?"

"Andrew's dead."

She didn't say anything. She got up, walked to me and took my hand.

"What happened?"

"Gabriel and I were looking around his house. There were some things that bothered him and we were getting ready to leave, to call the police. It had gotten dark outside from the clouds and I saw a light from his pantry. I opened the pantry door and he was hanging there."

"Oh my God, Noah, that's terrible. Why would he…"

"That's the same thing I asked. I just don't think he would do it. Kill himself, I mean."

"Are they sure?"

"They're having the Mount Pleasant Police look at things and a deputy sheriff was coming as we were leaving, but I think they want to believe it."

"You knew him better than me, but killing yourself over an election?"

"I know. I can't stop wondering if something other than the election was going on."

She hugged me. I put my arm around her and told myself that I didn't need to get emotional. We sat in silence.

Everything from the day played out in my head, again.

"Listen, I need to run out for a bit. I should to go tell his assistant, Rebecca. I don't want to just call her and if I don't tell her, she'll find out from the paper and Andrew wouldn't want that," I paused. "Want to come with me?"

"No, you go and you're right, she needs to hear it from someone she knows."

"I'll be back as soon as I can."

I stood and pulled her up from the couch, pulling her close to me as I did.

"I love you."

#

The day, after threatening rain, had turned out to be beautiful. The sky held a hue of deep blue. The temperature drop cut the late season humidity. None of that was going to make the next ten minutes anything other than painful. I'd parked at my office hoping the walk would give me time to decide what to say to Rebecca, but nothing came to me. I stood before Andrew's office as a crowd of tourists walked by, oblivious to was about to occur just feet away.

I walked through the front door into what had been Andrew's office. Rebecca looked up from her desk and immediately stood. She was looking over my shoulder, eager anticipation painted on her face. She was looking for something, for a face, a face that wasn't there and wasn't going to be ever again.

"He's not there."

"Where is he?"

"Gone."

I walked in and stood a few feet away from her in front her desk. She stared at me in silence, her eager look fading.

"What do you mean gone?"

"He's dead, Rebecca."

As I said the words, I realized that before today I'd never told anyone that someone they knew were dead and now I'd done it twice in the same day.

Rebecca stared at me then a tear ran down her cheek. Her hands went to her face and she collapsed into her chair and began to sob. I stepped around her desk and put my hand on her shoulder. A million thoughts ran through my mind about what to say or what to do, but I kept them all to myself and stood there in silence.

I stood beside her until her hand came away from her face and touched mine. She stood and without saying a word wrapped her arms around me and buried her face on my shoulder and continued to sob.

We stood like this for a very long moment. Suddenly, she pulled away, wiped her eyes and quickly walked down the hall toward Andrew's office, disappearing inside without a word. I waited by myself, then, partly out of curiosity, partly out of concern, walked down the hall and stuck my head in Andrew's office. No sign of her. I walked in and sat on the couch until Rebecca appeared from Andrew's bathroom. She walked across the room and sat in a chair opposite me.

"Noah, I'm sorry about how I acted."

"Rebecca, there's no need to apologize."

"I shouldn't have behaved like that. I'm sorry I cried."

"Stop it. He was our friend. I'm upset and you can be too. You should be. I'd be worried if you weren't."

"That's sweet of you, but you don't need me crying on your shoulder."

"I'm actually glad it was my shoulder you were crying on. I'd rather it was me and not a stranger who told you, or worse, heard it on the news."

She wiped her eyes again and sat up in her chair.

"What happened?"

"What will you hear happened or what do I believe happened?"

"Both."

"You'll be hearing he killed himself. I believe that's the last possible explanation."

"There's no way he would've killed himself. Not with everything going on," she slammed her clenched fist against her knee.

"I completely agree …"

"No, no, no, he wouldn't have done this. There's no way," she had risen from the couch, her hands both clenched, held tight against her side.

"You and I feel the same way, we both knew him, we both knew what he was like, and, I…"

"Noah, I need to go."

"Sorry?"

"I have to leave."

"Is everything okay? I mean I know everything isn't okay, but, well, you know what I mean."

"No, I, I just need to be alone. I have to go. You can stay, but I guess I need to lock up."

"No, I'll go. You sure you're okay."

"I just need to be alone."

I followed her in silence out of Andrew's office. The late afternoon sun shone brightly in our faces. Rebecca raised a hand to block the light.

"Thanks for coming by. That means a lot. You're right, I wouldn't have wanted to hear about it from a stranger."

"Call me if you need anything. I mean that."

She hugged me again and kissed me lightly on the cheek.

"Thank you."

She turned and walked down the street. I watched her until she disappeared around the corner. At least she knew about Andrew. I found myself wishing she'd been at the election party so she could've seen him one last time. Odd, I thought, odd she hadn't been there. I contemplated going after her to ask her but thought better of it. I'd ask her another time.

I turned and walked back to my car and headed home.

SEVENTEEN

Anna Beth was waiting for me. "How is she?"

I sat down on the couch, careful not to disturb the large canine napping to my right.

"I really don't know. I walked in and wasn't sure how to tell her, so I just did. She stood up and started to sob, then hugged me before she ran off to Andrew's office and disappeared into his bathroom. After a bit, she came out and we talked for a few minutes. I expected her to be upset, and she was, but there was something else, something odd. I can't really put my finger on it, but something was a little off."

"What did she say?"

"Basically, the same thing I've been thinking. There was no way that Andrew would have killed himself. Anyway, after a few minutes of talking, she left."

Anna Beth walked over and shooed Austin off of the couch. He left with a grunt, jumping onto the other couch, lying down with his usual sigh. Anna Beth kissed me on the cheek.

"Noah, she's what? Twenty, maybe twenty-one? It wouldn't be a stretch to have this be her first experience with someone dying. I've been thinking some too. Want to hear?"

"Of course I do."

She shifted to face me as she always did whenever she was about to get serious.

"Maybe Andrew did do this to himself. Not for the election, some other reason. People let all kinds of things bother them and everyone handles it differently."

"Gabriel said the same thing."

"Whatever it was, it wasn't your fault."

"Gabriel said that too. It's just such a shock."

"The police, they'll look at other things he had going on, won't they?" I just nodded my head. "Maybe you'll still find out what it was that he wanted to talk about."

"Maybe."

"It's never easy to lose a friend. I couldn't imagine it if I lost you, I …"

"I'm sorry?"

"I just mean, well, I'm happy now. With us."

"Me too," I said.

#

Rebecca didn't show up at Andrew's funeral, which was odd, but then again there are a lot of people who don't like funerals. Me being one, but I was there.

The turnout was overwhelming. Our new solicitor and his wife were in attendance. The church, St. Michael's, was overflowing.

To add what I felt was insult to injury, our new solicitor spoke at the funeral. His words were kind and resonated of a life cut short, of a dedicated advocate who worked tirelessly for his clients. Sincere, but for the politician who, except for Andrew's death, would have lost an election, the words sounded hollow. He even mentioned that in the balance there was little that would warrant the loss of such a life, particularly not an election.

Listening to him, I was left with the feeling he believed Andrew had been murdered. I found it interesting. He seemed to be the one person who agreed with me. Andrew's death wasn't a suicide.

After the service, graveside, they moved from small group to small group. In each, the solicitor let it be known he was going to get to the bottom of what happened and, if it wasn't a suicide, see Andrew's killer in jail. I thought it rather offensive he was practically politicizing Andrew's death, but what could I do?

Anna Beth and I were talking with several attorneys who knew Andrew when she squeezed my hand and whispered in my ear.

"Noah, he's coming this way."

I spied the solicitor and his wife walking in our direction. I looked to escape but as he saw me look away, he quickened his pace.

"Noah. Noah. May I have a moment?"

I smiled as he stopped in front of me. The other attorneys walked away.

"Certainly. I'm not sure if you've met Anna Beth Cross. Anna Beth, our new solicitor."

"The pleasure is all mine, Ms. Cross. Allow me to introduce my wife, Tamara Michaels."

"Pleasure, Ms. Cross, Mr. Parks," she said. "Such tragic circumstances. A tragedy. I understand you and Mr. Stephens were close, quite close."

An odd comment, I thought.

"He was my friend, one of my oldest friends. He'll be missed."

"Oh, just a friend," she said.

There was an awkward moment. Anna Beth smiled, nodded and was about to speak when the solicitor suddenly turned his attention to me.

He stepped closer, placing a hand on my shoulder.

"I want you to know I'm truly sorry about Andrew's death. He was a great man, a fine attorney and an excellent candidate."

"So you said."

Anna Beth gripped my hand tighter and pulled closer to me. I glanced to her and saw a look in her eye that said, 'Smile, he'll leave soon.'

The solicitor tightened his grip on my shoulder. His wife's stare was fixed directly into my eyes. I was caught completely off guard by the encounter.

"Noah, don't you worry, I'll soon tell the story of what happened to Andrew," then he stepped even closer, placing his mouth near my ear. "I will tell the story."

He paused a moment stepped back, turned and walked away. His wife was on his heels, but stopped and turned.

"You two take care now," she said, then turned and followed the solicitor.

"What was that about?" Anna Beth said.

"I have no idea."

#

I'd hoped after the funeral things would start to get back to normal, but such thought was little more than folly.

The news outlets were still reporting suicide. Though Andrew's death happened in Mount Pleasant and was in the jurisdiction of their police department, the solicitor wasn't content having only a sheriff liaison. He now had them handling the entire investigation. His justification was that as Andrew had been a candidate for his office, a county agency needed to investigate, with his office coordinating. He didn't have any authority to do this, but with all the attention being focused on the case, the Mount Pleasant Police didn't blink an eye when he took the case.

Nothing like exploiting tragedy for personal gain.

Little did I know things were about to escalate in ways I couldn't even imagine.

PART THREE

EIGHTEEN

I was arrested.

I was arrested for Andrew's murder.

I was booked into the jail.

And there I sat.

I shared my jail cell, a six-by-eight concrete-and-steel box, with three other men. The cell offered zero comfort. The concrete wall protrusions that served as beds were already occupied by two other inmates upon my arrival. A third had arrived two days later. After five days, I didn't know their names. Didn't want to.

I slept on the floor under the bottom bunk.

I'd seen the cop shows like everyone else. I thought I knew what jail was like. The reality wasn't even close.

Lots of correctional officers, or COs, complaining about long hours and low pay. Lots of pissed-off inmates complaining about how they shouldn't be locked up, blaming everyone else. Spending every moment of their time trying to target some other inmate to exploit. Add to that bad food and boredom and, well, you get the picture. There's lots of cigarette smoke. So much cigarette smoke. And the smell, you can't imagine the smell. To counter the aroma, the temperature was kept at around sixty-five degrees. It was always cold.

And every day is the same as the one before. My head was starting to hurt from looking over my shoulder.

On the morning of my sixth day inside, the new arrival sleeping in the middle of my cell's floor, rose, stretched and then started to urinate into the stainless-steel toilet. Feet appeared on the floor from the lower bunk above my head and walked towards the toilet. I stayed below my bunk, gazing out. The man from the bunk looked down at me, making momentary eye contact. I held his gaze till he looked away.

"Look here," Bottom Bunk said, "Floor Boy's up."

"Seems like they'd clean this place up a bit," I heard a voice from above say. That would be Top Bunk. Bottom Bunk turned and punched Floor Boy even though he was still urinating. This caused Floor Boy to double over in pain as he collapsed to the floor.

Bottom Bunk stepped over him taking a place at the urinal.

"Used to be some attention to detail around here," Top Bunk said as he jumped down and landed beside the crumpled man on the floor. I noticed a tattoo. I'd seen it earlier and wondered why someone would have a computer monitor tattoo on his bicep, but I wasn't about to ask.

#

My first night in the detention center, the "House" as it's known in Charleston, had been spent in an intake holding cell. The House has an open booking process, meaning while you're being processed, if you behave, you wait in what looks pretty much like a garden variety lobby, albeit it with guards and bars.

The guards are there to enforce what amounts to two rules: sit still, and be quiet. Simple as they were, they gave some people difficulty.

That group included me.

I was pretty vocal when I arrived at the jail, having gone from disbelief to really pissed-off on the ride from my house. Turns out I was vocal and uncooperative enough to completely ignore both rules. I ended up in a holding cell with about twenty other equally pissed-off recent arrivals, a lovely bunch.

I decided it was necessary to bang on the door and announce my innocence. A man who was easily the largest in the cell approached me.

"You wanna shut the fuck up?" he said.

Mistaking the man's question as interest, I took a deep breath to better summarize my innocence but before I could say word one, he punched me in the Adam's apple. I know it was a punch because I saw his fist on the way back from colliding with my throat. I sank to my knees, clutching my throat, gasping for breath.

"You got anything else you wanna get off your chest?" he said to a cell full of laughter.

Since then, other than my single phone call, I hadn't uttered a word.

NINETEEN

I'd been sitting in the jail for near a week doing what most everyone else did inside. I was thinking about what got me here.

Andrew Stephens was, or had been, my friend. The idea I could kill him was, or should have been ridiculous. To anyone.

When news broke that Andrew's death had been reclassified a homicide, the solicitor made a huge production out of prioritizing the apprehension and prosecution of his former opponent's killer. After all, that's what the solicitor was supposed to do and who was I to fault him for doing his job?

Trouble was, I was completely unprepared for where S. Bart's prosecutorial crosshairs came to rest. Perhaps the scene at Andrew's funeral with his wife should have clued me in.

The reality in most murders is that most killers are quite close to their victims. And here is where the reality of the situation began to impact me. Andrew wasn't married. Andrew didn't have nearby family.

But he did have a close friend.
Me.

The combination of my close relationship and two otherwise seemingly innocuous facts – an election night exchange between Andrew and I, and my having been the last to see him the night of his death – took me from being a friend to murder suspect in the span of a few days.

The solicitor wasn't interested in my thoughts on the case. He didn't care about anything but being able to spin his theory of a murder into probable cause for my arrest.

And he'd done just that and once you're charged with murder, it takes more than an expression of disbelief or a proclamation of innocence to make it go away.

#

The feel of handcuffs being placed on your wrists is something for which you can never fully prepare. The scene outside of my house had changed in the time Gabriel had been inside. All three police cars had their lights on and two television vans had arrived and bright lights from several cameras poured into my yard. More than one neighbor was on their front porch to watch. Why wouldn't they be? It's not every day the lawyer next door gets arrested.

One of the deputies reached for me, but Gabriel pushed his hand away and lead me to one of the police cars with the back door open.

"Keep your head down and your mouth shut." Gabriel said.

I could still hear Austin barking as we drove off. Hopefully Anna Beth would get back soon to take care of him.

And me.

#

I moved from under the bunk to the back of the cell as the door opened. Top and Bottom Bunk strutted out. Floor Man rose and scurried off without looking at me. I followed, careful to avoid the urine on the floor.

Breakfast. Eggs and bacon with dry toast. No surprise. I quickly ate, then wandered out into the common area, taking a seat at an unoccupied table.

"Let me see your bracelet," a voice said.

A guard stood over me. I raised my arm and he scanned my jail ID bracelet.

"Come with me," the guard said after consulting his scanner.

I stood and followed. He escorted me to a door and moved aside as it opened. He put handcuffs on me before he shut the door behind me.

After a brief walk, we stopped at a drab cinder block wall punctuated with a row of doors. Over one was the word "Legal." The guard opened it to reveal a small room, empty but for a cheap plastic chair. The far wall had a small ledge and from the ledge almost to the ceiling was a thick pane of clear glass. Sitting beyond, in a mirror image of my room, was my attorney. I stepped inside and the door shut behind me.

"I've always wondered. How's the view from that side?" Warren Brady said.

"Crappy. Tell me I'm leaving soon."

Warren Brady, a local Charleston criminal defense attorney, was widely considered one of the best in the state. Being considered the best also meant one of the most expensive. He was tall and slender with a friendly smile. Juries loved him. Outside the courtroom, Brady was aloof and perhaps a bit arrogant. There were whispers around the courthouse that despite being married, he was a womanizer, but he knew criminal law, got results and, best of all, was one of the few who worked well with the solicitor. It wouldn't surprise me if he had aspirations to the solicitor's job or perhaps elected office beyond even that. He was exactly what I needed.

"I'm flattered you, or should I say, your girlfriend, contacted me. I did some background for you and I won't sugarcoat things. You're in a bit of a pickle here. Though I must say, I never thought I'd see Noah Parks on the wrong side of the House. Candidly, I thought there had been a mistake when the paper reported your arrest."

"Makes two of us, but we can get into the details later. For now, I'd like to see my girlfriend, my dog, my shower, and my bed."

"Fair enough. I've already requested a bail reconsideration hearing. You know as well as I you're not guaranteed bail, but without a record, I'm pretty sure your days here are numbered, and a small number at that. The solicitor isn't holding back, but I don't think that will keep us from bail. He's being a bit dramatic at the moment, that's the reason you've had a "no contact" hold keeping visitors away. Ms. Cross asked that I let you know she was on the next flight back and Austin is well. She would've told you herself, but wasn't able to do so."

"Thought that may be the case with no visitors or phone calls. When's my hearing?"

"This afternoon."

"Anna Beth knows?"

"She does and I'll make sure she's there."

TWENTY

After I returned from meeting my attorney, I was transported along with fifteen other inmates to the Charleston County Courthouse. So we'd be missing lunch. No big loss. I'd never liked bologna sandwiches. I couldn't speak for the others.

From the transport, the prisoners were placed in the courthouse's secure basement holding area and there we waited. After several hours, two deputies chained us all together, then led us upstairs to our assigned courtroom. They moved us through a somewhat private section of the courthouse, but I still passed several attorneys and judges I knew. Thankfully no one seemed to recognize me.

Or at least they were considerate enough not to stare.

Courtrooms aren't loud places, but there is almost always a background buzz. However, when I walked in, the buzz immediately ceased. The attention I didn't get on the way to the courtroom was more than made up for as I felt the eyes land upon me as I made my way to my seat. Brady was sitting at one of the two counsel tables. In the gallery behind him was Anna Beth. She moved forward in her seat and flashed a nervous smile as we made eye contact. I tried, but could barely muster a grin.

A quick glance around the courtroom told me the usual suspects--other attorneys and courthouse personnel--weren't the only ones interested in my bail hearing. Generally, for these hearings the gallery was all but empty. That wasn't the case today. Seemed an attorney being charged with murder is enough to draw a crowd. I did a double take as, in the back, I spied Tamara Michaels. Odd she would be here. I looked around but didn't see S. Bart.

Apparently, a simple matter such as a bond reduction hearing wasn't enough to bring S. Bart down from his office several floors above. An assistant solicitor sat at the opposing counsel table.

I looked to the bench and saw Judge Paul Sutcliffe. I hung my head in embarrassment. A month before I'd been a guest at his daughter's wedding.

A deputy approached the judge's law clerk and whispered in his ear. The clerk in turn spoke to the judge who looked my direction.

"Noah Parks," the Judge said.

It had been law school since the sound of my name stoked fear in the pit of my stomach.

I was shocked back to reality as another deputy sprang to his feet, unlocked me from the rest of the prisoners and escorted me to a chair at Brady's side.

"Mr. Brady," Judge Sutcliffe said. "I see we're here on your motion for bail reconsideration. Murder case I see. Andrew Stephens."

"Yes, Your Honor, that's correct," Brady said.

"Very well, does the solicitor have any objection to bail?"

"Your Honor, if it please the court," the assistant solicitor said. "Albert Norris for the State. We don't oppose bail, per se, but feel due to the nature of the crime, the public attention that's been drawn to this matter, and the fact there's substantial evidence connecting the defendant to the crime, bail, if any, must be substantial. I would like to point out that the defendant is a member of the bar and all appearances of impropriety must strongly be avoided. Further, Mr. Parks is romantically involved with a woman of substantial wealth giving him access to significant financial resources. Additionally..."

"Sounds like you're opposing bail, Mr. Norris," Judge Sutcliffe said as Norris started to speak again, though he stopped as Sutcliffe raised his hand. "Let me ask you this. Did Mr. Parks surrender himself or did you have to go get him?"

"The sheriff had to go track him down, your Honor," Norris said.

That was a lie.

I shuffled in my seat then turned to Brady, but he stopped me with a hand on my arm just as I'd done with countless clients myself. It meant calm down and shut the hell up. I returned my hands to my lap and my gaze to the judge.

"Counsel, let me say I'm bothered the sheriff had to, how did you say it, Mr. Norris, 'go track him down?' Now, Mr. Brady, since this is your motion, tell me why your client deserves bail."

Brady rose and started to speak, but was cut off by the judge.

"I'm sorry, Mr. Brady. Mr. Norris, one more question," said the judge. "The sheriff's office did contact Mr. Parks and give him the chance to surrender himself, didn't they?"

"Um, I don't think they did, Your Honor."

"I see, so when you say the sheriff had to go track him down, we can't really say the defendant was avoiding arrest now can we?"

"No, Your Honor, we can't."

"Glad you could clear that up for us, Mr. Norris. The defendant have a criminal record?"

"No, Your Honor, no criminal record," Norris replied, a notch in volume lower.

"Thank you. So, Mr. Brady, I'll be happy to hear from you now."

"Thank you, Your Honor. Mr. Parks is a well-respected member of the local bar and a long-time Charleston resident with, as Mr. Norris pointed out, no record. While the solicitor may say there's strong evidence, the solicitor is the only one who knows what this evidence might be. Mr. Parks owns property here in town and presents zero flight risk. When the police visited Mr. Parks at his home, without advance notice, in the middle of the night, he let them inside and went without incident. Seems someone was thoughtful enough to let the press know about the arrest, so should Your Honor have any questions about the arrest, I have a DVD."

Sutcliffe looked at Brady and then at Norris, who had taken a sudden interest in his notepad.

"DVD of the arrest you say?" Sutcliffe said.

"Yes, Your Honor," Brady said, then paused as Sutcliffe looked back to Norris again.

"Please continue, Mr. Brady," The judge leaned back and made a temple of his fingers under his chin.

"Thank you, Your Honor. As a result of Mr. Parks' being an attorney, he'll be instrumental in his defense and, if forced to remain incarcerated, his defense will suffer. We aren't asking for him to be released on his own recognizance, but we feel the totality of the circumstances should allow for Mr. Parks to have the opportunity to post a reasonable bond."

"Thank you, Mr. Brady. Mr. Solicitor, if I look at that DVD, what time will I see that the sheriff went to get the defendant?"

"I'm not sure, Your Honor."

"It was just before midnight, Judge," Brady said.

"Your Honor, if I may," Norris said.

"No, you may not," Sutcliffe said. "Is there any family here on behalf of the victim?"

"No, there's no one here, Your Honor," Norris said. "The victim's closest relationship outside of work has been charged with his murder."

"That'll be enough, Mr. Solicitor."

"Yes, sir." Norris took his seat.

Sutcliffe retrieved a sheet of paper from an accordion file folder and started to write.

"Bail's set at $250,000. Cash, surety, or bond. Good luck to you, Mr. Parks."

The courtroom buzz returned and continued to grow in volume though I couldn't tell if the buzz was support for me or disdain at my being granted bail.

Brady turned to face me, and with a smile placed a hand on my shoulder.

"You know the drill. Hold tight till you get back to the jail," Brady looked over his shoulder to Anna Beth. "I'll have you ready to go by the time you get back and I'm sure you'll have a ride waiting. Take a day or two to let things settle, call my office, then we'll meet."

"Thanks, Warren. A lot."

I looked to Anna Beth who smiled at me. This time I was happy to smile back. Behind her stood S. Bart. He met my gaze, then turned and left the courtroom. I didn't see his wife.

#

The balance of the afternoon was spent in the courthouse holding area. It was uncomfortable and painfully silent. Not a lot of conversation. Some of us were going home, others not. After several hours, a deputy appeared at the door and not a word was spoken as we lined up and headed to the transport van.

On the way back to the jail, as I watched the city move outside the window. I wanted to smile--knowing I would be out of jail soon--but I couldn't, I wouldn't. I was going home, but, I'd lost a good friend and Charleston had lost a good man. The city didn't feel as alive today as I was used to and it was certainly nothing to be happy about.

#

I was placed in a small holding cell at the jail. After several hours, I was starting to think I'd been forgotten when the door unceremoniously opened.

"Parks," a deputy said in monotone as he thrust a small stack of papers in my direction. "You're being released on bail. Conditions set out by the court apply. Follow all instructions and appear at all hearings. If you have an attorney, make sure to stay in touch with him. Gotta put on the cuffs to escort you out. We'll stop by Property to pick up any of your items we have."

I took the papers, he turned me around and put handcuffs on me. I felt their uncomfortable bite for what I hoped was the last time.

He led me to the property room where he opened the door and motioned for me to go in. The property clerk inside pointed to a chair. The two deputies exchanged papers and my escort was gone.

"Sit tight and I'll get your property."

He disappeared and soon returned carrying a large paper grocery bag with my name and inmate number handwritten on the side.

"Take this and go into that room there. Hands through the small door and I'll uncuff you. Change and put your prison issues in the chute. When you're done, I'll buzz you through to the exit chamber and let the door guard know you're ready to go."

I picked up the bag he'd tossed at my feet and walked through the door holding the bag behind my back. I dropped it and put my hands through the space in the door where he removed my cuffs. I quickly changed from the prison clothes into the clothes I'd been wearing when arrested. I found a quarter in the bag. When I was through, I banged on the door and yelled.

"Done."

A moment later, I heard a buzzing sound. The door in front of me opened revealing another small room with doors to my left and right. A camera was mounted over each door. I closed the door behind me. A light flashed on the camera to my left. The door beneath it opened, I stepped through. I found myself in the lobby of the jail as I rubbed my wrists.

There were children screaming and running all about. People were crowded around the information desk. Another line formed behind a single pay phone in the lobby off to the left. Now I knew what the quarter was for. I stepped towards the line for the phone when the crowd cleared slightly.

Anna Beth stood not ten feet away. I rushed to her and took her in my arms, kissed her.

We were soon back home. Austin greeted us at the door, but as soon as we walked through and I shut the door, Anna Beth wrapped her arms around my neck and pulled me close.

"I missed you."

"Me too."

With Austin in tow, we moved into the living room and collapsed on the couch.

"Noah, what's happening?"

"Right now I don't know. The solicitor's decided that I killed Andrew and, well, that's what Brady's going to help us with."

She pulled closer to me, burying her head against my shoulder. Austin rested his chin on my knee. With one hand I brushed Anna Beth's hair and with the other I petted Austin's head.

Now, if I could only keep things like this.

TWENTY-ONE

The next morning I was lying on my back looking at the trees outside the bedroom window. The morning's light painted the oaks a golden shade of amber. Anna Beth lay to my side.

"That's beautiful."

"What?"

"The sun on the trees. It's gorgeous."

"Noah, it's the same that it's always been."

"After a week as a guest of Charleston county, it takes on a whole new meaning. I can't even imagine what it's like to someone who's been in for even longer."

We stayed in bed through the morning. Austin must have sensed we didn't want to be bothered because he stayed quiet, not even whining for food. I wanted to ignore all of the problems facing me, all of the things that were happening.

Finally, I rolled out of bed.

"Be right back."

I went down stairs and called Brady. He was in court, but I was told that he'd left instructions that I be given an appointment the next day. I hung up the phone and dialed Gabriel. He answered on the first ring.

"Good morning."

"I heard you were out. How you doing?"

"I'm out of jail. Appointment with Brady tomorrow morning. You hear anything?"

"Hang on a minute, let me walk out of the squad room." I heard footsteps as I waited. "There, that's better. I haven't heard anything other than the solicitor's going full steam, but as for news, it's all crickets. Glad to hear Brady's on your side. He's good."

"That's what I was thinking when I went with him. Alright, I wanted to call and let you know I was okay. Thanks for taking care of Austin."

"Anytime."

"And Gabriel?"

"Yes?"

"Thanks for not asking me if I did it."

"Thanks for not saying you didn't."

#

Anna Beth was still in bed when I got back upstairs.

"Everything okay?"

"I wanted to let Gabriel know I was back and we have an appointment with Brady in the morning."

I sat on the side of the bed, my back to her. She rose up to her knees, moved behind me and wrapped her arms around my shoulders.

"What was it like having Gabriel arrest you?"

"Strange, but that really didn't bother me. I mostly spent the last week wondering how the solicitor ever put together enough evidence for an arrest warrant. Gabriel didn't know much then and doesn't know much more now."

"When he told me, I thought he was joking."

"No one knows S. Bart as a solicitor, but if he goes about it anything like he did in private practice, he won't make it easy beating this thing."

"I can handle tough, just as long as you win and he loses."

She put her head on my shoulder and I pulled her close.

#

I was in no rush for the meeting with Brady. I was happy to be home, but despite being in my own bed with Anna Beth, the little sleep I found was not peaceful. While I was eager to start my defense, I was also dreading the appointment. I was supposed to counsel, not defend myself.

The ride to Brady's office took us the same route I traveled each time I drove to my office. In fact, his office was only few blocks away, so Anna Beth and I parked at my office. I hoped the walk over would help to clear my head and focus.

When Charleston first emerged in the 1700's the downtown existed largely to support the shipping trade and the downtown area then hadn't been exactly what you would call postcard fodder or even family friendly—think sailors with money in their pockets. The main commercial goal was to separate the two as quickly as possible and the tried-and-true formula for this was wine and women mixed with gambling, then more women and wine. Not exactly the kind of activities that drew the mainstream tourist crowd.

But the times had changed.

While the goal was still to separate visitors from their dollars, the merchants liked to impress and give value for those dollars. Many of the shops were in historic buildings that had been converted from shipping warehouses, trade shops, and the like, to more modern uses.

After a short walk, Anna Beth and I found ourselves standing outside of one of the more historic buildings as we headed down Atlantic Wharf towards Prioleau Street. Visually it probably hadn't changed much since it was first built. The street was still cobblestone.

Beside a pair of large imposing mahogany doors was a nondescript brass placard with raised lettering, a hallmark of Charleston attorneys, reading, "Warren Brady, Attorney and Counselor at Law."

"Why don't you have one of those outside your office?"

"I wanted one, but when I first opened my office it was a bit more important to have electricity as opposed to a fancy sign, so I opted for lights and a hand-painted shingle."

Anna Beth was studying the building's door.

"This was a shipping office?"

"It was. How did you know that?"

"I'm trying to learn all I can about my new home." She reached out and touched a carved inlay around the door that looked like a rope. "This. Shipping offices bordered the doors and windows with rope-shaped wood."

"Impressive. It was their way of saying 'I've made it and have extra money to spend.' Architectural bling so to speak."

I held the door open and we entered a large and opulent waiting area. There was a lot of brick. The floor was finished brick, the walls exposed brick that rose to a ceiling of at least fifteen feet that highlighted the exposed original timbers. The walls were lined with photos of Brady, awards he'd won, people who he knew, and framed magazine and newspaper articles featuring my attorney. It was an impressive wall of fame. However, despite the brick, the dominant theme of the reception area was nautical. The place could have been a maritime museum. It also said "success." That, and a history of large legal fees.

"Looks like your attorney knows every politician who's ever come through Charleston."

"He has a reputation for befriending them. He donates down both sides of the aisle. I've always been curious why he never ran for office."

A door to the side of the room opened and a smartly dressed young woman emerged.

"Mr. Parks and Ms. Cross. Welcome. Mr. Brady is just finishing up reviewing some material for your meeting. If you would follow me, I'll show you back to his office."

She held the door open and motioned for us to follow down a hallway off the reception area that was a continuation of the décor and style of the room we'd just left.

I took a deep breath and, despite having lost count of the number of meetings I'd done myself, got ready for my first meeting with my attorney.

TWENTY-TWO

It was my experience in Charleston you generally found three kinds of law offices. There was the minimalist: nothing shabby but nothing extravagant. There were those with ostentatious reception and conference rooms with a behind-the-scenes look more form than fashion. The final category was what I was presently witnessing. Everything polished and trimmed in near regal fashion. I'd always been of the opinion if you're over-the-top in the décor of your office you risked putting off--or even worse--scaring off potential clients.

Brady however, ran no risk of that. His office just said, "I win." And his success was a good bellwether for mine.

For the first time in my legal career I understood why my clients, when they first came into my office, were anything but calm and collected. For the first time I could remember, I was nervous at the prospect of a client meeting. It didn't take long for me to realize I didn't like the feeling. Though I knew exactly what was about to happen, I didn't like it one bit.

The receptionist opened a door to an office that transitioned in style with the reception area, but the best of the best had been saved for the inner sanctum of my new attorney.

Brady looked up from one of the largest and neatest desks I'd ever seen.

The maritime theme continued. From a look at the photos, relics, antiques, and decorations, it seemed Brady's family shared a part of Charleston's seafaring past.

"Noah. And Anna Beth." He rose and rounded the desk to greet us. "Please join me."

He walked around his desk and sat in an ornate high back chair across from a leather couch where Anna Beth and I sat.

"Warren, thank you for seeing us so soon. I can't tell you how happy I am to be in your office rather than jail. Nice work at the bond hearing."

"You're welcome, but I'm sure you've heard that exact same thing from many a client for whom you've performed the same service."

"That's nice of you to say."

"I'm sure it's true, but I gather you have other things on your mind."

Right to the point. Good.

"You're right and I'm quickly realizing things are dramatically different from this seat as opposed to yours. I know exactly what's coming next and I still feel completely lost."

"Noah, I'm not going to give you dog food and try to convince you it's filet mignon. We both know what happens next and what we have to do to be prepared. I'm not going to cut any corners. You know a lot more than most people who sit in that seat. Ask questions whenever you like, but I'm going to focus on one thing and one thing only. Doing all I can to bring about an acceptable conclusion for you. I'll make no promises or guarantees other than I will use all the resources at our disposal to give you a decision between two things: either a resolution without trial, or a trial to make S. Bart prove his case to a jury. It's that simple."

"Fair enough."

"Mr. Brady."

"Ms. Cross. Call me Warren."

"And call me Anna Beth."

"Certainly, Anna Beth. A question?"

"I know just because someone didn't commit the crime, that won't stop the prosecutor, or solicitor, from seeing things differently. I want to make sure you're not going to just work to get a deal to make this go away."

Brady contemplated her for a moment, shifting his gaze from Anna Beth to me, then back.

"As Noah will tell you, most criminal cases end with plea agreements. Few go to trial, but even fewer still end with an outright dismissal. I think the best course of action is to look at what we know so far and talk about the main strength in your case as I see it. Noah's alibi, simply put, is you, Ms. Cross. However, I'm not going to make a blanket promise it's simply a matter of making a phone call to get things taken care of. As you know, absent a credible attack on an obvious weakness, an alibi is a formidable hurdle for any solicitor to overcome."

"Just to add a thought or two. I'm fine with that, but I can't imagine the solicitor having evidence pointing to me. I don't want to oversimplify things, but I'm pretty confident when we see his case there won't be much there. And, with nothing, what can he prove?" I said.

"And that is the question of the day. What can he prove? You're innocent so how does he send an innocent man to jail?"

I paused for a moment, intrigued at Brady's choice of words.

"Alright, what does he have against Noah?" Anna Beth said.

"At this point, all I've seen is Noah's arrest warrant."

He opened a folder and handed me a copy of a warrant that was virtually identical to the countless number I'd seen from clients, that is except this one had the caption, "State of South Carolina v. Noah Parks" printed across the top.

I scanned it and saw nothing earth-shattering or the least bit different than what I already knew. But I wasn't going to fool myself into thinking there wasn't more than what was in the warrant. If the solicitor tried to prosecute his first big case on solely what I was seeing in the warrant, he'd be off to a poor start in office.

"Not that I like seeing my name there, but nothing here that I wouldn't expect to be in a murder warrant, but the way he's set out the facts, for it to happen so quick with nothing out there by way of public knowledge tells me he's jumping the gun …or he has some really compelling evidence."

"How does that tie together with resolving this?" Anna Beth was puzzled.

"It brings into play several different concerns."

Both Brady and I were silent. I closed my eyes, sighed, and rubbed the bridge of my nose as I shook my head. Anna Beth looked back and forth between us.

"I'm not a mind reader here."

I looked at Brady who was looking back at me. He started to speak. I raised my hand, stopping him.

"No, let me. It means they have to be sitting on some pretty compelling evidence. Probably something he thinks shows premeditation, that I planned to kill Andrew. It means if they arrested me for what will have to be a profile case, the solicitor's first case, he'll be using me to show he won't be soft on crime. It means I'll be an example."

We sat in silence for several moments.

"Tell her the rest."

"What rest?"

"It means they have something big and that when they do offer me a deal it will be one that includes a lot of jail time. And by a lot, I mean decades."

"What kind of deal is that?"

"One where the solicitor takes the death penalty off the table."

TWENTY-THREE

We stopped by my office, though as we walked in the office door I realized I didn't recall the walk over. Mrs. Laye handed me the largest stack of messages I'd ever seen. I scanned through them. There were a few from friends saying to contact them if I needed anything and offering their support. There were messages from virtually every newspaper, radio and television station in the state asking for me to call.

There were also messages from what seemed to be most of my clients. Well, from the look of the messages, former clients.

Mrs. Laye looked from me to Anna Beth, "There's mail on your desk. I opened and organized most of it. There's a lot of requests from clients asking for their files. After all you do for your clients ...."

I looked back into my office and saw a desk that was a stark contrast from the one I'd just seen in Brady's office.

"This also came today. I didn't open it."

I took the letter from her and looked at the return address.

"South Carolina Office of Disciplinary Counsel." Below, in bold capital letters were the words, "Personal and Confidential"

An attorney never wants to get a letter from the Office of Disciplinary Counsel. In the best of cases, they're writing concerning another attorney and want information from you. In the worst of cases the news is always less than stellar. That was the case here and Ms. Laye had been around long enough to know that no good news awaited me inside the letter.

I opened it.

"Dear Noah Parks," it began.

"Based upon criminal charges recently filed against you by the Ninth Judicial Circuit solicitor's office, your license to practice law has been suspended effective as of the date of this letter.

A formal hearing will be held within sixty days of the date of this letter where you will be given the opportunity to be heard regarding the ongoing and permanent status of your license to practice law in the State of South Carolina."

The letter went on to caution me to immediately cease any activities involving the practice of law. I couldn't say I was surprised; after all, the idea of an accused murderer practicing law didn't sit well even with me.

Mrs. Laye reached out and placed a comforting hand on mine.

"I'm so sorry," she said. "I guess this means you won't be needing me around here for a while?"

"Oh, quite the opposite. I imagine the phone will continue to ring off the hook and the clients will be coming by for their files. Why don't you plan on staying to see this through?"

"Thank you, Noah." She paused for a moment, wiped at the corner of her eye and took a deep breath. "I'll just get back to work now."

I smiled as she walked away. I looked around the office, turned and headed out with Ann Beth.

For the time being, my work was going to happen elsewhere.

As soon as we got home I called Gabriel and asked him to come by after work hoping he had some good news or perhaps some thoughts that would part the clouds that had settled on the day.

Not long after, I heard Austin's bark announcing Gabriel's arrival.

"Did you use the lights and siren?"

Austin was alternating sniffing Gabriel's pants and looking out the open door for Rudy, whom I'm sure he thought was close behind.

"I was in the area and since it's a rare day you ask me to come by, I figured it was important."

I motioned for him to come into the house and sit with me and Anna Beth in the living room.

"Care to fill me in?"

"We met with Brady and not that we thought it would be a great meeting, but it's becoming abundantly clear the solicitor is going for the jugular."

Gabriel looked at Anna Beth.

"How bad is it?"

"Given how quickly he's come out swinging, Brady's pretty sure the solicitor's sitting on something big and that it won't translate into a very attractive plea offer. He certainly doesn't expect this to just go away at this point."

Gabriel didn't say a word. Seemed I was bringing a lot of silence into the world lately. Finally, he spoke.

"Brady thinking jail time?"

I looked to Anna Beth and back to Gabriel.

"He's thinking at this point jail time and thinking it was a good deal. Brady thinks he'll leverage jail time to take the death penalty off the table."

"Death penalty? What the hell does he think S. Bart has?"

"Honestly, right now I don't know. Brady's requested the solicitor's file. Other than that, I'm basically at a loss though."

"Meaning?"

"I have a rock-solid alibi in Anna Beth. We were at the party and then here all night. Yes, we're involved but she's very credible and I think it would be a stretch to bank on a jury not believing her, especially when it was balanced against the death penalty."

"Either they're going off half-cocked or they have some evidence I had planned to kill Andrew. It almost means a witness or some pretty incriminating evidence and none of that exists. Have you heard anything?"

"Nothing. The Sheriff's Office is being as tight-lipped as I have ever seen. They even disciplined one clerk for talking about the case to a friend at the Mount Pleasant PD. There's an investigator from the solicitor's office heading things up. Don't know anything about him, Norton Gaines. Apparently, he did all of the solicitor's investigation when he was in private practice."

"Can you see what you can find about him?"

"Of course, but this isn't looking good."

"So now what?"

"We prove Noah didn't do it," Anna Beth said.

"Careful. I know you're a wizard with research and grassroots, but the last thing you two need to be doing is messing around with a murder investigation. I've been doing this a long time and I've yet to see an accused win the day on their own. Does Brady have an investigator?"

"I'm certain he does," I said.

"Then start with him. Have him review the solicitor's investigation. How long can it take? Stephens was murdered and you're arrested, what ten days later? We found his body four days after the election and they needed a day for the warrant. A total of five days to investigate and charge you with a death penalty offense? That's pretty quick."

"That scares me but encourages me, too. He's either on to something or has made a huge mistake."

"Let's hope it's the latter," Gabriel said as he rose from the couch.

Anna Beth joined us as we walked down the hall to see Gabriel off.

Gabriel opened the door.

"What's that?"

He pointed at an envelope on the front porch.

I bent over and picked it up, turning it over in my hand.

"Odd, nothing on it," I showed it to both Anna Beth and Gabriel. "Did you see that when you came in?"

"Nope. It wasn't there when I got here." Gabriel stepped around me and looked towards the street.

I slid my finger under the unsealed flap that had been tucked into the envelope to close it. I opened it.

"Noah, wait," Gabriel said.

I pulled out a single sheet of paper. There were three words printed on the page.

"Noah is innocent."

TWENTY-FOUR

All too often in my legal career I've received unexpected calls or visits from clients who had the pressing need to tell me their case was suddenly resolved.

In their minds they'd uncovered some event, fact or evidence tying everything together, or course, in their favor.

Or so they thought.

There'd been more of this than I could count through the years. With each of these situations, I had the difficult task of explaining to the client their revelations simply weren't enough or the facts they'd uncovered just wouldn't stand up to any degree of scrutiny. Part of my job was delivering perspective to clients who simply couldn't accept their efforts weren't the keys to salvation.

Worse than this was the client that had a "feeling."

Early in my legal career I'd struggled with how to handle these situations, often spending time running down leads, ideas, or nonexistent witnesses, only to end up exactly where I started, in a situation where a client had false hope and I still had a case no closer to being resolved.

"You need to tell the judge or solicitor, they'll understand," clients frequently pleaded.

131

If the attorney couldn't, or wouldn't, see the client's logic or couldn't make good with their excellent gift-wrapped information then how could the attorney possible provide effective counsel?

I'd learned to handle these situations delicately, letting clients know a case was built on facts and evidence, something apart from theory or feeling, and if we had that, well, then we would have something to work with. While this was generally met by a blanket statement something along the lines of, "I can't prove it, I just know," this paved the way for me to explain that generally in our legal system if you couldn't provide some proof, a witness who could look a jury in the eye, a document to be shown to judge and juror, then that situation simply might just as well not exist.

Now the roles were reversed.

Three sets of eyes stared at the paper as it fluttered in the early fall breeze. Gabriel spoke first.

"That's not something you see every day."

"Where did it come from?" Anna Beth said.

I looked outside. The street was deserted.

I looked back to see Austin sniffing at the letter in Anna Beth's hand. I walked back up the steps to join them.

"What do we do with this?" I took the letter from her. Austin's nose followed the letter.

"Not a lot you can do. Might be nothing more than a cruel joke. There's no way to tell." Keep your eyes out for anything else unusual and let me know if you see anything," Gabriel paused. "You know, that's not your smartest move. Opening a strange letter not knowing what's in it. No chance for prints either."

"Pretty sure you wouldn't find any. If someone's going to be this covert."

Anna Beth and I stood on the porch with Austin who barked as Gabriel got in his car and left us.

"Who would do something like this?"

"I've no idea," I said.

"Are we going to see what Brady has to say?"

"No," I folded the letter and turned to go into the house. "Nothing he can do with it. It's just false hope."

#

The days started to roll by. I wasn't going to the office and Ms. Laye called a few times a day to check in. Most of our time was spent trying to keep our minds occupied with something else.

Anna Beth walked into the den where I was sitting, staring at the television.

"You need a motive for a murder, right?"

"Yes."

"Then what's your motive?"

"My motive?"

"Your motive to kill Andrew. Follow me for a minute."

"Ok, but we already know there isn't a motive."

"Exactly. Wouldn't the solicitor know that? He'd have to, or make up a motive."

"No, you're looking at it just like I would. Without a motive and with you as my alibi, the case gets weak fast. I can't recall many cases I've seen like this that were brought at all.

Usually you have a solicitor telling a police department there wasn't enough for a case."

"Then what are some of the motives you've seen for murder?"

"Money's a good one."

"Hopefully that's not what they're going with."

I smiled at her.

"What else?"

"Revenge, jealousy, a variety of insane reasons, voices in your head and the like, murder for hire. There are more, but past those it's basically variations on a theme."

"What can they say? You don't need money, you'd already told Gabriel and me you didn't want the deputy solicitor's job, you're pretty sane. And revenge? Really?"

"I see your point and I can't say I haven't thought the same thing."

"Noah, this is driving me crazy. We have to do something."

"Don't disagree with you, but until we hear Brady's got the solicitor's evidence, there's not a lot to do."

"Unless we were to look around a little ourselves."

I looked at her a moment. There was a voice in my head that was sounding a mantra. 'Bad idea. Bad idea. Bad idea.' I was surprised how easy it was to ignore.

"I'd love to."

"Where do we start?"

PART FOUR

TWENTY-FIVE

Anna Beth was a go-getter, and I was all for it, but deciding to take matters into our own hands proved to be easier said than done. After our decision to become our own private investigators, we just continued the same discussion we'd been having since we'd met with Brady holding to the theme I didn't do it and we needed to prove it. Having received the strange note bolstered us, but I knew we needed more.

This line of thought continued until I decided to check the mail. The front door opened to an unusually humid fall day where the moisture in the air made one thankful for air conditioning. As I walked down my drive toward the mailbox I heard a car door slam and tires squeal. I looked towards the sound but caught only the faintest glimpse of a car bumper going around the corner a block up from my house.

I retrieved the mail, hoping for something in the mailbox other than the usual fare of bills and junk mail. As I stood going through the mail a thought occurred to me about Andrew's mail. I wondered if he had received anything that might help me. I knew exactly who would know. Rebecca.

I hadn't heard from her in almost a week. Not that I regularly heard from her, but given all that had happened, I would've expected something, even if it was only to confront me over the murder charge.

I turned to go back to the house.

I knew where we'd start.

#

Anna Beth was quick to agree Rebecca seemed the logical starting point and we should've both come to that conclusion a little sooner. Over lunch we talked.

"Tell me about Rebecca," she said.

"She's been with Andrew about two years. Student at the college, his usual pool for assistants. He's always hired college students, well, female college students, though she's been around longer than any before. Generally, they stay for a semester and usually his hires come and go with the school year."

"Then she should know him pretty well."

"Yes. She's also super protective of him, who gets in to see him, who gets through on the phone. She was more personal assistant than receptionist."

"Then I'm thinking this: If she was that involved, I'd bank on her being just as involved in his campaign, at least knowing who was calling, coming, going, donating money or asking for favors, wanting something after the election. And if not, she would be the best place to start so we could talk to who did know. We find that, then we've got a roadmap for Brady to use."

"That's more than a good idea, that's perfect. You know, with Billy Litman as determined as he was, I bet he called all the time. You asked me about motive, Litman, he has motive."

"I'm hoping you still have her number?"

"I do."

Straight to voicemail.

"She probably thinks I did it."

"Noah, I don't think anyone besides the solicitor and his people think you did."

"Why hasn't she called back?"

"With all that is going on, probably the last thing she wants to do is talk on the phone."

"Then let's go talk to her."

She was on her way out the door, Jeep key in hand before I had a chance to stop her.

TWENTY-SIX

Out of habit I parked at my office and we walked to Andrew's just a few blocks away.

At Andrew's office, we found the front door locked even though it was the middle of the day. No sign, no notice. I pulled my phone and dialed the office number. We could hear the phone ringing inside. It went to voicemail.

I placed the phone on speaker. We heard Rebecca's voice.

"Thank you for calling the law offices of Andrew Stephens. We are unable to come to the phone at the moment. If you are reaching this message during business hours, we are out of the office or with other clients. Please leave your name and number and we'll return your call as soon as possible."

"Haven't changed the message."

I peered in the small window at the side of the door. No sign of anyone but I could see mail spilling away from the door where it had landed after being put through the mail slot.

"Don't see anyone and from the look of the mail on the floor it's been a while since anyone was here. Interesting though, I would have thought the solicitor would've searched here as part of the investigation and sealed the place."

"This doesn't really fit with how you described Rebecca, so focused on Andrew and his practice."

"You're right. That surprises me. Not like her to not be here. Let's look around back."

We headed a short distance up Broad Street and turned onto Church Street to get to the back of Andrew's office. We passed several shops and turned down Elliott Street, which, not being a main thoroughfare, wasn't much wider than the wagons for which it had been designed a century before.

Andrew's building wasn't as deep on his lot as those to either side and the extra space gave him two parking spots in back, a rarity in downtown Charleston. The lot was empty. As was the norm with the rear of Broad Street buildings, there were no windows, only a single door. I tried it.

Locked.

"Now…," Anna Beth said only to be cut off by me mid-sentence.

"Hi, Rebecca."

Rebecca, who had been staring at her phone as she turned the corner into the lot, stopped and looked at Anna Beth and me, clearly surprised.

"Noah, I mean, Mr. Parks. What are you doing here?"

"Rebecca, I'd like you to meet Anna Beth Cross."

"Um, hi, Mr. Stephens and Noah mentioned you. A lot."

"Rebecca, you look a little nervous. Is everything okay?" Anna Beth said.

"No, it's not. Why are you here? I'm not supposed to talk to Noah. I'll get in trouble if I'm even seen with you."

She stepped back, looking up and down Elliott Street.

"Rebecca, you know I didn't do what they say. But someone killed Andrew."

I followed her but she kept backing up, extending the distance between us.

"Rebecca. Wait. Who said you weren't supposed to talk to me? Who will you be in trouble with?"

"Noah, I can't."

"Rebecca. Who told you to stay away from me?"

She looked up and down the street again then at Anna Beth, then back to me.

"I'm so sorry. Mr. Gaines. The woman. They told me to stay away from you or I'd be just as guilty as you."

She turned and ran down the street, around the corner on Church Street. I looked back at Anna Beth and threw my arms in the air as she disappeared.

"Norton Gaines. That's the guy heading up my investigation in the solicitor's Office. But did she say woman? Who was she talking about?"

"I can't imagine, but whatever they told her they have her scared. That makes me think we might be onto something," Anna Beth said.

"Clearly. Now we have to decide our next move."

"I think we need to see your attorney."

#

Not being one to just barge into an attorneys' office-- after all, I've been on the receiving end of it on more than one occasion--I called and asked for an appointment for the following morning. I learned Brady wanted to see me as well. Turns out Brady had received all of the solicitor's evidence against me and Brady wanted me to go through it with him as soon as possible.

Contrary to popular belief, criminal cases don't always play out as one may see on television. There simply aren't surprise witnesses or evidence that just happens to mysteriously appear or disappear. There are scores of guarantees and rights in place that provide protection for those accused of a crime–of any degree. From jaywalking to murder, the rights are the same and an individual is presumed innocent until proven guilty.

As a result of this, a defendant, or in this case, I, could ask for all of the evidence and the solicitor was required to turn it over, even if there was evidence that supported my innocence. There were no exceptions to this. I had a right to know what his evidence was, what he was trying to prove and who his witnesses were.

Period.

That was what was surprising about my conversation with Rebecca. To prohibit a potential witness from talking to me was akin to witness tampering in reverse. It also made me wonder if what she really had was something that would help my case. What did Gaines not want me to know? And a woman. Maybe someone from the solicitor's office.

The one thing I knew for certain was that now more than ever, I had to talk to Rebecca.

Brady's office was only blocks away and we were shown into a conference room as soon as we arrived. He arrived not long after we sat down.

"Noah, Anna Beth, good to see you. Please sit."

Despite the size of the room, it was typical of the traditional Charleston legal conference room–a large table surrounded by bookshelves filled with legal treatises, case summaries, and codes of laws, though the nautical theme continued. However, there was one unique feature that had me puzzled.

One wall was, from just above the waist-high bookshelves, a large chalkboard that extended to the ceiling. It was divided into scores of uniformly sized small boxes making it look more like a spreadsheet. Brady noticed the chalkboard had captured my attention.

"It's a holdover from the building's past. The office was once a shipping house and this was the nerve center so to speak. Runners would travel back and forth between the docks and customs house and report the prices on the various goods traveling through our port. The buyers would track the prices on that board so they would know what to buy and sell. Now we use it to map out cases. Your case will be up soon."

We sat in silence for a moment. While history had always been a curiosity of mine, given that the present held such deadly potential, history could wait.

"We understand you received the solicitor's information."

Brady motioned to a small stack of papers to his right.

"Yes, I did."

"That's it?"

"That's it."

A pause lingered only to be broken by Anna Beth.

"I'm pretty much stating the obvious, but that doesn't look like much."

"That's surprising," I said with a glance to Brady, "Very surprising."

"As usual, Noah, you've hit the nail on the head. Though 'odd' may work just as well."

"Maybe drop the attorney code for the non-lawyer in the room," Anna Beth said.

Brady and I looked at each other.

"Go ahead, earn your keep," I said.

"As we discussed the last time we were together, Noah has been charged with murder. The State can even seek the death penalty if certain factors are met. I can tell you now that the solicitor has alleged a number of facts that would support his seeking the death penalty, but he has not yet issued a formal declaration that it will be sought. However, he does have time remaining to do this. Given that the cause of death was violent blunt force trauma, this will only help the death penalty aspect."

Brady paused and looked each of us in the eye. When his gaze was met with silence, he continued.

"Cutting to the chase: Noah and I, I'm sure, share a common belief when presented with this small amount of evidence. Generally, in murder cases the information produced is voluminous to say the least. It's not unusual to have a moving van with a team of men deliver all of the information. Quite the opposite here. There's simply a dearth of information and while they have a duty to supplement these disclosures if new information is received, the solicitor has attested that what you see here," he motioned again to the small stack of papers to his right, "is all that they have. And when you add to it the speed at which their so- called investigation was conducted, and the charges that have been levied, this is where I come to use the word, 'odd.'"

Again, there was silence, which I decided to end.

"What that means is that either the solicitor hasn't turned everything over to us yet, or he is posturing, hoping that the speed of his case will scare me into a plea. He very may well be hoping that if he hints at the death penalty I may be quick to jump at a deal."

"My thoughts exactly."

Anna Beth looked back and forth between us and the stack of papers. She reached towards them then stopped.

"What makes the solicitor believe the case is so strong against Noah?"

"The theory is this. In the days leading up to the election, Noah coerced his friend to make a place for him on his staff by threatening to expose Stephens' sordid sex life. Stephens initially acquiesced and offered a position as his chief deputy. Noah, to cover the coercion, told some folks, likely Anna Beth, he was going to decline the position. This was to make it seem that Stephens really had to twist your arm to get you to take it. However, at the election party, when he sensed victory, he told you that you are out. He even showed you a list where he had crossed out your name. You and he struggled at the party–this was witnessed by virtually everyone there. Some even heard you threaten to kill him. Then you waited until everyone had departed and you did just that. Though it wasn't the murder weapon, they have your print on a broken glass that no one saw broken at the party. He will use this fact to establish you were there after the party ended and that there was another struggle. Under their theory this establishes several of the factors necessary for the death penalty."

"Lovely. Half-truths mixed with evidence we can't refute."

"Wait, wait a minute. You're forgetting one thing. Noah has an airtight alibi. Me."

Brady didn't say a word.

From his silence, I immediately knew I'd lost my alibi, but I had no idea how.

"No, Anna Beth. That's the nail in the coffin."

"Meaning? Because there's no way they could get me to say otherwise."

Brady slid a single sheet of paper across the table.

"What are these?"

"It's a lab report showing a wine glass that was found at Stephens' house with traces of a powerful sedative in it."

"And?"

"And two fingerprints on the glass. One belongs to Noah and the other belonging to you Anna Beth. Their theory is that Noah drugged you, killed Stephens, then drove back to your house where the next morning Ms. Cross woke up with a murderer, a custom-made alibi and probably a nasty hangover."

TWENTY-SEVEN

Brady left us alone with the news of Anna Beth's discredited alibi. He told us to take a few minutes but we needed to discuss options. What he hadn't said, what I already knew, was the options were limited.

We sat, not speaking. I heard a grandfather clock.

I noticed movement beyond the clock. There was a seagull on the terrace. A set of French doors opened to a balcony that most certainly overlooked the Charleston Harbor. Odd, I hadn't noticed the doors or the terrace before.

A phone was ringing somewhere in the office.

"Noah, Noah."

Without turning my head, I shifted my gaze from the terrace to Anna Beth who had reached out and was lightly touching my arm.

"You haven't said a word."

"I was just thinking."

"About?"

"That seagull out on the terrace. What Brady's going to tell us in a few minutes."

"What's he going to tell us?"

148

"Brady's going to come back in, sit in that chair." I pointed at the chair across the table. "He's going to tell us what we talked about on our first visit, the plea deal, jail time and no death penalty, and we can expect that deal to soon come our way. He'll tell us the simplicity of the solicitor's case is the weakness. He'll tell us he won't recommend a plea, but he'll also caution us about the uncertainty of a trial. He'll explain how there just isn't enough evidence to justify the death penalty. He'll tell us to try and not let that consume us. And he'll be right."

"But?"

"He'll downplay the fact that even if we win and the solicitor loses his bid for the death penalty, our 'win' will likely mean only one of two things. I walk away a free man or I spend the rest of my life in prison. The term 'roll of the dice' or something like it will probably be used. Defense attorneys love that term."

"You're sounding a lot like you are about to throw in the towel and I won't for a minute believe that," she said. "Or let it happen."

As her words were hanging in the air, Brady walked back in the conference room.

"Do you need a few more minutes?"

"No, come in. I know we have things to discuss."

He stopped momentarily to put his hand on Anna Beth's shoulder then rounded the table where he absently adjusted the small stack of papers that apparently were to be instrumental in determining my future.

"Not easy news to hear so I'll cut to the chase. Noah, you could probably recite what I am about to say, so I'll just say it. There's no plea offer yet, but because the solicitor has been so careful to track the death penalty factors in his warrant, a plea offer is on the way. Expect an invitation to meet with him soon. For a variety of reasons, he'll want to deliver the deal in person. He'll offer you a plea to a lower charge in the murder family, perhaps even manslaughter, but the offer will likely be accompanied by no recommendation on sentencing which would mean a court could order the maximum twenty-five years which would mean around twelve to thirteen years of actual time in jail. Though there are scenarios where a court's sentence could be less that would require what I call complete contrition. You'd have to admit to everything and express supreme remorse. You'd have to admit that you killed Andrew."

We stared at him in silence.

"That being said, at this point I'll not recommend we take any offer that involves jail time. There simply isn't enough evidence here." He once again motioned with his hand towards the small stack of papers before him.

We continued to stare in silence.

"Warren," Anna Beth said. "It sounds a lot like what you are saying is that a trial is in Noah's future."

"Possibly. Unfortunately, it would be a very public trial. The solicitor would see to that. Promises are not possible, but in my experience, I believe there would be a low likelihood a jury would convict and hand down a death penalty on what we have here. That leaves two choices: guilty or not guilty. If it was not guilty, you walk out of the courtroom a free man. If it's guilty, it's likely guilty of murder and as you know guilty of South Carolina murder means life with no parole. At the moment, as harsh as it seems, this is our reality. Of course, this would all change if he was to actually seek the death penalty.

It's a crap shoot. But with the alibi gone, well, his case gets stronger."

Silence.

"Did the name Rebecca Martin come up anywhere in that?" I pointed to the stack of papers on the table.

"It did."

"In what context? Witness, statement, what?"

"There was a list of Stephens' employees. Her name was there as the most recent. Her name was also a reoccurring entry on his credit card and bank statements. That's about it."

"About it? Or completely it?"

"Completely. Why do you ask?"

"It's actually why we called to see you, before you sad to come in ASAP. We ran into Rebecca at Andrew's office, and ..."

"Noah, what the hell were you doing at his office? Please tell me I don't have to remind you that you've been charged with murdering him and right now your life," he looked at Anna Beth, "and future hang in the balance and you're out playing detective? I thought you of all people, you would be the one I didn't have to have this talk with."

I probably deserved being chastised, but not in quite so cutting a fashion. I ignored his scolding.

"Regardless, I ran into her and tried to talk to her. She's always been friendly in the past, but she would barely look me in the eye and ..."

"You're charged with murdering her friend and employer. That's not always a quality friends and family respond well to."

"Indulge me for a moment. Rebecca didn't completely avoid me. She told me she couldn't talk to me because Norton

Gaines had talked to her," I said as Anna Beth caught my eye. "Actually, she said Gaines spoke to her and had a woman with him. Thought that sounded odd. She said she was told that if she talked to us she would be just as guilty as me. If the solicitor's been talking to her and telling her not to talk to me and they haven't listed her as a witness, that's concerning. If she's not listed as a witness then what would be the problem with me talking to her?"

Brady contemplated me for a moment.

"Alright, I'll give you that it's odd," he made a note on a legal pad. "I'll have my investigator look into it. You know not to get your hopes up, but it merits some attention."

"And there is something else," I said.

"Noah, you know it's never something an attorney likes to hear when his client says that. What have you done?"

"Nothing. Someone dropped a letter off at my house. We didn't see who it was, but it said I was innocent."

"And you believed it?"

"Of course I believe it," I said as I straightened up in my seat. "But I wanted to mention it to you."

He looked at me without speaking for a moment. A long moment.

"Someone is likely having a laugh at your expense. Careful you don't invite more attention."

"I know. Where's your investigator at on looking into what was provided to us?"

"Making progress. There are a lot of folks from the party, but otherwise there just isn't much to go through. We're going to look at some alternate theories. Billy Litman for instance. Seems there was something between Stephens and him in regard to Littman's son. We will be looking at him."

"That's one way to put it. Everyone at the party had to see what was happening. Not only between Litman and Andrew, but between Dave Litman and his father's new wife. The son even went after me."

"You're paying me to do a job. Rest assured we will do it, but also keep in mind, and I'm not telling you anything you haven't told clients before, leave the legal work to me. Nothing good can come from you working on this case. Even if you think you start to see a way out."

I nodded my head in response.

PART FIVE

TWENTY-EIGHT

The momentum changes quickly when you're defending a murder case. The answer to the questions I had been asking before had been answered. From my perspective, the solicitor was going to gather the pieces of conjecture and assemble them in a way that created a picture of me as a murderer.

Suddenly I had no alibi and my best-case scenario was looking as if it would have me behind bars for a decade if not more. If I hadn't hit bottom yet I was pretty sure a glance over my shoulder would show the floor fast approaching.

But I wasn't reaching for a towel just yet.

I'd had no intentions of following Brady's instructions. No way was I not going to try to find Andrew's killer, no way was I going to sit this one out. This was my life and it appeared the sum total of my future had been condensed to a stack of perhaps 150 sheets of paper assembled by a man who thought I was a murderer. If the solicitor would be able to strengthen his case by my efforts to show my innocence, I was happy to have him try to do so. I might fail, but I would never let him defeat me without some effort on my part.

I needed another perspective. That and help. Gabriel. I needed Gabriel.

We got in the Jeep and I looked at Anna Beth as I reached over and took her hand.

She looked at me. "Tell me you're not about to listen to Brady."

"No way, no how. I'll just be more careful about what I tell him. We're making a stop on the way home. No more sitting on the sidelines and damn what Brady said about staying out of things. If my best shot is a decade in jail how bad can we screw that up?"

"Good. We're on the same page. Though one thing he said, I can't stop thinking about."

"What?"

"The day after the party, I did wake up feeling sorta hung over. Not hung over, but like I was. I only had two glasses of wine. I fell asleep at the party. I don't ever do that."

"Then that means someone did put something in your drink. Add that to the list of questions we need answered."

#

It was Gabriel's day off. We pulled into his driveway, parking behind his unmarked cruiser.

I climbed the steps in two strides and knocked on the door with the large wrought iron door knocker that Gabriel's great-grandfather, a blacksmith, had made. Gabriel told everyone his grandfather had the knocker and then built the house around it. From the time it was built, it had been in Gabriel's family. Family was important to Gabriel. I was glad we were like family given what I was about to ask him.

No answer at the door, which meant we'd find him with the bonsai. Rudy met us at the backyard gate, tennis ball at the ready. I picked it up, threw it and Rudy was off. We followed him to the garden where Gabriel greeted us at the arched entrance.

"Thought I heard Rudy rustling around. To what do I owe the pleasure?"

"We have some news and I wanted to make you an offer."

"This should be interesting."

"We just met with Brady," Anna Beth said.

"And?"

"Long and short of it is there's no plea offer. Not yet anyway, but Anna Beth's alibi is shot. There's evidence of a sedative in a glass they believe was her drink. She even woke up feeling off so she couldn't say otherwise if asked. Theory is I wanted the chief deputy position, Andrew and I argued. I drugged Anna Beth so she wouldn't be a witness but could give me an alibi and then, this is the good part, I confronted Andrew with murder on my mind. Brady's thought is to reject any plea and try the case. If I win I'm home free. If I lose, you and Anna Beth get to visit on weekends."

"Oh, that's all? Not a problem. Remember, police get to visit whenever they want. And I could probably bring a guest."

"My, you have a way of making a guy feel great, don't you?"

Anna Beth actually laughed at the exchange.

"How are you doing?" He gave Anna Beth a hug.

Plainly a rhetorical question.

"I've never seen you hug anyone before. Ever."

"Rarely do. But makes it all the more special, don't you think?"

"Thanks, Gabriel," Anna Beth said.

"Well, what's your attorney going to do? Or should I ask what are you going to do?"

"His thought is for me to let him to do what he does best and take advantage of the solicitor's inexperience, but I speak that language and it has plea deal written all over it."

"And I'm about to hear you won't be taking any plea."

"That would be correct. We're going to find out who killed Andrew. Which leads use to needing your help."

"Of course it does."

#

"Andrew's assistant, Rebecca, well, something is going on with her," Anna Beth said.

Good, I thought it better coming from Anna Beth.

"Meaning what?"

I looked at Anna Beth for a moment.

"What did you guys do?" Gabriel said.

"We went by Andrew's office. We didn't go in, but were surprised by his assistant, Rebecca, who, by the way, was very nervous. She said Gaines and a woman came to see her and told her not to talk to me. From what she said, it sounded like they threatened her. Said if she did, she would be in the same boat as me. And then, best part, she left as suddenly as she arrived. In a huge hurry."

"When we met with Brady, he said she wasn't listed as a witness," Anna Beth said.

"Gaines again. That guy's a ghost. Everyone knows he worked for the solicitor as an investigator, but apart from that, I've got nothing. And why would it be a problem talking to this Rebecca if she isn't a witness. You can't tamper with a witness if they aren't a witness."

"Exactly, but that's where we'd like your help. Brady wants me to stay out of looking into my case, but I can't do that. I'll be careful. I just can't sit on the sidelines."

"And who better than a detective to talk someone like Rebecca? Right?"

"She's not a witness," I said.

"No, and that's why I'll help you, but remember, if I find out anything major, I have to take it up the chain. Even if you don't like it."

"Thank you," Anna Beth said. "Thank you."

"You think this Rebecca person's the key."

"I hope so, because there's really nothing else. Of course, the solicitor, or at least Gaines, not wanting me to talk to her makes me really curious."

"You're banking a lot on a little Parks."

"Maybe. I don't even know where she lives, but I'm guessing you can take care of that. Right?"

"Shouldn't be a problem and if it gets to be one, we'll sort it out then. I'm actually surprised someone at the department hasn't gotten word to tell me to keep away from this, but then again, like you've said, S. Bart isn't the most experienced when it comes to prosecuting."

"Then that's what we'll do. Alright, we should go and, thank you, my friend, thank you."

We walked toward the gate leading from Gabriel's backyard to the front of his house."

"I'll call you soon, regardless of whether I find anything."

Gabriel opened the gate turning to face us. He gave Anna Beth another hug.

"You keep strong. You'll get through this."

"Two hugs in one day. I fear you're going soft on me."

"Just don't do anything stupid, Parks."

Anna Beth and Gabriel parted from their hug. She looked around him out of the gate.

"Noah, what's that on your car?"

Gabriel and I looked past the gate towards my Jeep. There was something under the windshield wiper.

I walked over and returned with a plain white envelope. Remarkably like the one from the house, the flap unsealed and folded into the envelope. Inside was a tri-folded single sheet of paper. I took it out and unfolded it:

"Noah didn't kill Andrew. He wasn't the last one to see him alive. He wasn't the last one to leave the election party."

TWENTY-NINE

The day had been one big curveball. Anna Beth's alibi was gone. Then another mystery letter appears making us believe there may actually not only be an alibi out there, but maybe someone who knows about the real killer. That or someone was taking a mind game way too far hoping I would help the solicitor put the nails in my coffin.

We spent some time staring at the letter. Then we spent some time over takeout and a bottle of wine ignoring the letter. At least Anna Beth and I did. Austin kept going over to check on it. That, we found amusing.

After we ate, Anna Beth took Austin for a walk.

I went back to the letters and stared at them.

Side by side on my dining room table they sat. I was staring at less than thirty words that said I was an innocent man. Question was how could I leverage the messages to convince those who mattered.

Another question I couldn't answer.

I realized I'd lost track of time when I heard the door open and Anna Beth and Austin come in. Anna Beth walked into the dining room, took my hand and kissed my cheek.

"I'll be upstairs. Come to bed."

The letters would be there in the morning. I turned and followed her up the stairs.

#

It seemed like no sooner had I closed my eyes than I was wide awake thinking of the letters. Morning was not that far away and I quickly realized I wasn't getting back to sleep, so I got up and went downstairs.

The letters and empty wine bottle were right where I left them. Of the letters, I still had no idea, but I decided the Paso Robles Cab had been a winner.

I heard footsteps and dog paws on the floor behind me followed by a cold nose against my hand and a warm touch on my shoulder.

"Tell me I wasn't dreaming about someone getting in bed with me."

'No. Couldn't sleep and had to come stare at this again."

She looked at the bottle in my hand. "It was good wine, so at least the evening wasn't a complete loss."

Austin rose up on his back paws, sniffed at the letters then wandered out of the room.

"I don't want to over analyze or get my hopes up, but I have to believe there's someone out there who has something that could help us."

"Or someone with a sick sense of humor. You're awfully interested in that wine bottle."

I was playing with the wine bottle and had started to stare at it.

"Good wine. Has me thinking."

"About?"

"The label. Look at the corner there," I said as I handed her the bottle.

"It looks like maybe a barn or a house or maybe a little symbol."

"Exactly. That's what I was thinking."

"You're losing me."

"It makes me wonder how many wineries put something on their label for people to find. It's there, but not exactly obvious."

"Hiding in plain sight," she said.

"Exactly."

Anna Beth was silent for a moment."

"Someone somewhere you wouldn't expect knows you didn't do it and they don't want to come forward for some reason."

"Precisely."

"Okay," she said. "Who? Who would hide trying to help?"

I thought about it for a moment. I took the wine bottle from her and turned it over in my hand as if the answer was somewhere on the label. Then it came to me.

"I'm thinking it has to be someone in the solicitor's office. Someone who knows there's more to the case than the solicitor is telling us or someone who wants me to take a thin case and make it stronger by, well, doing what I'm doing."

"What about a police officer?"

"Maybe someone who knows me who saw how evidence was handled or put together."

Anna Beth turned and walked across the room and leaned against the doorframe. Her thinking pose. "But wouldn't that mean if it was someone at the solicitor's office there would have to be some evidence there you didn't do it?"

"Maybe. The solicitor and his deputies get to decide what to turn over. If it's a close call, it may not get sent my way. Maybe there is someone over there who hasn't been happy with the decisions they've made on what to give me. Someone in the office sees that or sees not everything has been sent over and they send the first note. Then to make sure I know they're serious then the second comes. They want to make sure we keep looking."

"But would the solicitor keep something from you?"

"I want to think he wouldn't. But then again, maybe he would. Or it could just be someone differs in the opinion of how they see certain evidence."

I headed to the phone and got Gabriel on the line.

"We've had another idea."

"And a good morning to you, too. Tell me what you found."

"Anna Beth and I were talking. We narrowed the letters down."

"I'm listening."

"Someone is just messing with my head or someone close to the investigation knows there is more going on than what we've been told."

"Someone in the solicitor's office?"

"Or maybe someone responsible for collecting evidence. Someone who knows the solicitor hasn't turned everything over. Someone who's seen something they think would help me."

"Interesting theory. But you really think the solicitor is withholding evidence?"

"I hope not, but he was quick to charge me and now he has to make it stick. It would make sense. At a minimum, he blurs the line on what he gives me."

"Maybe, maybe. You sure you're not just reaching here?"

"I still have friends over there, at least I think I do. That's where I need your help."

"Meaning?" he said.

"I need to know who was let go from the solicitor's office, particularly the ones who were shown the door around the time I was arrested. Attorneys, support staff, really anyone."

Silence.

"That might be a bit more than I can do without looking like I am digging around where I shouldn't be. I think we'd have to go through the back door so to speak. If we start asking for employment records that would draw attention. Maybe we could talk to some of the people we know worked there, the ones who knew you. Why don't you put together a list of people you knew and we can look at it, see if anything jumps out."

"What about..."

"Noah, it's a good idea, but remember, I want to help and I will help. I'm your friend, I'm Anna Beth's friend, but I'm also a police officer and this is getting close to where the police officer/friend line starts to get a little blurry."

"I know, I know, it's just that this makes sense."

"It's not a bad idea, but keep this in mind. If a person wants to remain anonymous, then count on them staying that way, maybe even after you figure out who they are. If these letters are going to help you then I'm pretty sure that the biggest help will be that they get you looking somewhere you're not already, but I'm thinking the solicitor's office may not be the place. If you out and accuse the solicitor of withholding evidence, that can't help your case, now can it? Think like a lawyer, not like a defendant."

"Okay. I get it. We don't look at the solicitor's office. So then what's next?"

"You and I do some thinking and then get back together to see what we come up with? Did you tell Brady about the second letter?"

"No. I spoke to him on the phone about the first one and he wasn't too happy with it. He told me what I'd have told me if I was the lawyer on the case. It'll take more than letters to get him interested."

"You can only use what you can prove."

"I did find out that the coroner's report on Andrew's death is going to be released today or tomorrow. Thought you'd want to know, he is ruling it a homicide. Death was the result of blunt force trauma."

"What did you say?" I said.

"The Coroner's Report is about to be released."

"Not the cause of death?"

"Blunt force trauma."

"So good. Well, not so good, but not a suicide."

"It appears that way."

"Good. Talk soon."

I put the phone down and turned to Anna Beth.

"And?"

"He wasn't quite as excited as we were, but he's going to help. Getting the records without arousing suspicion will be tough. He and I are going to make a list of who we both knew in the solicitor's office and see if one jumps out at us. That and Andrew was murdered."

"That's it?"

"At the moment, but it's twice as much as we had a few minutes ago."

I stepped towards her but stopped as my cell phone rang and vibrated on the counter. I smiled at her and turned to answer it.

"Noah Parks."

I looked at Anna Beth who had walked into the kitchen and was staring into an opened refrigerator.

"That's fine. Okay, see you then."

I ended the call.

"You're not starting to get anonymous calls, are you?"

"No, that was Brady. The solicitor wants to meet tomorrow morning. He wants to discuss a plea."

THIRTY

All I had done was support a friend and I was witnessing the fabric of my life slowly being unraveled. No matter how hard I worked, how hard I focused, the more I tried the faster it crumbled.

I had Anna Beth's love and support, I had Gabriel, and I had a professional in Brady who also believed in me. A professional who was at the top of his game and he could do little other than stand beside me as the thread piled up at our feet. His hands were tied by what could be proven in a court of law.

I was still holding the cell phone as I felt Austin's damp nose nuzzling my other hand, once again pulling me back from my thoughts. He took a step back and slowly wagged his tail from side to side looking up at me with what I interpreted as a "What now?" look.

"I don't suppose you have any ideas do you, boy?"

He woofed and sat, keeping his eyes on me. Anna Beth had walked over to the window where she stared out into the backyard.

"You're not in Chicago anymore, are you?"

"No, but you wouldn't think a move south would be this hard."

"Call me crazy but the idea of a conjugal visit doesn't do it for me."

She turned, wrapped her arms around my neck and put her head on my chest.

"I thought we'd have a little time to sort things out, to decide what to do. Why is he moving so fast?"

"He's convinced I killed Andrew and nothing is going to change his mind. Seems the solicitor wants to announce his presence with authority and show he's tough out of the gate with no thought of quarter. And I'm going to be his example."

"Wonderful."

"I'm not excited about this meeting, but at least we'll know where we stand, and if we have to get ready for trial, so be it. But that doesn't mean we can't do something about it. It also makes me more convinced someone close to the investigation knows something is off."

#

When I opened my eyes the next morning, we went through the normal motions of getting ready, neither of us talking about the meeting that was looming just hours away. Austin was none too happy when we left him at the house.

We drove downtown in silence, parking at my office once again.

"We're early."

"I thought we'd walk over and maybe linger in the office, maybe say hello to some old friends in the solicitor's office."

"Not a bad idea," she said.

As we headed up Broad Street towards the courthouse, the location of the solicitor's office, I thought about going in my office, but I stopped just short of the front door. For some reason, today the idea of entering the realm of what was starting to look like a testament of my former life didn't sit too well. The thought occurred to me I might actually have to sell the building. I turned away.

"Come on, it's a beautiful morning."

The city was just coming to life, the merchants opening their stores, the tourists wandering around and people going to work. I was starting to see what clients meant when they said it would be the little things they'd miss when they went away to prison.

The solicitor's office was located in an annex to the main courthouse off Broad Street. We walked a short way up Meeting Street, taking another turn down a small alley beside the Hibernian Hall, a local civic organization whose home was as regal and elegant as one would expect in Charleston.

We entered the annex, called the O.T. Wallace building, and took the elevator to the fourth floor, the realm of the solicitor. We waited in the lobby, me paying close attention to the staff. I saw a number of familiar faces, but none offered anything other than brief 'hello's.' Brady soon arrived and an assistant escorted us to the solicitor's office. The office was empty.

"Please have a seat at the table, the solicitor will be along shortly."

Charleston was a city of few tall buildings. From the solicitor's office, we were able to gaze over much of the lower

Charleston peninsula out to the harbor, the bridge and Mount Pleasant beyond.

His office was exactly what one would expect from a Southern prosecutor. A huge mahogany desk with two padded leather chairs took a large portion of the room. The desk was positioned so those sitting before it would be confronted with the view of the downtown through the window beyond. It made for an interesting juxtaposition. If you were sitting before the desk, your view through the window behind it was a beautiful picture of what would be lost if a deal couldn't be struck with the solicitor just across from you.

A rectangular conference table for eight sat to the rear of the office. The walls were lined with grip and grin photos of the solicitor covering his career. There was a photo of him with nearly every South Carolina politician of note from the last quarter-century. Mixed in among these were certificates, plaques, and other recognitions. Central to it all was his weathered law degree beside his ornate certificate showing he had been admitted to practice before the highest court in the land, the United States Supreme Court.

Not many Charleston County solicitors had appeared before the U. S. Supreme Court and I was sure the current solicitor would not be included on this rather small list anytime soon. I was also sure he'd furnished the office as the county's decorating budget was most assuredly not in line with what we found in his office.

The office door opened and the solicitor entered. I had to work to hold a poker face. My efforts failed.

Miserably.

THIRTY-ONE

"Jesus Christ, what's he doing here?"

Dave Litman made his way into the room behind the solicitor holding several files. No one answered my question.

"Guess he's glad to see me."

S. Bart glanced at Litman who muttered, "Sorry" under his breath as the solicitor turned his attention to Brady.

"Warren, pleasure to see you today. You may know Dave Litman. He's come on as one of the new solicitors in the office. He'll be second chair on the case. Please. Sit."

He motioned to the conference table at the back of the office. He didn't greet Anna Beth or me. Old prosecutor's trick. If you have the occasion to meet with the accused, treat them like they aren't there. Dehumanize them.

I let Brady and Anna Beth sit first. Brady took a seat at the head of the table. I joined Brady to his left. The solicitor and Litman sat at the other end of the table.

"Thank you for coming today. I felt that given the attention this matter was receiving, it might be prudent to discuss a resolution sooner rather than later. Closure is always best in cases such as this. Closure for all. I know concessions will be necessary on each side, but this office is prepared to do just that, perhaps even more so than we would regularly consider. I've always been a firm believer that matters such as this are resolved to everyone's liking when we avoid the uncertainty of a jury."

Brady didn't look at me, but placed his hand on my tense forearm. S. Bart was trying to get under my skin by acting like he was the seasoned prosecutor. Why not let him think it was working? I took a deep breath and leaned forward so as to better hang on his every word. Time to let Brady earn his fee.

"We're certainly happy to be here, but please don't construe our presence as anything other than curiosity as to what you're thinking and where you're headed with this case. Cutting to the chase, we'd love nothing more than to have closure, but I believe our idea of closure may be a bit divergent from what you have in mind, Solicitor."

"Warren, you've been at this a long time and your reputation is pristine. I can't say that I'm surprised this defendant sought your services, but you've seen our evidence, I hate to use the term "slam dunk" but I'm assured we have your client dead to rights."

I felt Brady's hand return to my forearm where he allowed it to rest for a moment as the silence set in over the room.

The urge to speak my mind was stirring in my gut and I was pretty sure I wasn't going to be able to contain it much longer.

"Solicitor, thank you for your commentary on my reputation, but our focus here is simple and I'm not sure if it's a good use of my or my client's time to have you patronize and gloat. If you decide to…"

"If we decide what?" Litman said, interrupting Brady.

Brady looked at Litman pausing momentarily before returning his eyes to S. Bart.

Litman wasn't done. "I asked you a question. If we do what?"

"Solicitor, do you need a moment with your junior solicitor?"

"Watch it pal. You'll do well not to press the government."

Litman rose from his seat as he spoke.

Anna Beth slammed her hands down on the conference table.

"Excuse me."

Litman was standing and the solicitor was in the process of joining him but as Anna Beth spoke, all eyes turned to her, which was nice, as I certainly didn't want anyone to see me grinning.

"Could everyone please sit down? I thought we were here to talk about a way to end this. I'd like to get on with that. Please."

Litman started to speak but the solicitor raised his hand. Litman lowered himself into his chair, glaring at Anna Beth.

"The young lady is correct. You've come to learn the terms of how we would, and I would say graciously, resolve this case."

"Go on then," Brady said.

"Certainly, so why don't we cut to the chase as you say. The defendant is charged with the murder of Andrew Stephens, a prominent member of the local bar. He planned this murder in a cold and calculated fashion, motivated by a personal vendetta that stemmed from a desire to be included on the staff of this very office," he paused and stared at me. "And for other personal reasons. Reasons that I'm sure the defendant would rather keep from the public as these were perhaps an even stronger motivation to silence Mr. Stephens."

We sat in silence.

"Questions?"

More silence.

"Very well then. Mr. Litman, please."

For a moment, I thought he was going to have Litman go over the offer, but he only pulled a thin manila file from a larger file folder and slid it across the table to the solicitor.

For a moment, he considered the folder, shifting his gaze not to Brady, but to me, where he locked onto and held my stare. I couldn't believe it, he was going to try to stare me down, to intimidate me. Wasn't going to happen. I refused to break it, even shifting in my chair to move slightly closer to him. He held my stare as an uncomfortable silence started to build.

Then he blinked. At that moment, I knew.

I knew even before he opened the folder to tell us his offer I wasn't going to take. In that moment, I realized I was no longer Noah Parks, attorney at law, I was Noah Parks, accused murderer and the accused was starting to think less and less like the attorney.

His stoic expression became a bit unfocused as if he might be confused. He looked at me again and saw the grin on my face.

He started to speak, but there was a knock at the door. We all looked on in silence and the door opened. A face I didn't recognize appeared.

"Sorry to interrupt, but I was delayed."

"Mr. Gaines, please join us. Everyone, this is the lead investigator in my office, Norton Gaines."

I hadn't counted on meeting Mr. Gaines today. Lucky me.

He nodded to everyone, but let his stare fall on me. He held it. Then I looked away.

Damn it. Why did I do that? Just what I needed, him thinking he was getting in my head. Then again, he already was.

S. Bart continued.

"As I was saying, you are aware, the charge of murder allows this office to seek the death penalty. I want to assure you it is not without great consideration and deliberation that I've approached this decision. It is not lost on me I could not have a more public case with which to start my prosecutorial career. I also want you to understand I'm keenly aware the public may be under the incorrect impression you will somehow receive special treatment as a result of your former position within the legal community and any deal must show that a member of our bar will be as responsible as anyone else. Rest assured that you'll not receive any consideration that would not be afforded any other defendant being prosecuted by this office. We aren't going to be harder on this defendant, but we must proceed carefully and there will be no special considerations."

His words were once again met with silence. He briefly met the eyes of Brady and Anna Beth while avoiding my stare.

"This case has also been the topic of many a discussion among myself and my senior staff. It was and is my opinion that simply removing the death penalty from consideration should be incentive enough to induce you to enter a plea; however, my staff has convinced me the proper approach would be to remove the death penalty and also offer a lower charge. I can't say I initially agreed but in the end, I felt it appropriate to embrace their suggestions. Accordingly, I am prepared to offer you a plea to the reduced charge of manslaughter. Obviously, this would mean the death penalty is off the table but the balance would be a recommendation for the maximum amount of time as to a sentence. Actually, that would be a condition of the plea. That is, as you may know, thirty years. Not bad as the defendant would be out and perhaps able to enjoy his retirement."

He again paused and looked to Brady.

"Anything else?" Brady said.

"In fact, yes, one other matter. We would also require that the defendant voluntarily surrender his law license and agree never again to practice law in South Carolina or any other jurisdiction."

I rose and took a step toward the door.

"Where are you going?" Litman said.

"Are you guys coming?" I said.

Anna Beth rose from her chair. Brady kept his seat.

"Noah, join us for just a moment."

I walked back over to the table but stood behind Anna Beth rather than sitting.

"We want to make sure the solicitor knows we understand his offer, that he is crystal clear on our thoughts and how we intend to handle this case."

"Warren, that's fine, but we would like an answer now. This offer does have a rather limited shelf life."

I once again felt words rising in my throat but they halted when Brady raised his hand sensing I was about to speak, likely to say something I would regret.

"Solicitor, thank you for taking the time to meet with us and for relaying your offer. However, I believe that we will have to respectfully reject it."

"You'll want to consult with your client I would imagine, to explain to him the attractiveness of this offer. There's no need to be hasty."

"Noah. Any need to talk?"

"Nope."

"Then Solicitor, you have our answer."

THIRTY-TWO

Warren stood, pulled Anna Beth's chair out and we started for the door. The solicitor rose to his feet. We stopped. I was certain he was about to command us to leave his office, rather he stood in silence for a moment and then walked over to his desk, leaning back against it looking towards us, forcing us to turn to face him.

"Warren, I'm surprised. Certainly, I realize this is my first major homicide as solicitor, but I would have hoped you thought better of my abilities than to think that merely because this is the first I would somehow bend to your cheap lawyering and other petty charades. My evidence is overwhelming and you certainly realize the true nature of our offer. In fact, some in this office would call it a gift given the personal nature of the crime."

He looked towards Gaines, who up to this point had not said a word.

"Solicitor, certainly you didn't expect me to come in here within weeks of my client's having been charged and dive all over your first offer. I'm also a bit puzzled. I've seen this information you've been calling 'evidence' and if what you've produced is sum total of your evidence, the term 'overwhelming' certainly doesn't come to mind. Unless you have more information or witnesses you haven't told us about," he paused. "But you wouldn't have withheld evidence, now would you? If you want us to engage in serious consideration, make a serious offer."

I realized why Brady commanded the fees he did. He knew this whole plea offer was just for show, the solicitor wanted to see how we reacted. He had me come back over to the conference table for the sole purpose of letting the solicitor see him ask me about the deal. He wanted to let the solicitor know he had client control. He was also testing the waters to see if the solicitor had withheld any evidence. I was getting my money's worth. It was brilliant, almost like he knew how the solicitor had the script sorted out. I started to smile again.

I saw Litman looking at me and apparently the smile was enough to set him off.

"Oh, that offer was serious and it won't get any better."

The solicitor raised his hand again and as he did, Gaines rose from his seat.

"Mr. Solicitor, may I?"

"Certainly."

Now this was odd.

"Mr. Parks. Take the offer. I'm sure you don't want everyone, particularly your little lady, to know about your boyfriend and the problems the two of you were having. Lover's spats can get downright embarrassing. And I think you'll find that there's not a lot in the way of evidence to help you end it without a plea. Be smart."

"Screw you, Gaines," I said.

"Noah, don't." Anna Beth grabbed my arm.

Gaines took a step towards me, a creepy smile formed on his face.

"Yes, Noah, stop. Listen to your little lady. Don't want to make it worse now do you? Imagine what she'd think if she learned all about your boyfriend, all that time the two of you spent together. Early morning meetings. It could get messy, we'll see to that."

I stared in silence.

"Once again, solicitor thank you for the meeting. You have your answer."

Gaines held my gaze as he returned to his seat.

We moved towards the door. S. Bart followed.

"Warren, you walk out that door it might not be open next time. He was at the murder scene. People saw him fight with Stephens. You can't stop me, I'm going to tell the story."

We were in the hall outside of his office. He followed us, raising his voice as we walked towards the reception area.

"His name was marked off Stephen's list. He had a key and no alibi. He laced her drink. Don't think we won't bring out the homosexual relationship. I'll tell the story."

The solicitor's office support staff was starting to stare.

"Just walk on Noah."

"Oh, I'm enjoying this."

"His reputation will be ruined. I promise it." His closing shot. It missed. Completely.

The elevator door opened as soon as we pushed the call button. I half expected the solicitor to come running down the stairs after us as we reached the front door of the building.

#

"That was interesting," Anna Beth said.

"Not sure what that was."

"That, I believe was the sign of a new solicitor with an unflappable belief in his case. I am however, a little surprised at the offer," Brady said.

"I'm going to take that to mean that you were surprised he could think his case could ever support that. That's not an offer. Jail time? Never going to happen and what was that business at the end about never practicing again. I mean if I go to jail, my legal career is over so why even mention it? And a relationship with Andrew."

"He wants you to grovel. Grovel and get upset. Don't take this the wrong way, but he got half of what he was looking for. Remember, he's convinced you did it. He wants, hell, needs, you to validate his thin evidence and be able to say not only was he able to get you to admit to murder, but that he was so tough on you he had you walk away from the practice of law saving the State a great deal of time and money taking your law license from you. Though that was just his first offer, he'll follow with something more attractive."

"Wait a minute, you're not telling me you're actually considering his offer, are you?"

"Consider it? No, not at all. However, I'm curious to see how it evolves. There's room for improvement."

"Improvement?" Anna Beth said.

"He's yet to reach his final offer. All of that about the death penalty, that was purely for show. And his little outburst there at the end was his tell. That exchange with Gaines was staged and was purely to put us on the defensive. They wanted you to shy away from the homosexual angle and essentially fold before you have all the cards in your hand. Litman was there just to piss you off. He wanted us to scramble to a deal today and our leaving has the solicitor unnerved. They wanted to negotiate today and I believe if we came back with a counteroffer we might actually gain significant ground. Though I admit I am a bit puzzled how he thought any of that would work on me. He knows me better than that."

"Could we keep Noah out of jail?"

"I don't think we could gain that kind of ground, but I believe his time would be much less than what they are offering. I'm thinking involuntary manslaughter. Perhaps four or five years. Then with good time, you may be out in as little as three years. A little time for a crime you didn't commit is bad, but life for the same crime is even worse."

I stopped and turned to face him.

"You have to be kidding me. In less than five minutes you've decided I can do three years. Let me make this clear, a plea will only be acceptable with zero jail time. Period. End of discussion."

"Noah, you may be an innocent man, but you have to know this reality, well, it's not unexpected. You know as well as I we have to look at the big picture."

"Paint any picture you want, but it ends the same way. I'll never hear a jail cell door close behind me ever again."

"Very well. Then that makes our task straight forward. I'll make that known to the solicitor at the appropriate time and continue the work on your defense. No reason why his first homicide can't be his first murder trial."

We were interrupted by the most unexpected of people.

"Well, Mr. Brady, Bart mentioned he had a meeting first thing today, he didn't say it was with you," Tamara Michaels said.

"Mrs. Michaels, what a surprise. Yes, S. Bart and I had a meeting today. Do you happen to know Mr. Parks and Ms. Cross?"

The cheerful smile on her face instantly disappeared as she looked first to Anna Beth and then to me.

"Oh," she said as her eyes darted back and forth between Anna Beth and me. "I, no, we, have met, but no, I do not know this man. I do not know him, but I certainly know who he is. Mr. Brady, a pleasure to see you. You'll excuse me."

She turned and headed away from the courthouse looking back over her shoulder twice as she walked away.

"Can't say she was happy to see you Noah."

"Apparently not. I hope the solicitor doesn't add on time for running his wife away from the courthouse."

#

Neither of us liked how quickly Brady jumped to the idea of me doing jail time. Sure, he was thrilled to have the chance to resolve a death penalty case for three years, but it was my three years he was playing with.

We rolled into the drive and immediately I knew something wasn't right.

The front door was open.

"Call Gabriel and stay in the car."

I ran up the steps and peered inside, listening carefully. From my front porch through the open door to the left I could see into my office to the left and to the right, the dining room.

Chaos everywhere. The house had been ransacked. Great. But at the moment that was the least of my worries.

I didn't hear a thing. The silence was deafening. My chest tightened as a sense of panic rose. This was the first time in years I'd come home and hadn't been greeted at the door by Austin. I glanced around the outside the front of the house but there was no sign of him.

I moved to the right side of the open door. The dining room was a mess. I looked over my shoulder to my office. It was a disaster. Drawers dumped on the floor, books, papers, photos thrown about. No sign of Austin.

Then my heart fell to my stomach.

THIRTY-THREE

He was on the floor.

Lying.

Still.

"Oh shit," I said aloud.

Not caring if someone was in the house, I raced to Austin.

He was on his stomach, his legs splayed unnaturally as if he had just collapsed. His tongue fell ungracefully from the side of his opened mouth. A pool of saliva surrounded it. His eyes were half opened. His eyelids drooped.

"No, no, no, no."

As an Australian Shepherd, Austin had a lot of fur. That made it difficult as I searched for a pulse or a heartbeat or any sign of life. I found nothing. He was limp, his chest still. He wasn't moving. I raised a paw and let it go. It fell to the floor where it remained still. His nose was cold.

I felt helpless. Someone had come into our home and taken him from me, from Anna Beth. I saw a part of my life lying dead on the floor and I could already feel an emptiness grow inside of me that Austin had once filled.

Earlier in the day I had wondered what else could happen to drag me lower.

Now I knew.

I felt the sting of the salt as tears welled in my eyes. I had to go tell Anna Beth.

I started to rise when I noticed something – the slightest ripple in the pool of saliva on the floor. I looked around and reached for a picture on a nearby table. I cradled his limp head and put the photo less than an inch from his nose.

"Come on, come on buddy, you can do it."

Condensation appeared.

He was alive.

I reached to the couch for a blanket, gathered him and headed to the door.

Anna Beth was standing outside the Jeep's door looking frustrated. Her expression changed to panic as she saw me carrying Austin down the stairs.

"He's alive. Call the emergency vet and tell them we're on the way."

#

"How is he?" Gabriel said.

Anna Beth had called him after we discovered the break in and then again when we arrived at the emergency vet, which was thankfully only a short drive from home.

"The vet still has him. He was barely breathing when we got him here, but no word yet. It's been more than three hours. ..."

"He's going to be fine. Positive thoughts. You guys need anything?"

"We're fine. Just worried about our little guy," Anna Beth said.

"What happened?"

"We had a less than productive meeting with the solicitor, suffice it to say we weren't in the best of moods on the way home. We drove up and the front door was open."

"And you never use the front door unless you're home and the bell rings."

"Right we go out through the garage. Anna Beth was calling you and I went up the steps. I saw the office and dining room had been trashed but was more concerned Austin was nowhere to be seen. Even with the door opened he wouldn't have run off."

Anna Beth moved closer to me and took my hand in hers.

"I know I shouldn't have gone inside, but when I looked down the hall and I saw him on the floor, I didn't think twice."

"Don't worry about that. Did you touch anything? Move anything?"

"I went to him, knelt beside him. And let's see, I touched a photo that's probably still on the floor and I grabbed a blanket off the couch. I picked him up, pulled the door shut and came here. I probably wasn't inside more than ninety seconds."

"Did you go in?"

Anna Beth shook her head. "No. I was about to when Noah came out with Austin."

"Good. We've got our guys over there now going through everything. I did a quick walk-through before I came over here. Your computer's gone, and they tried to pry up your

190

safe from the pantry, but looks like they gave up when they couldn't get it loose. Most of the downstairs drawers and cabinets have been opened or emptied. It's a real mess, but nothing else obvious is missing. None of the other electronics were touched, which is odd. But that gives us a good chance of getting prints. Those letters, where were they?"

"I had copies on the dining room table. Are they gone?"

"Let me check."

Gabriel turned and walked out of the emergency vet's office. I saw him speaking into his radio. I was watching him when I heard a voice.

"Mr. Parks?"

"Yes." I turned to find a woman in scrubs standing in front of me.

"I'm Dr. Colven and …"

"How is he?"

"Austin? He's likely going to be fine. He…"

"Thank God. What's happened?"

"He's had a very high dose of a sedative called Acepromazine."

"But he'll be okay?"

She looked to Anna Beth. "He's going to be a little groggy for a few days. Do you mind if I ask how this happened?"

"Someone broke into our house and poisoned him."

"Now why would someone do that? I take it you've called the police to report this? Or if you like I can call them now for you."

She motioned towards the phone at the front desk and took a step that direction.

"Wait, what?" I said.

"Mr. Parks, this drug isn't something you just go to the store and pick up. It's a controlled narcotic, primarily a canine sedative. We use it to relax patients after surgery or to calm them for travel, but only in very small doses. Austin was lucky. We ran a blood test and the dose was perhaps five times the recommended level. With his breed, even small doses can be potentially fatal. You got him to us with very little time to spare. This drug isn't something you would just have lying around, if you aren't a medical professional or a dog owner who has a prescription, I wouldn't expect someone to have it. Let's just say I'd be surprised to have it be a coincidence someone decided to use this drug by chance to poison Austin."

"Hang on a minute. Are you accusing me of trying to poison him?"

"I'm saying when with overdoses of this drug it's almost always a result of an intentional dosing which is considered animal abuse. Thankfully it's a crime in South Carolina and..."

Gabriel appeared at my side. "Doctor?

"Yes?"

He held out his badge.

"I'm Captain Emmett Gabriel with the Charleston Police Department and we have several investigators at Mr. Parks' residence going through things. I generally don't discuss investigations, but there's no question he was the victim of a break-in. We also found residue of what I believe to be some form of meat at the scene. I'm guessing whoever did this shoved some of this sedative into the meat and gave it to Austin."

"The police are already looking into this?"

"We are. Do let me ask you a question. You say this isn't a drug someone would just stumble upon. Is it primarily a canine sedative or does it have other indicated uses?"

She looked at Anna Beth and me for a moment.

"Look at it like this. If you have a headache, you generally known to reach for a pain-killer. That's common knowledge. Most people, if they want to overdose a dog have no idea where to start so they reach for a human sedative: Valium, Percocet, even aspirin, something they would use themselves, something they know. Given we found a canine sedative, I'd be surprised if the person who did this didn't have some specific knowledge about this drug. It's generally our go-to sedative for canines. I'm comfortable saying someone planned to sedate Austin today. Or worse."

"You said the levels were quite high. Can I take that to mean whoever used this would likely have had some knowledge it was a commonly used canine sedative and also know how much to have given Austin to incapacitate him?"

"I think whoever did this wanted to quickly knock him out and really didn't have any concern what it would do to Austin. And I don't think the drug choice was an accident."

"Any idea how long the drug's been in his system?" Gabriel said.

"At least an hour, no more than three. If it had been any longer, well, you got him here in time so we don't have to worry about that."

"Thanks Doctor. I may call if I have any other questions."

"Certainly, please do. And I'm Kathy. Kathy Colven." She picked up a card from the reception counter and after writing on the back, gave it to Gabriel. "You can reach me here and my cell's on the back."

"Thanks for answering my questions Doctor. It's a big help."

"You're welcome and please call me Kathy," She turned to me. "And Mr. Parks? Please forgive me for insinuating you harmed Austin. The idea of a break-in seemed a little too convenient and we do see some terrible things here. I apologize for jumping to that conclusion. I'm not used to having patients with police officers who are interested in their well-being."

"No offense taken, I'm just glad he's going to be alright."

"He will be. They'll be bringing him out in a little while. He's had a lot of fluids to flush his system of the drug so he'll need to go out frequently. He'll also likely be out of sorts for a few days. Don't worry if he sleeps for most of the next forty-eight hours and doesn't have much of an appetite, but he should be good as new in three or four days. Call anytime with questions."

"Thank you, Doctor. Thank you so much," both Anna Beth and I said.

She turned and disappeared back into the clinic.

#

"The letters aren't there and I'm going to be surprised if this isn't related to your troubles of late. Who knew about the letters?"

"You. Brady. Some people in his office probably."

"Any concerns about Brady?"

"I don't see how. If he wanted them, all he had to do was ask?"

"Did you have copies?"

"Those at the house were copies. And I had scans on the computer, so whoever has that has all the copies, but the originals should be safe. They weren't at the house. The computer's encrypted, but the letters are so vague that doesn't really bother me. What does bother me is that if it was for the letters, well, then it gets really confusing because the people on my end who know about them aren't many and I trust all of them."

"There is one more person who knows about the letters," Anna Beth said.

"Who?"

"Whoever sent them."

"Meaning?"

"Meaning if someone wants to really mess with your head, they send you cryptic letters. Get your hopes up. Then they break in your house and steal them. Then not only are you hoping there's a miracle get out of jail free witness out there, but now you're thinking there is a big conspiracy afoot. It would be enough to really drive you crazy."

"She's not too far off there."

"Great. I guess this means the office was trashed too?"

"Soon as Anna Beth called I had a unit check it out. Having someone there may have saved it, though you may want to do something nice for Mrs. Laye. I hear she was a little surprised when three officers came in with guns drawn. You probably want to go by later to be sure and take anything you can't live without. I'll have a unit stay in the area and keep an eye on it, but I think we are a step ahead."

"Did you find anything else?" Anna Beth said. "At the house?"

"The techs found a big stain on the back porch. They were confused at first because it had traces of blood, but when they tested it turned out non-human. Just guessing, but I bet they shoved something in some hamburger or a steak, tossed it on the deck then opened the door for Austin after they trashed the lock."

"That would certainly explain how they got him. He'll eat anything."

"You know if the doctor is right on the time, someone may have been waiting for you to leave this morning."

"Means they were probably watching the house," Anna Beth said.

Gabriel looked at the business card the doctor had given him.

"Something bothering you about the doctor?"

"No, she just seems like she really cares."

"Yes, and it also seems like she is hoping a certain detective will need to ask some more questions," Anna Beth said.

THIRTY-FOUR

Gabriel returned to the house and we waited until a vet tech brought Austin out on a leash. He was standing, but very unsteady on his feet.

Anna Beth and I knelt at his side.

"How are you boy?"

He nuzzled against me and lightly licked Anna Beth's face. He sat and yawned, barely able to hold his head up. Finally, he gave up and slowly sank until he was on his belly, head on the floor. Anna Beth lightly rubbed his head.

"Poor little guy, he doesn't have any idea what's going on? Let's get you home."

He lay at our feet as the vet tech went over his discharge instructions.

I picked him up and carried him to the car.

#

Several cruisers, along with Gabriel's car, awaited us as we returned. We walked up the front steps, me carrying Austin. Gabriel and two other officers were inside talking. He broke away from their conversation.

"We'll go over things in a few minutes, but I cleared off a spot on the couch for Austin. Why don't you have a look around and we can talk when you're done."

We helped Austin onto the couch where he immediately went to sleep, oblivious to the strangers in his house. Gabriel walked into the room.

"Is it okay to start cleaning things up?" Anna Beth said.

"I'm sure it is. I'm going to go upstairs. Let me know if you find anything," Gabriel said.

Anna Beth went into the kitchen and started to straighten up.

I looked around the house and the clutter everywhere. I grabbed a trash bag and started loading it up. I figured if what was on the floor held no attachment then it was a perfect candidate for the trash. Soon I had three bags by the front door. Gabriel and the other officers had come in and out several times and were currently in the garage looking around. So far, other than my iMac, iPad, and the letters, nothing was missing.

I carried the fourth bag of trash to the porch and heaved them over the rail where they each landed with a "whomph." I walked down the steps and lifted them each into a large curb garbage can. As I walked back up the brick steps and my eyes came level with the porch, something caught my eye along the front edge of the doormat. Something white. I knelt and looked behind me to the street. Empty. I lifted the mat and beneath it saw an envelope. Just like the others before. I folded it and put it in my rear pocket without looking inside.

As I was rising to my feet, I heard the door from the garage opening inside the house and looked up to see Gabriel and the police officers.

"Find anything?" I said.

"Not much. They came in the back door from the looks of the lock. That means they had to have come through the back gate or over the fence. There's nothing that indicates they came over the fence, so we're thinking the gate. They probably drove into the driveway, walked through the gate and forced the rear door open. Looks like a garden variety crow bar in the door jam."

"No prints or anything?"

"Lots of prints. Mostly yours, Anna Beth's and even mine. No others and nothing seems obviously cleaned which means gloves. The only thing out of the ordinary is the stain on the back porch. I think they came up, opened the door, gave Austin a handful of drugged meat and waited for it to kick in. Once he was out whoever it was went through the house and walked out the front door. You have to really give your front door a pull to shut it so they probably just didn't pull it hard enough. Means they've probably never been to your house before. We've checked with the neighbors. No one saw anything."

"Great. I'm sure the neighbors will just love me."

Anna Beth had joined us from upstairs.

"We let them know to keep an eye out. Try not to worry, clean up. Try to put this behind you."

"Captain," one of the officers said.

"Yes?"

"We're going to head back to the station and talk with the crime tech guys to compare notes. Let you know if we come up with anything."

"Thanks guys. I'm heading out too," he looked over his shoulder as he walked towards the front door. "I'll see you guys soon. Call if you need anything."

"Do you have a minute? I want to talk about something."

He turned and looked at us, then to the officers walking down the steps.

"Sure."

"Get the front door and let me show you something."

I waited for him to walk back into the living room. Anna Beth joined him at my side. I pulled out the envelope from my back pocket.

"This was under the front door mat. No idea if it was there when I first got home, but I noticed it just now when I was taking out the trash."

"You touched it I guess?" Gabriel said.

"I did."

"Another letter? And they left it while the police were here. I'm starting to be more worried about the letter writer than the burglar. I'm starting to think whoever is dropping these things off is a ghost. Maybe it's Andrew," Anna Beth said.

I stared at the letter then looked to Gabriel who rolled his eyes.

"Oh, go ahead. Though I'm a little curious how my guys missed it."

I opened it and, like before, found a single sheet of paper.

"Andrew was murdered. You need to understand what Andrew knew. There are things they don't want you to know."

Both Anna Beth and Gabriel read the letter over my shoulder.

"What the hell does that mean?" she said.

"Not a single idea."

"You think the killer is doing this?" I said.

"Couple of things are starting to look clear. Seems someone knows something and we don't know who it is or what they know."

"Then let's find out," Anna Beth said.

THIRTY-FIVE

Finding out who was sending the notes was similar to investigating my case. It was a great idea, but we really had nowhere to start. Gabriel was going to think of options, Anna Beth and I were going to do the same.

After several hours of cleaning, the condition of the house had returned to one of general clutter and the chaos of earlier was thankfully gone. I wanted the internet to look up the drug Austin had been given, but with no iPad or Mac, my only option was my phone. Then I remembered the old laptop. I went up to the bedroom and into the master bath. Don't ask me why I decided to put a laptop in the bathroom, but that's where it ended up. Sure enough, under a stack of towels was the old MacBook.

I plugged it in and it started right up.

Then suddenly, without fanfare, a doorway appeared.

The lone icon on the screen read, "A. Stephens Remote Server."

When I first met Anna Beth and ended up devoting the entirety of my legal efforts to helping her, Andrew essentially stepped into my practice. To keep me in the loop, so we could easily communicate, he'd given me remote access to his office server. The portal was set up to allow complete access to all of his files, records and calendars. Though I had not used this in more than a year, actually having forgotten about it, I was hoping Andrew hadn't closed out my access.

I knew Andrew was in the process of switching over to a paperless office so theoretically, I'd be able to see what Andrew had been doing, who he'd been meeting with, what he'd been working on in the days leading up to his death.

Or I could call Brady and have him follow up. That would be the smart thing to do.

I paused for a moment and considered the options.

I launched the icon and was asked for the login information. I entered my name and the password I had selected, smiling as I typed in "Austin#1." The screen went blank.

Then suddenly I was looking at the desktop for Andrew Stephen's office server.

I wasn't sure where to start. All of his files were there, as was his calendar. There was a file folder related to the election. I started there.

There was a file for campaign contributors, copies of speeches, a file called "Transition" and a host of others. I opened the file labeled "Possible Deputies."

It was the exact list that Andrew had showed me at his house.

Print.

"Is that you printing something?"

"It is. Down in just a minute."

This one had my name on it unlike the one produced by the solicitor's office. It was also in a different font. This put a smile on my face. It didn't mean I was out of the woods, the solicitor could say Andrew created the list at his house separate from this list from his office, but all I needed to do was find some reasonable doubt.

This meant I also needed Rebecca now more than ever. She was the best witness to testify that Andrew did all his printing at his office. Maybe that was why the solicitor didn't want me to talk to her, why she been threatened. I talk to her, she effectively tanks the solicitor's theory of the crime and creates reasonable doubt for me. That was a pretty good reason to keep her off the stand. Made me wonder if the solicitor had been to Andrew's office.

As I looked at other files, I was amazed Andrew's server hadn't been removed. The solicitor's mistake was my gain. Of course, he'd say if I had access to the files, it gave me an opportunity to spy on Andrew and know what he was doing. He'd find a way to add to my motive. Maybe he'd been to the office and was waiting for me to do this. I pushed the thought from my mind.

I accessed Andrew's calendar. The answer had to be here. I started the day before the election and went back day by day. Andrew wasn't practicing much law in the weeks before the election. I saw my name on the calendar a few times.

The eagerness at my discovery started to fade. There wasn't a lot of new information. Most of it I already knew. Perhaps the most interesting thing I'd found other than the list of possible deputies was a list of people who were to be invited to the party. I wasn't finding my get out of jail free card anywhere.

As I went back further through his calendar, I saw nearly every day he had some amount of time blocked out with no description. Always in the afternoon or evening. Odd, Andrew was meticulous about noting how he spent his time

Clearly he was doing something, but what?

The pattern continued back month to month. I kept going backwards, printing each page as I moved back through Andrew's life. Then on a random day nearly a year before, the notations for the mysterious time stopped or I guess I should say they began.

I'd found the first day, a random summer day. Still the time was shown busy with no explanation. I stared at the screen a moment and happened to move my hand across the touchpad. The mouse moved over the bottom of the blocked-out time notation and as it did, a file name flashed.

I went back, slower.

"Journal–Day One" appeared as a link on the screen. I clicked it and a Word document launched. It was simply entitled "Journal."

I held my breath as it loaded. A screen appeared.

"File password protected. Enter password."

I started moving forward through the calendar again, checking a number of the blank calendar entries. They all had a hidden link to the journal as did the first.

I went downstairs to get Anna Beth, computer in tow.

THIRTY-SIX

"I think I may have something."

"Good something?"

"Definitely not bad," I placed the laptop on the coffee table in front of the couch. Anna Beth moved over so I could join her.

"I remembered I could access Andrew's server back from when I was working your case. I looked around and found this file. I can't get in it and I've got to think maybe there's something, something that could help us. At least I hope so."

We stared at the message on the laptop's screen.

"File protected. Enter password."

A dialogue box with a flashing cursor awaited our next move.

"What would he use as a password?" she said.

"No idea."

"He kept a journal?"

"Appears so. That couldn't hurt and it'll shoot the homosexual motive out of the water."

She hugged me tight. "You know that's just the solicitor trying to upset you."

I smiled.

"We've to get into that file. But I don't want to just start trying passwords, it may lock us out and I've got no idea how to reset the system if that happens."

"Do you know anyone who could get around the password?"

"No, I've never needed to get past someone's password."

"I have an idea."

"Please, share."

"Call Gabriel."

#

"You've had access to his computers and files all along?" Gabriel said.

Gabriel sat on my couch with a cup of coffee, staring at the laptop. We had opted to wait till the morning to call Gabriel.

"I have, I just didn't remember it. It's been more than a year since we set it up and I'd never used it. Yesterday was actually the first time. Probably wouldn't have remembered I had it unless my computer had been taken."

"You mentioned this to anyone else?"

"It's just us."

"Let's keep it that way. Someone knew you were going to be out yesterday and they tore the place apart. If someone finds out you have access to Andrew's computer, well, I'd rather not chance it."

"Okay. How do we get into the file? I'm certain that's where we'll find answers."

"Don't get ahead of yourself. You don't know what's in there and there's no telling if someone hasn't already left you a trail of breadcrumbs to get further into your head. The solicitor could be watching the server for all we know."

"Okay, okay, I get your point. Just tell me you have someone who can get past this password."

"I do. We've got a great computer guy at the department, but he's the last person we can use."

"Because he'd have to file a report," Anna Beth said.

"Exactly right. We use him, or anyone at the department, it's the same thing as calling the solicitor and telling him. It's one thing for me to help you on my own time, but I can't start using other people at the department. Don't take this the wrong way, but maybe you planted something there or maybe it's the evidence that says you did it."

"I know you're playing devil's advocate but keep in mind, I didn't do it. Any of this."

"Nothing makes me think you're anything but an innocent man. But look at it this way: You've been charged with murder and you get a crappy plea offer from the solicitor. Then, suddenly you remember you had access to the victim's computer and you find a get out of jail free card."

I sat back down on the couch.

"Noah. He's right. We can't rush this. If there's something there to help you then the last thing we want to have happen is to not be able to use it. Or, worse, to have it used against you and have it look like you orchestrated it. If Gabriel can't help us, maybe we take it to Brady," she paused. "I see the gears turning. Do you know someone who can help?"

I looked back and forth between both of them.

"I do have someone. Maybe. I just don't know his name or where he lives. And I'll need your help."

"Of course you will."

Surprisingly it had only taken a few phone calls and Gabriel had the name and an address I needed.

"I guess you want me to drive you over to talk to this guy?" He stared at the scrap of paper in his hand before handing it to me.

"No, you probably shouldn't go. No offense, but I think he'll pick up that you're a cop pretty quick. Probably won't even talk to me, but I have to try. But if you guys don't hear from me in a couple of hours, you know where I'll be."

"Parks, this isn't the best idea you've ever had."

"We don't have a lot of other options. I'll go and ask and if he can't help, I'll leave. Simple as that."

"Simple as that, huh? You don't even know if this guy knows a thing about computers." he said.

"Give me an hour or so, alright? I have a feeling."

Anna Beth was sitting on the couch with Austin, rubbing his head.

"Are you sure about this?" she said.

I looked at her and reached to scratch Austin's chin.

"No, but I have a feeling and, well, we need a break, something. And this is all we have."

"I'm pretty sure the right thing to do is to tell you to sit down, forget about this and let Brady deal with it," she said.

"Is there a but in there?"

I looked from Gabriel back to her. He was staring at her with his hands on his hips.

"Not exactly. It's just that all of this is crazy. It's something I'd have never have thought for a moment we would have to deal with ever again. It shouldn't surprise me we have to push the envelope a bit to get a handle on this. I just don't like it."

She looked to me, then to Gabriel. He spoke.

"You've got an hour. I'm not really excited about this."

"I know, but right now, it's the only option we have."

THIRTY-SEVEN

I turned from my neighborhood onto Highway 17 and headed towards the address Gabriel had given me. It was in North Charleston and, while the miles were few, it might as well have been a half a world away.

I turned off the Crosstown and headed through the Charleston peninsula leaving downtown behind me. The stately buildings of downtown Charleston, some dating as far back as the 1700's, gave way to Rutledge Avenue and turn-of-the-nineteenth century homes around the Military College of South Carolina, also known as The Citadel.

Further down, Rutledge turned to Highway 52 and the scenery changed from charming Southern neighborhoods to crumbling factories and vacant storefronts punctuated by tattoo parlors, liquor stores, and strip bars. The pattern was broken only by the occasional overgrown vacant lot, abandoned building, or home. It would make a good set for an apocalyptic movie.

Lately, whenever I found myself alone, I began to think about the unknown. And that was perhaps the worst part of this process, the not knowing. In the past, I'd had clients tell me about this and I thought I had a handle on it, but I was quickly learning a little bit of perspective went a long way. I had on more than one occasion, told a client not to worry, to let me as his attorney handle his case, that they would drive themselves crazy wondering about the "what if's." I could recall exactly what I would say to these clients to address exactly the same thing I was thinking at this very moment and not one word of what I had said in the past was doing me the least bit of good. If given a few moments, my mind raced to worst-case conclusions, conclusions with ominous questions marks.

Would I end up in jail?

Would I lose Anna Beth?

What if we just left it all behind?

On and on it went, each scenario worse than the one before.

Up until now I'd been sitting on the sidelines watching as the game, the game of my life, unfolded before me. But now, accused of a murder I didn't commit, my legal career perhaps over, a lawyer who was thinking jail time. It was time to get in the game and take control.

Now, to start this, I was going to talk to a stranger in hopes he would be able to help put the pieces of my life back together. This stranger was also a criminal.

As I drove towards the unknown, I believed the potential reward far outweighed the risk. After all, if I didn't take a few chances, how was anything ever going to work out in my favor? And if I got caught, what would they do? Arrest me?

#

Spruill Avenue is the main artery through one of the worst crime areas in Charleston County. Drug activity was the most apparent crime, but any other sort of illegal activity was just a short stroll away.

The area would be a goldmine for a police reality show.

No matter how hard the police tried to it clean up, the drug dealers seemed to stay one step ahead or at least bounce back, time and again. There were plenty of hardworking people in the area, but the drug dealers preyed upon them and, more troubling, upon their children. In a neighborhood where there was little to offer by way of incentive to stay in school, children were all too easily impressed by a teenager with a roll of cash, a shiny necklace, and a new pair of kicks. Lots of children were recruited into a dangerous lifestyle.

If you didn't live in the area and you were there, chances were slim you were there for any good reason.

Yet here I was.

As I traveled along, the eyes of street dealers studied me, hoping for a sale as I turned onto the street where the address was located. I followed the numbers, those that I could find, to the house I was seeking. Fortunately, the address was clearly marked on a post to the right side of the porch. I parked my Jeep on the street.

A child across the street eyed me suspiciously through the fence surrounding his yard. I turned to face the house. My eyes followed a chain that emerged from the shadows below the porch. It snaked towards and up the steps, to where it was attached to a bolt in the wall. I shut the Jeep's door.

I took several steps up a dirt path worn hard in the grassless front yard. An old rusted grill was partially hidden in

213

the weeds that grew along a fence. Two worn kitchen chairs were all that occupied the front porch. I glanced to the other side of the house where a row of bushes formed a barrier to the next lot over.

The house was adorned with old, faded clapboard, one of hundreds gracing this part of town. What paint remained was dingy and peeling away, several shutters were missing and most of those still present hung precariously, looking as if the slightest breeze could cause them to fall away. A screen door banged softly in the fall breeze. The windowless front door was shut.

A growl rose from under the porch.

"Easy boy," I fished a dog treat from my pocket. Fortunately, I always had them in the Jeep for Austin and had grabbed them when I saw the chain.

I threw it in the direction of the growl.

The growling stopped and a black and white dog head appeared from under the porch. I smiled. He eyed me for a moment and, with his teeth slightly bared, walked towards the treat, still watching me. It was an Australian Shepherd mix. Finally, something was going my way. He sniffed at the treat and then swallowed it in a single bite.

No more teeth.

I threw him another which he caught in mid-air. I kneeled but avoided making eye contact as he came over and sniffed my outstretched hand. He didn't have a tail, but the nub where the tail should have been was going crazy.

"Good boy."

"He's a she," I heard a voice say.

THIRTY-EIGHT

I looked up and saw a tall black man standing on the porch, the door now open.

I rose and the Aussie leaned against my leg, her nose pushing my hand away as she sniffed at the pocket containing the treats, her nub wagging so eagerly it caused her entire backside to swing.

"She's friendly."

"Not usually."

"I have one myself. What's her name?"

We stood in silence.

"What's yours?" the man said.

Her nub continued to wag and she gave a 'woof' as she raised a paw to my pocket. The man on the porch moved to the top of the steps. He was tall, easily over six feet. He had on socks, Nike shower sandals and basketball shorts. He was shirtless. I looked to him and then to his right forearm where a computer monitor was tattooed.

"Nice ink there. I'm guessing you're Melvin Jones."

He stretched out his arm and rubbed a hand over the tattoo.

"Guess all you want, but it might be a good idea for you to do it from the front seat of your Jeep there with me in the rearview mirror. Gettin' smaller."

"We've met before."

"So?"

"We shared a cell about a month back."

"So?"

"So, I need your help?

He stared at me, my hand absently rubbing the dog's head. "Wait a minute. I know you. You're that lawyer killed the guy running for solicitor, right?"

"I'm that lawyer they arrested for it. I didn't kill anyone and my name's Noah. Noah Parks."

He laughed and sat on the top step.

"That's funny. Innocent and arrested. Never heard that before. Come here, Gracie."

She didn't move from my side. I gave her another treat.

"You're cheatin," Melvin said.

"Maybe."

"She usually don't let people this close. She ain't good with strangers."

"Maybe she likes me."

"Maybe. Tell you what, cause I'm curious, I'll give you a minute. One minute. What kind of help you need?"

"I'm hoping that tattoo on your arm means you know something about computers."

"If it does?"

"Then maybe you can help me."

He stared at me in silence. I gave Gracie another treat. He said nothing.

"Okay, maybe I've wasted your time. Sorry to bother you."

I tossed a treat towards the steps and Gracie trotted over to it. I turned my back to Melvin and took a step towards the Jeep.

"Hold up. You still got some of your minute left. How'd you find me?"

I looked back at him. He looked at me then up and down the street. I followed his eyes and could see drapes and shades moving in almost every house, those that weren't burned out or abandoned.

"Tell me and maybe I'll find another minute or two," he said.

"Don't worry about that. I've still got friends and it's not too hard to find out who's been locked up."

"Maybe. You feel all those eyes staring at you?"

"I figure you getting an unannounced visit from a white guy who's feeding your dog might get a few looks."

"True, but you'd have to be a fool to just drive over here. I know you know 'bout this neighborhood. Half those eyes are thinking how they can get that Jeep in their front yard or your shoes on their feet. The other half, well, I'm guessing you know what they're thinking."

"I know this isn't the safest place for me. I didn't kill anyone. And maybe I'm hoping you can help me with that."

"What? You do something all crazy like come up over here just cause of a tattoo on my arm?"

"Short answer is yes."

Melvin stared and glanced at Gracie as she lay at his feet.

"She's not much of a guard dog."

"No, she ain't. Not today anyway."

He knelt squatted down beside her, looking at me for a moment then shifting his gaze to her as he petted her head.

"I hate that chain probably more than she does, but if I don't keep her on it, someone round here'll steal her," he said more to Gracie than he did not me. "Damn crackheads. Alright, say I know a thing or two about computers."

"Then I'd like to talk."

He looked at me a moment longer.

"Ain't this some shit. If you're coming up over here, you must be down the dead end. Alright, I'll bite. What you need?"

"Where can we talk?"

"Well come on in?"

I hesitated a moment.

"Don't worry, no one's going to mess with your car. Heck, someone might even wash it," he said with a chuckle as he turned to go back in the house. Gracie rose and climbed the steps. Marvin unchained her and she followed him looking back at me as she went inside.

THIRTY-NINE

The inside of Melvin's house matched the outside, only less light. The walls were unfinished wood turned gray over time. The furniture, a couple of ragged chairs and an old couch, were covered with stained sheets. Two milk crates with a worn door placed horizontally over them served as a coffee table. Other than the front door, there were two other doors, one that led to the kitchen through a bedroom whose decor appeared to match that of the den. The other was closed. Gracie took up a spot on the couch.

I was beginning to think I'd made a mistake.

"What you need?"

"Straight to the point. Okay. I have a file on a server I need to get into. It's password protected. I need you to open it."

"You mean an innocent guy out on bail for murder's running around on a network ain't his. The police don't take too kindly to that kind of behavior, but I'm guessing you already know that don't you. Being a lawyer and all."

He laughed.

"Why's that funny?"

"Come on, it's funny. You're a Charleston lawyer, probably got an office on Broad Street. Bet you've told more clients than you can count 'Don't do this,' 'Be careful about that,' 'If you do it, I don't want to hear about it.' And here you are, get handcuffed and first thing you do is start looking the other way when it comes to those laws you swore to, how is it? 'uphold and defend.'"

"I didn't come for a sermon."

"No, you came for my help and if you want it you get a little sermon. I'm gonna enjoy this."

"I'm starting to realize that."

"Alright, what kind of password you need me to jump."

"It's a file on a remote server. I can get into the server, but not the file."

"How'd you get in the server?"

"I have my own password and username."

"This about your murder?"

"I hope so," I said.

"I can help."

"You can say that without even seeing the file?"

"Sure can."

"And you'll just help me? Just like that? No charge."

"No, not just like that. And certainly not for free, but I don't want your money. If the file's important enough to have you find me and come up over here in this neighborhood then you think it's pretty important, but I don't want to tell you some price and short change myself. If I open it for you, you'll need to do something for me sometime. Maybe a few somethings. If you can live with that, you'll get your file opened."

"That's asking a lot."

"Don't seem you've got a problem asking me to avoid a few laws. That's the deal, take it or leave it."

"Alright. When can you look at it?"

"Now," he said.

#

"Most of my friends call me 'It,' he said as he turned and stepped towards the closed door in the small living room.

"'It?' Why would they do that?"

"Cause most of 'em are just ignorant. My brother's an insurance agent up in Summerville and when we was kids, back when I started getting good with computers, he started calling me I.T. Said I was his own private IT department. When I started living back in here most of folks didn't know no better so ended up being just 'It.'"

"Ok. 'It.' Is that what I you want me to call you?"

"No, you can call me Melvin," he said as he pulled out his iPhone and held it to the door. "Or Mr. Jones."

I heard the faintest wisp of a lock mechanism.

"Step into my office."

He opened the door to reveal a modern computer work space. I stepped into the threshold and looked back over my shoulder into the living room. Gracie stopped momentarily as she crossed the threshold into the computer room. She went straight to a dog bed by a desk that looked like it came from IKEA.

There was no comparison between the two rooms. In Melvin's computer room, there were four iMacs on the desk. Several iPads were scattered about. Ethernet cables ran to a bank of servers and more disappeared into a junction box on the wall. The room was easily ten degrees cooler than the living room from where we had just come. A small bedroom adjoined with a bathroom beyond.

"This is surprising."

"What? Just because I was in jail you think I'm a criminal?"

"Stereotypes. I apologize."

"Remember, you get locked up for child support too. I was late last month and that bitch of a baby's momma had me picked up."

"Pardon the question, but what do you do?"

"I've got some people in the area I do computer work for. Nothing over the line, but let's say on the edge enough they want someone they can trust. It pays in cash so I need a little extra security around here. Everyone knows me, but sometimes the dope back up in here makes people forget they shouldn't come in without an invitation."

"Probably best I don't know anymore."

"Yeah, probably. Pull up a seat."

He motioned to a chair. I sat. Melvin sat at his desk and started to work.

"You got someone can turn the computer on at your place?"

"I do."

"Well, give them a call."

I called Anna Beth and had her turn on the computer. She was happy to hear from me.

Melvin scribbled something on a Post-it note and handed it to me.

"Have her send a blank email to that address."

I repeated the email address to Anna Beth.

I heard a ping from Melvin's computer and instantly he had my computer's desktop up on his screen.

"You need to get a little tighter on your internet security."

"Maybe I'll get you to come set it up."

He launched Andrew's remote access and I provided him the login and password information to the server. I then directed him to the protected file.

"Can you open it?"

He started off on a flurry of keystrokes, his eyes darting back and forth among the monitors. The monitor showing the remote connection to my computer stayed constant, the others were cycling through different screens so quickly I was unable to follow any progress.

As he continued to work, Gracie busied herself with a chew toy on a dog bed in the corner.

"Yep, I can get past it. Here's the thing though. I can get you in, but there's something watching that part of the server. Could be just the activity monitor. Could be someone waiting for you to try to log in. Can't tell past that. If I get you in, minimum there'll be a record. If someone's watching that file as soon as it's opened, they'll know."

"And it will lead them right to you."

"Nope, right to you. I'm doing all of this through your computer."

"Of course you are?" I thought a moment. "Do it and download the file to my computer."

"Already had it set up to do just that," he hit the 'Enter' key. "Done."

"That's it?"

"That's it. If I was you, I'd call back to where your computer is and have them put a password on your machine. Use something random. Something long. Harder to jump."

"I'll take care of that."

He reached for a business card and wrote something on the back.

"Don't use something simple like whoever set that one," he said as he handed me the card. "You'll need that to get in again. That's the password to that file."

"Thanks. I owe you."

"Yes, you do. We'll talk again, I'm sure. Who knows, I might need someone to help me with my child support if you ever get to be a lawyer again. You can find your way out?" he said with a laugh.

"Yes," I said not knowing what his laugh meant.

I walked out though the dirty living room looking back to his office before I headed out the front door. Gracie followed me to the porch. I reached into my pocket and fished out a handful of treats, dropping them on the porch where she started to devour them.

In my other hand was his business card.

"Melvin Jones – Private IT Consulting"

I turned the card over and found a single word.

"Vanderhorst2291"

It was a street in Charleston near the College of Charleston, but aside from that it meant nothing.

I called Anna Beth who was waiting with Gabriel at the house and told them the news. I told them to log off Andrew's server.

Then as an afterthought, I had her change all of our passwords.

I took Melvin's advice and put his house in my rearview mirror. He appeared on the front porch, rubbing Gracie's head, as he grew smaller in the rearview.

FORTY

Anna Beth looked wide-eyed as I recounted the story for her. Gabriel stared and shook his head.

I took out Melvin's card and showed it to Gabriel.

"Don't suppose that on the back means anything to you?"

He turned the card over.

"Street downtown near the college. The numbers don't mean a thing. It isn't a house number. The street's only four or five blocks long, numbers don't go up near that high. I don't think they even hit three digits."

Anna Beth reached for the card.

"He does private IT consulting?"

"He does and his street name is 'It.' "

"That's pretty amazing Parks. Meet a guy in lockup and he happens to be a computer guy."

"I had to look at his tattoo every morning for a week and he had a different air about him than the other guys in there. I had a feeling."

"Let's see what it says, the file," Gabriel said.

Anna Beth started the computer and we were soon looking at the log in screen.

"Melvin said the file was being monitored but he couldn't tell me if it was the server's activity log watching it or if someone else is watching it."

"You're telling me someone knows you have the file?"

"Melvin says at a minimum there'll be a record of my accessing the server and at most someone watched me do it."

"We've got the file now, let's open it and see what's inside," Anna Beth said.

I looked to Gabriel who shrugged his shoulders. I launched it and entered the password.

"Journal–Day One" were the only words we saw on the screen. The rest of the file was empty.

"That's it?" Anna Beth said.

I selected properties from the pull-down menu. A box appeared and I selected the "General" tab.

"The file was created over a year ago. Looks like it was modified about two weeks ago."

"Meaning what?'

Gabriel looked at Anna Beth, then to me. He shook his head.

"Someone's erased everything that was there?"

"It appears so," I said.

FORTY-ONE

NASCAR racing is one of the most popular spectator sports in the world. Rather amazing given that it's less than a century old and still a family-owned business. There are a lot of reasons to like NASCAR. Even with all of the restrictions and regulations, the cars still represent some of the most powerful machines one will ever see in action. The cars approach speeds of near 200 miles per hour and the environment on race day can be electric.

Plain and simple, the fans love the action. It's intoxicating and addictive because, even when an accident occurs and the race proceeds under caution, the race is still moving forward. Every fan knows at any moment the action could explode into chaos.

It's that unknown that keeps everyone's attention.

Even as the finish approaches, after hundreds of miles, the final few seconds may actually determine the outcome of the race.

I'd never really been a big fan myself, but I was beginning to feel as if my life was becoming a NASCAR race. As of late, my life had been high-speed lap after lap towards a finish where a checkered flag awaited. Then out comes the caution flag as that slowed progress to a crawl.

Once again, staring at a computer screen displaying a document with only a title, I felt I was on a NASCAR track approaching a dead end at 200 miles per hour.

"Now what?" Anna Beth said.

"I'm at a complete loss. Gabriel?"

"Looks like you might want to go back for a little chat with your friend Melvin."

"Really? Thought you didn't like that idea in the first place."

"I didn't, and still don't, but he's ...."

"I'll give him a call."

I reached for Melvin's card and my cell phone. Gabriel started to speak but stopped, chuckled and dropped his head, shaking it as he looked to his feet with a smile, hands in his pockets.

I dialed the numbers and waited. Nothing but rings. Then Melvin's voice.

"Leave a message."

"Melvin. Noah Parks. Please give me a call."

"Not there?" Gabriel said.

"No. He's out."

"Or isn't going to talk to you," Anna Beth said.

"I'm going over to Melvin's."

"No, you're not. You called him. Now wait for him to call you back. He helped you, or maybe dangled a little bait for you, but you don't know this guy. Ever think he erased the file after he copied it and is setting you up to be his bankroll? Classic long con."

I looked at him.

"No, I hadn't thought of that. Maybe you might have mentioned that before I called him."

"Maybe, but would you have listened? Didn't think so. And let me guess, he didn't charge you, did he?"

I looked at Gabriel, but didn't give an answer he already knew. I tossed my cell phone on the table. It landed with a loud pop causing Austin to jump.

"Then we're back to square one. You'd think I'd be comfortable here by now," Anna Beth said.

"I guess we'll wait on Melvin to call back."

"Yes. You wait. I'll check up on Melvin, look at his record and give you an update if I find anything. How's that?"

"What else can we do?" My hands raised in frustration.

Gabriel looked back and forth at each of us. Austin jumped up on the couch and with a sigh stretched on his side. I was glad someone here was able to relax. Next time around I was coming back as a dog.

"Alright, I'm going to go to work. You," he pointed to me. "You stay here and don't go back to Melvin's. My guess is he's setting you up for the long con. And you make sure he stays here."

"He won't go anywhere. We're going to spend the day inside talking about options."

"Call me if you hear from him."

We walked him to the door. Austin, who was acting a little less groggy, jumped down and trotted to the window where he watched him walk down to his car giving a 'woof' as Gabriel shut his car door and backed out of my drive.

"Now what?"

I sighed.

"I have no idea. I'm growing tired of dead ends and I'm fresh out of ideas."

I walked back into the den and collapsed on the couch. Anna Beth joined me.

"I might have an idea. Something to get our minds off of this for a little while."

I looked at her and grinned.

"What did you have in mind?"

"Well," she adjusted herself on the couch. "I thought we all might get out of the house and have an afternoon off from all of this."

"What did you have in mind?"

"It's Dog Days at The Joe."

The Charleston RiverDogs were the local minor league baseball team. Through the years, they'd enjoyed a variety of different names and had been affiliated with a number of different major league teams. Presently they were a class A affiliate of the New York Yankees. The interesting thing about the RiverDogs, and what set them apart from scores of other class A teams was their approach to the fans.

The RiverDogs were owned by a group whose members included the actor Bill Murray. It wasn't unusual to find him enjoying one of the games. One of the owners was Mike Veeck, the son of the legendary and innovative baseball marketing legend, Bill Veeck, Jr. The younger Veeck, a marketing master in his own right, was definitely carrying on his father's legacy. After all, how can you not attract a crowd when you book Tonya Harding to appear on a bat giveaway night?

One of the perennial fan favorite promotions was Dog Days when fans were allowed, even encouraged, to bring their dogs to the park.

"That's actually a great idea and I think it would be good for him to get outside for a bit after having been cooped up in here."

"Great," she said, grabbing Austin's leash.

Upon seeing the leash, Austin was already standing by the door waiting for us to head to the park. Clearly, he was feeling better.

FORTY-TWO

The RiverDogs stadium, The Joe, named after Joe Riley, Charleston's former mayor in near perpetuity, is situated along the Ashley River in Charleston, hence the name RiverDogs. At least that's what I gathered as I wasn't otherwise sure what a Riverdog might be.

After a short drive, we were early enough that parking wasn't a problem.

Austin was pacing around the back of the Jeep knowing he was going to a game. I would forever believe the dog loved baseball.

"Someone's excited," Anna Beth said.

I turned the Jeep into the parking lot and stopped in a spot just across the street from the front gate.

Anna Beth busied herself getting Austin leashed up and out of the Jeep. The two of us, and one excited canine, crossed the street eager for an afternoon of baseball.

The stadium seated close to 6,000 people and it wasn't unusual for it to be full on game day, but arriving early we found the park largely empty. After purchasing tickets, we walked up the few steps to the main concourse where there was a variety of food and beverage vendors located between the entrance and the right field line. We walked over to one of the ID stations and picked up our wristbands in case we wanted a beer. We decided to head on to our seats and let Austin meet a few other dogs on the way.

"Hang on a sec," I said as I paused to put my driver's license back in my wallet.

It slipped from my hand and I bent to retrieve it. As I was rising, I absently glanced across the concourse and noticed a familiar face around the corner. I turned back to Anna Beth.

"Did you see that?"

"What?"

"Over there by the beer garden?"

"No. What was it?"

"More like a who. Listen. Talk about coincidence. I think I saw Rebecca. Take Austin and walk towards the beer garden then take the tunnel to the left and meet me at the right field concourse. I'm going to go around the other way through the tunnel and will meet you there in less than a minute. Let's see if we can't talk to her here. In public."

"Okay." Though she looked a bit on the confused side.

She walked away from me as I turned the opposite direction towards the field. I quickly made my way to the walkway that bordered the field, paralleling the third base foul line. I looked over my shoulder to see Anna Beth disappear from view around the corner. Just a short way up, I turned to my right into a tunnel that connected the field level walkway to the main concourse. As I walked into the tunnel a familiar face was walking hastily towards me, though she was yet to see me.

"Hi, Rebecca."

Rebecca stopped in the middle of the tunnel as Anna Beth and Austin came up behind her.

"I didn't know you were a baseball fan."

"Noah, I, I like baseball. Andrew used to come here, and, what are you doing here?"

"Anna Beth, you remember Rebecca, don't you? From Andrew's office."

"Yes. Hi Rebecca."

"Hi," Rebecca said, as Austin walked up and sniffed her leg.

"Don't worry, he's friendly," Anna Beth said.

"Is this Austin?" Rebecca said, as she knelt to pet him.

"Yes, that's Austin. How did you know his name?"

"Andrew says he's a great dog."

"Andrew did like him. You know, someone poisoned him."

She turned her eyes up to me but said nothing.

"Someone broke into our house and poisoned him," Anna Beth said.

"I'm sorry about that."

"Rebecca, I'd still really like to talk to you."

"I know."

"But?"

"You know I can't talk to you, Noah."

"Rebecca. I know you've been told not to talk to Noah, but we really need your help," Anna Beth didn't press her, but her voice was firm.

"I can't Noah, I just can't."

Austin was being quite demanding, pawing at her hand for more attention.

"Calm down boy. Thing is Rebecca, you can. I'm sure you know that. No one can do anything to you for talking to me. Think about all the times Andrew had you run down witnesses to help with his clients' cases. This is exactly the same except I need, no, I *have* to talk to you. I just want you to help me understand what Andrew was doing before he died. I don't want to sound dramatic, but you may be my last hope. Tell me about Andrew's journal."

Austin pulled against his leash to reach Rebecca as she backed away. He lunged towards her, pulling Anna Beth along. For a moment, I had a concern he might bite her, but he was only interested in more attention.

"You know about the journal?"

"We do, Rebecca." Anna Beth said. "It has something in it that will help Noah, doesn't it?"

She looked at Anna Beth.

"Do you love him? Noah?"

Anna Beth looked at me then back to Rebecca. I could tell she wasn't expecting that question.

"I do, Rebecca, I do love him and that's why I'm asking you to help him, to help both of us."

She looked to the ground while she petted Austin's head.

"Noah, please don't make me."

She stood and faced me.

"Rebecca. Rebecca, please."

I reached for her arm as she backed away from me.

"No, just go."

Her voice echoed in the tunnel. As Rebecca spoke, a police officer passing the tunnel heard her and looked our way.

"Is everything alright here?"

Austin sat at Anna Beth's side and Rebecca moved a step further away from me.

"Everything's alright, officer."

"Wasn't talking to you, sir. Ladies? Everything alright?"

"Oh, yes sir," Rebecca said without a hint of the apprehension she was showing seconds before. "Anna Beth and Noah were just going to their seats and were asking me if I wanted to join them. I just told them to go on. Was I being too loud?"

The officer looked as if he was caught off guard.

"There's no problem here?"

"No officer, not a thing," Anna Beth said. "We'll see you later, Rebecca."

"Great. Is it okay if I go, Officer?"

"Um, yes, if there's nothing wrong."

I was sure she was headed to the front gate. She glanced back at me as she turned the corner and disappeared.

"Sorry to bother you, Officer," I paused to look at his name tag. "Best."

"It's okay, I guess these tunnels make things sound louder. You folks enjoy the game."

He wandered back down the tunnel and disappeared into the crowd.

"That's odd running into her here," Anna Beth said.

"Not as odd as that line she fed the officer."

"I'm guessing she didn't want to deal with him, but she's clearly afraid to talk to you."

The sun was reaching into the tunnel and reflecting on Anna Beth's hair which was moving with the slight breeze. She had on a sundress that came to mid-thigh. She looked beautiful. I walked over to her, took her head in my hands and kissed her.

"What was that for?"

"Just because. Let's go watch some baseball."

After all, everything was going to be here in the morning.

FORTY-THREE

We spent the game in our seats watching baseball, holding hands, flirting and generally acting as if we didn't have a care in the world. It was just what we needed. An escape. Austin alternated barking at the players, playing with a few dogs near our seats, eating boiled peanuts and napping.

Maybe it was the baseball, maybe we were both at our limit, but miraculously we were able to escape for a few hours. After the game the three of us headed through the twilight back to the car. I opened the rear hatch for Austin, shutting it after he was inside.

"I enjoyed that."

"So did I. We've got a lot to deal with, but forgetting for a few hours was nice."

She stepped closer, put her hand behind my neck and pulled my lips to hers.

Her hands moved to my hips and pulled me close to her. I ran my hands through her hair, down her sides and let them come to rest momentarily on her hips. Then I slowly moved one hand up the middle of her back letting it stop on her neck.

She pulled away from me enough to speak in a whisper.

"I'm not ready to go back to reality just yet."

I pulled her lips to mine.

"Let's go home."

"Let's."

We continued to kiss as we moved towards her side of the car. I opened the door and she got inside.

"Hurry," she said.

Somehow, I managed to avoid a ticket on the way home.

#

The sun came up the next morning to find us in bed. Anna Beth had her head on my chest and one leg draped over me. Austin was at the foot of the bed on his back, all four paws in the air, clearly feeling his old self.

I watched the ceiling fan, enjoying simply staying in bed for a bit longer before the day started anew.

Reality started to creep back in from the recesses of my mind.

What did the notes mean?

Who was sending them?

Had Melvin set me up?

What had been in Andrew's journal?

Was S. Bart involved in this?

My head started to swim thinking about everything that was going on. Clearly, the relaxation from the prior day was gone. The frustration started to set in. I started to think about NASCAR again. The caution flag was gone, but I was clearly back on the track traveling in circles.

I felt Anna Beth stir beside me.

"Good morning."

She stretched.

"Hi."

"Sleep well?"

"I did. Thank you very much."

She kissed me and rolled out of bed, picking up a T-shirt from the floor.

"Coffee?"

"Sure. I'll be right down."

She walked out of the bedroom with Austin at her heels. In a moment, I heard the back door open. That would be Austin heading out into the back yard.

I showered, dressed and headed downstairs.

"I'm going to run to the office and pick up the original letters so we can have them here at the house. Want to come?"

"Sure."

#

Early Saturday morning traffic in Charleston is nonexistent. That's one of the many great things about the city. We were in and out of the office in a matter of minutes. The sight of my cluttered desk didn't distract me at all.

It was a quick trip even with a stop for coffee.

When we got back to the house we set the letters out on the coffee table and stared. Austin came over and sniffed at them, staring at them with us for a moment before he stretched out on the living room floor with a sigh. I walked over and kneeled beside him. He rolled over, presenting his stomach for a belly rub.

"He seems to be feeling better."

"He does," she said. "I want to ask you a question," she said as she turned to face me.

"Yes?"

"Brady's good, right?"

"He is. Very good. That's why I, well, why we, hired him."

"Is he serious about the three years in jail?"

"Honestly, yes. He knows I don't like it, but being realistic, for a murder charge, three years is a gift. And he knows I know that."

"And innocence doesn't enter into it."

"Not at all."

"Then this is all about losing me as an alibi?"

"Innocence doesn't really have anything to do with it. It's all about what the solicitor can prove. I started with an alibi. Today, I don't have one. That doesn't mean it's a slam dunk, but the case is not as good today. Brady thinks the three years balances everything."

"Then that's the best deal we get? But, but isn't it happening way too fast?"

"Maybe to both. It's usually months before an offer is made unless the defense pushes for one. When he made this offer, the solicitor sped things up. The solicitor wants me to confess. Brady knows this and he knows the solicitor knows it. If he wants it so bad, Brady is going to make him pay for it, hence the three years. Trouble with that is I'm the one behind bars doing the time while Brady gets to say he did a great job and the solicitor gets a confession."

"Be honest with me, will you really have to go to jail?"

"I wasn't being all that dramatic yesterday when I told Rebecca that she might be my last hope. A trial really means only two options. I go free or a conviction and that means jail."

"Which would mean more than three years."

"Or worse."

"Well, Mr. Parks, that simply isn't an option."

I smiled.

"Come on, we're going for a ride," she said.

"Where to?"

"We're going to see your Melvin."

"We are?"

"I'm not going to sit here and feel helpless. You're not going to jail and that leaves the two of us to figure this out. Melvin may be trying to con you, but if he is, then we push back and find out what was on the file he erased. If not, then maybe he can us his computer know-how to tell us who did erase it."

I smiled.

"Don't make me talk you into it, just come on. Okay?"

"You don't have to talk me into it anything. Let's go."

FORTY-FOUR

The ride over to Melvin's didn't seem to take as long as before.

Yes, I was ignoring Brady's counsel and Gabriel's instructions. I knew both of them were looking out for me and I understood that Melvin may be conning me, but I was done sitting on the sidelines waiting for results.

Through the years, the law had provided structure and guidance as I represented clients. I thought back to the times I counseled them, times I told them I understood. I had understood as their lawyer, but until you've been charged with a crime, until you are facing the reality of prison, you can never understand. Never.

Funny thing wasn't that I realized this change; rather I was surprised at how quickly I had abandoned the structure and familiarity of the law when it was my freedom on the line. I guess self-preservation has a way of prioritizing perspective.

We turned off of Spruill onto Melvin's street. I watched the windows, blinds, and drapes as I moved slowly along. Faces and eyes followed us. I stopped in front of the white clapboard house I had visited only the day before.

"This is where you went yesterday?"

"This is the place."

"I see why Gabriel wasn't too excited about your coming here. And I'm guessing it's rougher than it looks."

"It is."

I could tell something was wrong as soon as I stepped into the yard and saw the front door opened and the screen hanging on one hinge. I walked to the porch and heard only silence. The chain leading under the porch was slack. I knelt and pulled. It gave with no resistance. As I retrieved it a broken collar was all I found on the other end. No Gracie.

"Noah, what's wrong?"

"Call Gabriel and tell him to get over here."

I rose and started to step onto the porch but thought better of it and walked back to the Jeep as Anna Beth was ending the phone call.

"He was at the office but he's on his way. Fair warning, he didn't sound too happy."

"No, I should imagine not."

It didn't take Gabriel long to arrive. He pulled up in his cruiser with two North Charleston police cars behind him. I knew without asking he was none too pleased with me.

"Listen...," I said but was quickly cut off.

"No, you listen. The last thing I said, to both of you, was not to go to Melvin's. I said that, didn't I? But still, here we all are, at Melvin's."

I started to speak.

"Parks. Keep your mouth shut. You'll just piss me off even more."

The police officers joined us.

"What are they doing here," Anna Beth said.

"We're in North Charleston. Gabriel doesn't have jurisdiction here."

"No, I don't. And neither do you. Anywhere. Alright, what's going on?"

"Yes, how about you tell us what's going on, sir?" one of the officers said.

I looked to Gabriel and back to the officer.

"Sir?" the second officer said to me.

Gabriel looked at me but said nothing.

"The man who lives here, Melvin Jones, I was speaking to him yesterday about some legal issues. When I couldn't get him on the phone today, well, when I didn't hear from him, I decided to drive out here to talk to him."

"Legal issues?" Gabriel said.

"Are you an attorney or something?" the first officer said.

"I'm an attorney, but not practicing at the moment."

"Alright, but why did you call Captain Gabriel?"

"I called him because I know him. I didn't think about the jurisdiction."

"Guess we know why you're not practicing, huh?" said the second officer as he turned and walked across the yard to the house.

"Listen. I came up and the door was opened and the screen was hanging halfway off. It wasn't like that yesterday. And the dog. The dog's not on her leash."

"Sir, do you know anything about this neighborhood? Usually when we find folks from your part of Charleston over this way it's for legal issues, well, illegal issues. This is crack alley central. The dog..."

"Tate. Come look at this," the officer who had walked to the house said.

"Stay here with the detective," Officer Tate said as he walked towards the house.

Standing at the bottom of the steps the officers looked at the porch. The second officer knelt and studied a section of the steps. Almost in unison both officers reached for and pulled their side arms, each quickly moving up the steps to opposite sides of the front door, their backs to the house. Officer Tate pointed at Gabriel and motioned to his cruiser.

"What's going...," Anna Beth said but was cut off by Gabriel.

"Move," Gabriel said as he quickly ushered us behind his car.

I saw one of the officers speak into his radio handset on his shoulder and almost instantly I heard sirens in the distance. The other officer pulled out his collapsible baton and extended it with a flick of the wrist. With it he moved the screen door to the side and then slowly pushed the front door completely open. I had a good angle on the front door, but I couldn't see inside. It was too dark. Officer Tate took out a flashlight and stepped across the threshold into the house. The second officer followed. Both officers had their guns raised at the ready.

"Anyone have any idea what's happening?"

"Did you go in the house today?" Gabriel said.

"No. Neither of us did. We didn't even walk up on the porch. What the hell is going on?"

"Nothing good. Nothing good," he said.

I looked over my shoulder as four police cars sped down the street, coming to a stop in front of Melvin's. Officers with weapons drawn rushed out of each car. Two slowly moved up the front steps to join the other officers inside. The other two disappeared around the back of the house. I heard radios crackling from all around.

I looked up and down the street. People were on the porch of every house. Even the burned-out ones. The police may not have been too popular in the neighborhood, but it certainly didn't seem that was going to stand in the way of some good ole' fashion live entertainment.

FORTY-FIVE

"Don't you have a gun?"

"Not on me."

"What kind of cop doesn't carry a gun?"

"The kind that doesn't think he'll need one when his best friend calls."

"Would you two stop it please. Why all the police?"

We turned and saw that Anna Beth was standing between the Jeep and Gabriel's car looking at the house.

"Would you get over here behind the car?"

"I can see better from over here. Wait, look over there. There's something moving in the bushes across the yard."

The last of the officers on the porch had moved into the house. The others were in the back. It was only the three of us standing on the street with dozens of eyes staring at us from up and down the neighborhood.

I moved to Anna Beth's side and guided her behind the Jeep. I peered around the corner in the direction she'd been looking. I saw the bushes move slightly.

"Gabriel, she's right. There is something over there." Though when I turned the movement had stopped.

I looked back and Gabriel was behind his car. He emerged with a bulletproof vest emblazoned with the words "Police" in yellow letters on the front and back. A pistol grip, pump shotgun was slung diagonally across his chest, muzzle down, a pistol on his belt.

"I thought you didn't have a gun?"

"On me. I keep it in the trunk. You guys wait here."

Gabriel moved to the front of the Jeep, spoke into his cell phone, racked a shell into the chamber of the shotgun, leveled it against his shoulder and pointed it in the direction of the bushes across the yard. I looked around the Jeep and saw movement again. I heard the officers' radios crackle and then saw movement on the porch. One of the officers stepped out of the house, gun drawn, and looked towards Gabriel.

Gabriel pointed the index and middle finger of his left hand at his eyes and then pointed to the bushes. As he did they moved again. The officer nodded and leveled his gun in the direction of the movement. The officer quickly crossed the yard and joined Gabriel at the Jeep.

Gabriel moved quickly from the cover of the Jeep to a telephone pole at the edge of the yard where the row of bushes began a few yards from the area of the movement. The other officer was flanking Gabriel against the Jeep's front tire.

Gabriel and the officer locked eyes. The officer nodded.

"Show me your hands," Gabriel said, shotgun still pointed in the direction of the movement.

The movement in the bushes stopped.

"Show me your hands. Last warning then I shoot." he said again.

I saw Gabriel motion for the officer to stay put then he disappeared around the row of bushes out of view, shotgun at the ready.

A radio crackled, a dog barked in the distance, I heard a child scream. Then I heard Gabriel.

"Noah, come here quick. Now."

I moved behind the Jeep and jogged behind the bushes to join Gabriel. The shotgun was on the ground and he was kneeling, peering into the bushes. I joined him and saw a bit of fur through the leaves of the bush.

"It's a dog. I think it's hurt."

I moved closer to the bush.

"Let me see. Gracie?"

The fur moved and a nose appeared. I reached out.

"Careful, you'll get bit."

"Gracie." A pink tongue appeared and licked my hand. "Come here girl. Come here."

Gracie slowly moved towards Gabriel and me, dragging her back legs. As she cleared the bushes, I saw her fur was matted with blood.

"She's hurt. Go get a blanket out of the Jeep."

Gabriel picked up his shotgun and disappeared. He appeared moments later with Anna Beth in tow. The other officer was clearing the bushes ensuring there was nothing else we weren't seeing.

We spread the blanket out and coaxed Gracie onto it. Much to my surprise, she moved onto it and collapsed on her side, panting rapidly though her was breath quick and shallow.

"Let's take her to the Jeep."

Gabriel and I lifted the blanket and walked her to the back of the Jeep. Anna Beth poured some water into Austin's collapsible dog dish and then into Gracie's mouth.

"She needs to get to a vet," Anna Beth said.

I looked to Gabriel.

"Can we go?"

Gabriel looked to the house and back to us.

"You go," he said to Anna Beth. "Parks, you stay."

"Go, take her to the emergency vet. Gabriel will drop me there or home when we're finished. Hurry."

She kissed me, got in the Jeep and headed off.

Gabriel and I, along with all the eyes on the street, watched Anna Beth drive away.

FORTY-SIX

"Is that Melvin's dog?"

"Yeah, Gracie."

"Detective," Officer Tate said.

"Wait here," Gabriel said as he turned and headed towards the officer.

I watched as Tate pointed to the porch and motioned to the house. Gabriel stood with his arms crossed, nodding his head. Tate pointed towards me. Gabriel shrugged. Several times I saw Tate speak into his radio hand set. Finally, they both turned and looked towards me.

"Mr. Parks," Officer Tate said as he walked over to me. "I have a few questions for you."

"Is Melvin inside?" I said.

"You were here yesterday?"

"Where's Melvin?"

"Noah, answer his questions."

My next question about Melvin stopped before it came out of my mouth.

"Yes. Talking to Melvin about some legal issues."

"You said you weren't practicing law, why is that?"

"My license is suspended."

"Why's that?"

"I was arrested and charged with murdering Andrew Stephens."

The officer looked at me a moment.

"Where were you yesterday after you left here?"

"I went back home. Saw Gabriel at my house for a bit. Then my girlfriend and I went to a RiverDogs game. We went home afterwards. We went downtown this morning, stopped by my office, got coffee, then came here. We'd been here just a few minutes before you came."

"Anyone see you at the game?"

"Lots of people."

"Mr. Parks, don't be cute. Can anyone verify you were at the game?"

"Yes, a police officer. Officer Best."

"What were you doing talking to a cop at the game?" Gabriel said.

"Nothing. I was talking with a friend and for some reason he came up and talked to us."

Gabriel pulled out his cell phone turning as he spoke.

"Was the occupant of the house acting at all odd when you saw him yesterday?"

"I don't really know him, but no, not really," I said.

"How did you know Mr. Jones?"

I looked at Gabriel who had his back to me. What was I doing talking to a police officer when I had no idea what was going on in the house? I decided to be honest.

"I met him when I was in jail. We were in the same cell."

Officer Tate stared at me a moment, then scribbled on his notepad.

"Wait here."

Gabriel turned and put his phone back in his pocket. Officer Tate stepped over to him. I could hear every word they said.

"You said you know this guy?" Tate said.

"I do. Known him for years," Gabriel said.

"It's odd his being here today. You know for a fact he was here yesterday?"

"I'm pretty sure about it and I don't think he'd lie about it. No reason to."

Tate chuckled. That had to be a good sign, right?

"Any idea how long he was here?" Tate said.

"No more than an hour."

"You here with him yesterday?"

"Careful there officer, but no."

"Who did you call just now?"

"Duty officer from last night. Checked to see who was at the RiverDogs game. Checked to see if he talked to anyone. Turns out he did. Officer saw something he thought looked unusual but wasn't a thing. Remembers Noah."

"He happen to say what time that was?"

"Yeah, just before six p.m."

"Keep him here for a bit."

"I will," Gabriel said.

Tate walked away and Gabriel motioned for me to follow him to his car. He walked to the rear of the car and opened the trunk where he returned the shotgun in its case.

"You've stepped in it Parks."

"What the hell's going on?"

"Someone's killed Melvin."

#

Police officers were pouring over Melvin's. Crime scene tape circled his house. The street was clogged with first responder vehicles. The neighbors from the street had moved from their porches and windows and were congregated in the street just beyond the controlled perimeter. I waited at the car with Gabriel as officers came and went from the house. I was questioned several more times by several different officers and two detectives. They all asked me essentially the same thing and they got the same answers. Several uniformed officers began to ask questions of the crowd in the street. That caused them to scatter. The same officers began going door to door, but not a single knock was answered.

"Where was he inside?"

"And why would you possibly need to know that?" Gabriel said.

"He had a sort of safe room in the house. It's where he kept all of his computers. He said he had to keep it locked up because sometimes people in the neighborhood would break in looking for drug money. I was curious if any of his computers were taken. That's all."

"I'll check when it slows down."

Another detective approached us.

"Mr. Parks, what kind of car do you drive?"

"I drive a Jeep, Jeep Grand Cherokee. Why?"

"Do you have access to any other cars?"

"My girlfriend drives an SUV, an Acura."

"Rent any cars recently?"

"No, I haven't. Going to tell me why you're asking?"

"No, I'm not. I'm also going to ask you to go, and encourage you not to come back here again. I'm not sure I believe your story on why you were here yesterday, but it seems your alibi's solid. We know how to get in touch with you and since you're out on bail, you shouldn't be going anywhere. Detective, why don't you see Mr. Parks home?"

"I'll do that, but let's talk a minute."

They stepped away, out of earshot. Finally, Gabriel walked back towards me.

"Let's go."

I joined him as he turned around and got in his car.

"You want to tell me what's going on?"

"You're talking to that officer last night just saved you a world of hurt. Mind telling me what the hell you were doing over here today?"

"Honestly?"

"No, lie to me. Of course, honestly. That was one of the stupidest things you've done by the way. And I've got a lot of stupid to choose from."

"Maybe it was a little stupid, but I called you and didn't go in the house. What happened?"

"I told you, someone killed Melvin."

"You have any details?" My phone chimed with a text. "Let's head to the emergency vet. Anna Beth's still there."

"When the two officers came up to the house they saw some blood on the porch. That was enough to get their attention. They called backup and when they went in the house, they found Melvin in a closet in the bedroom. Single gunshot to the head. Up close"

"Was his computer room messed with?"

SEAN KEEFER

"They said no. Apparently, whoever was here didn't find the computer room so if he didn't have anything out it looks like whoever probably walked away empty handed. Other than Melvin's body in the closet and bloodstains in the bedroom and the porch there was nothing out of the ordinary. It's so dark in the house they missed the blood coming from under the closet door till the second time through."

"I'm guessing the blood on the porch will be Gracie's. Melvin said she didn't like strangers."

"You've got to get your head on straight and stay out of this investigation. Last thing you need is to be mixed up in another murder."

"Am I in the clear on this?"

"I think so, but forget about Melvin, alright?"

"My only question now is who killed him. That and was it because of me?"

Gabriel pulled into a parking space at the emergency vet. He looked like he was about to say something, but he shook his head and got out of his car.

FORTY-SEVEN

As Gabriel and I walked into the office Dr. Colven was talking to Anna Beth who was listening intently.

We walked over to them.

"Doctor."

"Oh, detective, nice to see you. Mr. Parks, you've been keeping us busy lately."

"I certainly thank you for your help, and don't take this the wrong way, but I wish we weren't here again."

"None taken."

"How's Gracie?"

"She was shot. Fortunately, the bullet was a smaller caliber. It went in the muscle of her left rear leg, passed through and stopped in the muscle of her right leg. From the angle, it looks like someone surprised her while she was sleeping or shot her when she was running away. She's lucky. The bullet didn't hit any major arteries but there was some blood loss."

"Have you taken the bullet out of her yet?" Gabriel said.

"No, we're about to start surgery."

"I'll need you to get that bullet to me as soon as it is out. I'll get an evidence bag for it."

"Dare I ask why?" Dr. Colven said.

"It's part of a murder investigation."

"If you catch whoever did this I hope you charge them with animal abuse as well. I need to get back to surgery, but she should be okay."

Dr. Colven disappeared back into the clinic.

"What did she say about Gracie?"

"Pretty much what she told you. She said she was in shock, but stable and it looked like she'll be okay. She really looks like a sweet dog. I was so scared when I was driving over here. I couldn't see her in the back and didn't know how she was doing. When I got here she was barely breathing and wasn't moving at all. I told them to do whatever they needed to make her better."

"I can just imagine what the vet thinks of us bringing in two dogs on death's doorstep in just a few days."

"What happened at Melvin's?"

Neither Gabriel nor I spoke.

"I'll take it that means whatever it was, it wasn't good. He's dead, isn't he?"

"He is," Gabriel said.

"Is it related to Andrew?"

"No way to know."

"I guess this means we have another dog for a while?"

"I was thinking that same thing," I said.

The same tech from before came over and spoke to us. She encouraged us to go home. They would call us when Gracie was out of surgery. Gabriel decided to wait to collect on the bullet.

"Not exactly what I expected for the day," Anna Beth said.

"Tell me about it. I seem to remember waking up in bed this morning with a beautiful woman, but after that it's a blur."

The garage door opened and we pulled in. We walked up the garage steps to the house. I opened the door expecting Austin to be in his normal spot to greet us as we stepped through the door from the garage, but he wasn't there.

Not again.

I panicked.

"Austin, come here boy. Austin." I turned to the left through the door and hurried into the den. He wasn't on the couch or his dog bed. "Where is he?"

"He's here."

I looked back down the hall and saw Anna Beth standing over him at the front door. He was lying with his nose pushed to the bottom of the door. Sniffing. He turned to look at us then returned his attention to the door.

"What is it buddy?"

Austin woofed and scratched at the door.

"What's he after?"

"No idea."

I knelt beside him and looked on the floor. He pushed his nose close to the bottom of the door and sniffed again.

"Come here boy."

Austin looked at me then moved from the door.

"Hold his collar."

Anna Beth reached for his collar and I opened the door.

There from below the doormat I saw the edge of an envelope.

I was starting to think Gabriel should just move in. I called after I found the envelope and he was there shortly thereafter.

"Have you opened it yet?"

I'd put the envelope on the table in the dining room and we were all staring at it.

"No. I've been waiting on you."

"Where was it?"

"Under the front door mat, same as the last one. Austin found it," Anna Beth said.

"Austin?"

"Yea, he was at the front door waiting when we got home," Anna Beth said.

"It was strange. Something obviously attracted him to the door and he stayed. He normally only does that when Anna Beth's gone."

"Who dropped this off, buddy?" Gabriel said as he scratched Austin behind the ear. "Too bad he can't tell us. Well, open it already."

I reached out and picked up the envelope. Austin sat and watched the envelope like it was a special dog treat, licking his chops. Like before, it was a normal envelope with the flap tucked in. It contained a single sheet of folded paper. I opened it.

"Gabriel can take it back to the start."

"Now there's a curve ball for you. Any idea what that means?"

I looked to Gabriel who was staring at the letter.

"What the hell is that supposed to mean? And why are they talking about me?"

"I've got no idea."

Austin was still extremely interested in the paper, standing on his rear paws to sniff it.

"Settle down boy." He sat, but whimpered as he continued to stare at the paper.

"Back?" Anna Beth said. "Do either of you have any idea what that means?"

"Actually yes. It's either that someone is still trying to get in your head and mentions me to make it sound better, or, and I can't believe I'm saying this, someone really wants to help you."

I was still holding the paper, puzzled as to why Austin was so interested in it. Suddenly a thought came to my mind. I left the room.

"Where's he going?" I heard Gabriel say as I headed upstairs.

#

I returned with several sheets of paper and a manila folder.

"Austin." He looked to me as I said his name. "Sit."

He sat directly in front of me, his eyes locked to mine as he was trained to do.

"I have an idea. Watch this."

I looked to Gabriel and Anna Beth. Neither said a thing.

Turning my attention back to Austin, I held a sheet of paper out to him. He sniffed it and showed no interest. I looked to Anna Beth and Gabriel again. I dropped the paper to the floor. He ignored it. I showed him another. Same reaction.

With the third, he again showed no interest either when he sniffed at them or when they floated to the floor.

I looked to Gabriel.

"No idea what you're showing me."

"That's okay, but if I what I think is happening is really going on, this next one should be interesting."

I opened the manila folder and took out the letter that had just arrived then held it out to Austin. He spun in a circle and stood on his rear legs, sniffing towards the letter.

I put it away.

"Sit." He obeyed, but was eager in anticipation as I opened the manila folder again. I took out the prior letter and Austin gave the same excited reaction. However, when I tried a blank sheet of paper there was no reaction. I tried all of the other letters we'd received. He showed the same excited interest.

"He recognizes the smell of the letters," Anna Beth said.

"That he does."

"Impressive, but how do we get him to tell us who sent them?"

"Gabriel, feel like taking a ride? I think I can get him to tell us."

FORTY-EIGHT

Vanderhorst Street consisted of about five blocks in downtown Charleston. It was almost entirely residential and most of the houses had been built more than 150 years ago. While they all had character and charm, they were far from mansions or of any real particular historical relevance. In fact, some years back the bulk of the residences on the street went through a transformation shifting from single-family homes to multi-occupant rentals rented mostly by students from the College of Charleston or the medical university, making Vanderhorst largely a street of privately owned college dorms.

Cars lined the street, surpassing the limited parking spaces afforded by the older homes. Trash cans overflowed with signs of the student population: beer cans and pizza boxes.

"Why exactly is it we're down here?"

"Just drive slowly to the end of the street and then turn around."

Gabriel shook his head kept driving. After our second pass down the street, he pulled into a spot in the middle of the street that had just come vacant. He turned off the engine and turned to face me. I glanced at him and continued to look up and down the street.

"You know if you tell me what we're looking for I might be able to help."

"Just be patient and get ready to drive."

He stared for a moment and began to tap his fingers on the steering wheel clearly anxious about not knowing what we were looking for.

The few people we'd seen had moved on and the street was empty. I continued to look up and down each direction. From where we sat, there was a good vantage point to see the entirety of the block.

I glanced at Gabriel who was clearly not happy about sitting in his car on the street with no clear purpose. He was about to speak when I saw a familiar face on the street ahead of us.

"There, drive up."

"Oh, tell me we aren't here so you can talk to coeds."

"Actually, that's exactly why we're here."

Gabriel pulled out onto the street and headed towards the person I'd pointed out. She hadn't seen us and was walking towards us.

"Pull up slowly in front of her and I'll take care of the rest."

Gabriel positioned the car a few car lengths ahead, I got out and moved to the back of the car.

"Hi Rebecca.

FORTY-NINE

"Noah. What are you doing here?"

"It's time for us to talk."

Rebecca hugged a book to her chest and looked up and down the street. I wasn't sure she was looking for anything particular or if it was out of some nervousness. It looked as if she might cry.

"You know I can't. The solicitor. His investigator made it clear. Not a word to you."

"Then why the letters?"

"What does she know about the letters?" Gabriel said.

Gabriel had gotten out of his car and walked around to join us.

"Gabriel. This is Rebecca Martin. She used to work for, well, with Andrew."

"Ms. Martin."

"This is Emmett Gabriel. He's a detective with the police department. He was a friend of Andrew's too. You probably heard him mention his name."

"Yes, I know who he is, but what's he doing here?"

"I actually think you're the best person to answer that, about the letters."

"I don't know what you're talking about."

"You sure?"

I stepped to the car's back door and looked over to Rebecca. I opened the door. Austin jumped out and rushed over to her. She took a step back as he jumped on her sniffing and licking her. She didn't try to stop him, rather she knelt down and he continued with his over the top show of affection.

"Rebecca you're sure you don't know anything about the letters?"

Suddenly her expression changed and I was pretty sure I saw a grin cross her face.

"This is how you figured it out? Your dog?"

"Yes." I looked over to Gabriel who was chuckling to himself. "Austin's a friendly dog, fiercely loyal, but only when he recognizes you. Till then he's standoffish at best. The first time he ever met you was at the RiverDogs game and he greeted you like he knew you. When the last letter appeared, he was just a bit too interested in it."

"How did you find me? Nothing's in my name."

Austin was on his back as Rebecca rubbed his stomach.

"Andrew helped with that."

"He did?"

"He had a password protected file on his computer. The password was ..."

"The name of my street."

"Pretty much yes. I took a guess and put two and two together."

"I guess you want the file."

"I do." I said.

"It was erased."

"I know. Do you know what was in it?"

Rebecca stood up from Austin. He wasn't too happy about this so he rolled over, stood, shook from nose to tail, then sat beside her and pawed at her for more attention.

We stood in silence, everyone waiting for someone else to speak.

"Yes. I know what's in the file."

"Does the solicitor?"

"I don't know. If he does he didn't mention it when he talked to me. And he didn't learn about it from me."

"Rebecca," I took a step closer to her and reached out to touch her, stopping just short I pulled my hand back. "I really need your help. I need that file."

"I don't really have a choice do I?"

"Rebecca, you always have a choice, but I'm really hoping you choose to help me and Andrew at the same time."

"Ms. Martin."

Without looking at him, she said, "Yes, sir."

"He's not being dramatic. He could really use your help."

"Rebecca, about the file. Can you give it to me?"

"Now? No. I don't have it, but, but, well, I can take care of getting you what you need so you'll understand what was going on, what happened."

I looked to Gabriel who had raised his eyebrows as he looked to Rebecca.

"You have a copy of the file?"

"Sort of."

"Sort of?"

"Yes, since I found out Andrew died, or was murdered, I thought I should have the information that was in there."

"Why didn't you tell me about it? This means you know I didn't kill Andrew."

"I've never thought you did. I just, I'm scared of the solicitor and the man named Gaines. Andrew's dead and he didn't do anything except run for a silly elected office. I don't want something to happen to me."

"Rebecca, it won't, if...."

"Can you promise me? Can you guarantee that nothing will happen to me?"

I looked at Gabriel then back to her.

"No. I can't. I don't think anything will, but I can't make a promise over something I don't control or understand."

"Ms. Martin, about the file?"

"Ok, the file. I don't have it here, but I can get the information to you. I'll need a day or so, but you have to promise you won't bother me anymore, that you'll leave me alone. I think I need to get away from all of this."

"Rebecca, if you're going to really help me, I'll probably need to talk to you again and will probably need you to talk to some other people."

"Noah, Andrew never had anything bad to say about you. I know he loved you like a brother and that's the reason I'll help you now, the reason I've been sending those letters. I want whoever killed him to be punished, but I can only do so much, and, and I'm not real excited about doing that. If whoever did this was able to get you arrested for a murder you didn't commit. If they were able to kill Andrew, I don't want to be around to find out what they can do to me," she said. "You really don't need it; Captain Gabriel can help you figure it all out."

"Ms. Martin, the more you can do to help Noah, it helps Andrew too."

She looked at us and we all stood in silence a moment.

"Promise me you'll at least think about…."

"I've already thought about it and I won't change my mind. After this, I'm going away."

"When can I have the file?"

"Soon. I'll get a message to you, but I want to go now."

I looked at her. I wanted to tell her this wasn't how to help Andrew's memory and it certainly wasn't the way I wanted her to help me, but I could tell she was scared and I didn't want to push her away. Gabriel, ever the astute cop, finally spoke up.

"Do what you think is right. Go on along now, but if you need us, call us, or me, for anything," he took a card out of his jacket pocket and gave it to Rebecca.

"I understand. I'll let you know what to do so you can see the whole picture."

We watched her turn and hurry away.

"That certainly wasn't what I'd hoped for."

"No, but that was pretty good on your part with Austin. I'd have never thought about that."

"Yeah, that was pretty good, wasn't it?"

"Doesn't make you a detective."

Rebecca didn't glance back as she turned up the walk to a Vanderhorst Street house. She disappeared inside.

"You think she'll give me that file?"

"I don't know, but the way she's been acting with the letters and all, she's definitely up to something. If she doesn't give you the file, you've no choice but to pull her in. I think you give her a little time but you need to tell your attorney

271

about this too. She's setting my alarms off. She's hiding something."

"You think?"

"I do. It's just too convenient for her to know to get that file and say that she knows you didn't kill Andrew. She's probably the one that erased it too. For her to have information you didn't kill him and not want to get it to you makes me wonder what is in it that hurts you."

We'd gotten back in the car and were driving off down the street. Gabriel slowed to look at the house Rebecca had gone into. As we drove by the curtain in an upstairs window moved.

"Yep, she's on edge. Something or someone has her spooked. She's wanting to see if we're going to follow her. You definitely need to tell your attorney."

"He's not going to do anything with the letters, he can't."

"Good heavens Parks. You're missing the point here. Rebecca may be your get out of jail free card. She knew Andrew. No one saw her at the party. She would've had access to his computer. She probably had a key to his house. She could've had that list. She said she's accessed that missing file. Heck, we know she sneaks around following you places dropping off letters, breaking and entering at your place isn't too far removed. Maybe Austin likes her because she gives him a nice big drugged up steak."

"You really think Rebecca could be behind all of this?"

"Maybe, maybe not, but there's enough there you need to talk to Brady about it. I've seen fewer questions make reasonable doubt. And that is a get out of jail free."

FIFTY

When you pin your hope and future on a twenty-one-year-old college student, prepare for frustration. This was the lesson I was learning; however, when options are limited there's little you can do but wait. Not that it was easy to wait, but I was fresh out of ideas beyond waiting for the legal process to grind to a conclusion.

Anna Beth and I weathered the frustration and the wait and on the second day after Gabriel and I saw her, Rebecca sent a text and it was only slightly cryptic which, given her past performance with the letters, shouldn't have surprised me.

"Calabash. 10283 Beach Drive SW. Under your favorite bridge. Information that you need."

I felt the frustration increasing. How hard would it have been to have emailed or even dropped off the journal? Even the mail would have been something. I immediately called her back, but she didn't answer. And she had turned off her voicemail.

I walked out onto the back deck where Anna Beth was watching Austin in the backyard. Fall was upon us and it appeared that the humidity had finally broken. I realized it was a beautiful day.

273

"I heard from Rebecca."

"Good news I hope."

"She told me where I could pick up Andrew's journal."

"Pick up? Are you meeting her?"

"I don't think so. She is leaving it out of town. Out of state actually. In Calabash. "

"Seriously? Why there?"

"It's a guess, but I seem to remember Andrew saying she was from up there somewhere. I'm guessing she's left town and headed home. It was probably convenient for her," I said. My voice must have trailed off.

"And?"

"And she didn't say where she left it specifically."

She stood up and leaned against the deck rail.

"What did she tell you?"

"We have an address in Calabash and whatever she left me is under my favorite bridge."

She stared in silence for a moment.

"I don't want to sound too negative, but she promises you his journal, reluctantly. Then instead of giving it to you she sends you out of state and tells you to look under the Cooper River Bridge when you get there? That's what she told you?"

"That's pretty much it," I said.

"Let me ask you a question."

"Ok."

"You're probably not supposed to leave, what, the county? Definitely not the state, while you're out on bail. Right?"

"No, I can't leave the state."

"Then we go to North Carolina, Rebecca waits until we get there then calls the police, tells them you're following her and I'm guessing it's back to jail for you. Right?"

She was spot on. If Rebecca was playing me, and—though I refused to believe it—if she was the killer, this would be the perfect way to set me up to be near one-hundred percent responsible for taking the fall. Problem was, I trusted her.

"I trust her. Maybe I shouldn't. But where we are now, it's take a chance or wait on Brady and, well, right now from Brady, a win is really a loss."

"Then we both go."

#

The drive to Calabash took me through Horry County where I'd grown up. The heart of Horry County, at least the largest part of it, is Myrtle Beach, which, in the not too distant days of my youth, had been little more than a sleepy beach community. I'd grown up in the sleepier-still town called Loris, tucked away from the glitz of Myrtle Beach in the northeastern corner of the county. Given that the Loris of my youth was less than exciting for most of the resident teenagers, we, in a coming of age ritual, learned every possible route to the Myrtle Beach area and spent virtually every free moment there either on the beach, in the clubs, or somewhere in between. While there was a lot more to Horry County these days, I knew my way around. I used back roads to be safe.

Calabash, where Rebecca had directed us, was just north of Myrtle Beach and the first town over the North Carolina line. Unlike Myrtle Beach, Calabash still had the charm of a small sleepy beach community. In years past

Calabash had been, and to an extent still was, a commercial fishing port. Supporting the local fishermen, the area became famous in the first half of the twentieth century for the local seafood houses specializing in Calabash-style seafood. This meant an abundance of fried seafood with hush puppies, potatoes of the baked or fried variety, and coleslaw. It was interesting that most every one of the still existing Calabash restaurants claimed, in some derivation, to be the "first," "original," or "oldest."

But we weren't going to eat seafood.

I'd driven into Calabash more times than I could remember and knew my way around as if I were a local. Problem was after so many trips through the years, I didn't remember, if I had ever known, any of the actual street addresses.

I was a little bit on the surprised side when, as Anna Beth was reading off street numbers, few that there were, we arrived at our destination and found ourselves looking at a rather large art gallery.

"Seaside Market Gallery" the sign read.

"You sure this is the right place?"

I pulled out my phone and looked at Rebecca's text once again.

"Calabash.10283 Beach Drive SW. Under your favorite bridge."

"According to her text, this is the place."

"Then let's go look around."

The building resembled a large corrugated warehouse with near floor-to-ceiling windows across the building's street-facing front, none anywhere else. We walked inside and, true to the sign, we found a sprawling art gallery that, now that we were inside, appeared to continue on without end. The entire place had a very comfortable, homey feel. The walls were covered with all varieties of what appeared to be original artwork. As I looked around I quickly saw the gallery was divided into smaller galleries within the gallery.

We must have looked a little overwhelmed.

"Can I help you?" a friendly voice said.

I looked to my right as woman appeared from a small room behind the front desk.

"This is quite the impressive gallery you have here."

"Well thank you, ma'am. Are you folks from around here or just visiting?"

I chimed in, "I grew up in the area, sort of, but we are just passing through and a friend suggested we stop by. They didn't warn us that your place was so, well, large."

"We get that a lot. Most of our pieces are on consignment directly from the artists. Pretty much everything you see in here is either local or regional. There are so many fabulous artists in the Carolinas and, well, we're honored to have their work here. Is there anything in particular you're looking for? Canvas, oils, sculpture, photography? We even have a section with books from local authors." She reached out to adjust a stack of books.

"I think we're just going to look around for a bit and see what we can find."

"Please take your time and if you need anything, I'm Virginia. I'll be up front."

"Thank you very much," Anna Beth said.

Virginia disappeared behind the desk. I turned to find Anna Beth had wandered further into the gallery. I followed. As I passed through one section to another, for every separate room I entered there seemed to be at least more adjoining it with no end in sight.

Each different section was a floor-to-ceiling display of flowing styles. The inventory was near overwhelming. However, as we roamed from room to room, the one thing I wasn't seeing were any bridges. There were sculptures, prints, photos, and pretty much any other medium you wanted, but no bridges.

"This is quite odd," Anna Beth said as she was looking at a wall of images of sea turtles.

"I wasn't sure what I was expecting to find, but this is a little overwhelming."

"Haven't seen any bridges, have you?"

"Actually, not a one."

FIFTY-ONE

"Let's hope that this isn't a wild goose chase. Hang on a second."

I pulled my phone from my pocket and glanced around to make sure there was no one nearby. I dialed Gabriel. He answered on the first ring.

"Hey. I need a favor."

"It's afternoon, I was thinking I had a chance to get a day off."

"Could you swing by the house and make sure it's okay?"

"Me needing to swing by tells me you're not close by. Tell me you haven't left the state."

"Rebecca sent word where the journal was and we went to get it near Myrtle Beach."

"Near?"

"Yes, near."

"Why do you need me to go by the house?"

"Rebecca. I want to make sure she isn't trying to get us out of town to go to the house."

"I'll go, but get back here soon," he said as the line went dead.

"You didn't call him and tell him you were going out of town, did you?"

"I didn't want him to have to tell me not to go, but he's going by the house, and ..."

"You folks finding anything you like?" Virginia approached with a smile.

"You have some really great pieces here," Anna Beth said. "I love the coastal feel."

"Where are you folks from if I can ask?"

"I'm from Chicago but I've recently relocated to Charleston."

"Charleston, such a lovely town. Relocated. That's nice."

"With me," I said.

"Of course, dear," Virginia said. "You know, we have several beautiful prints of the Charleston bridges. Some of the new bridge and several really striking examples of the older ones."

As she spoke Anna Beth and I looked at each other.

"Oh, I didn't see them as we walked through."

"Here, follow me, I'll show you. This place can be a maze, sometimes I'm surprised people don't ask for breadcrumbs."

She turned and walked out of the room. We followed. She navigated through several adjoining rooms, all of which we had visited on our first trip through, but then she turned behind a partial wall that deceptively hid the fact there was a room, or as we learned, two rooms beyond.

We followed her through the first one that contained a plethora of aerial coastal photographs and moved on to a second room. I realized why I hadn't seen any bridges before.

The room was full of bridges - paintings, photographs and even reliefs and sculptures of various coastal bridges. We were in the bridge room, if there was such a thing.

"Wow," was all I could say.

"That's the normal reaction. There're a number of really impressive ones in here and several--there, there, and there," Virginia said as she pointed. "From the Charleston area."

She walked over to a print of an old-fashioned swinging drawbridge.

"This is one of the more popular pieces. It's the bridge into Sunset Beach just up the way, before the work was done on it. Anyway, look around and let me know if you need anything."

"Certainly."

We stood still as Virginia disappeared yet again.

"She's right, the place is like a maze. What are we looking for?"

"I'd say something related to the Cooper River Bridge. Rebecca said, 'under my favorite bridge.' Andrew probably told her that so I'm guessing we look under an image of it."

"Sound's as good as anything."

We split up and started looking for paintings and photographs of the old and new Cooper River Bridges. There were a number of them in the room, but as far as under them, there was only the floor below those hanging on the walls. In total, we counted fourteen different images and nothing was to be found anywhere below the bridges. We'd gone through the room two times without success, even looking behind the prints, when I looked to see Virginia was back. She had a wonderful way of keeping tabs on us without seeming to hover.

"Any of the Charleston Bridges strike your fancy? There are some really nice works here."

"Yes, there are. Is it only paintings and photographs of the bridges you have?"

"Well, yes and no. As to depictions of the bridges, yes, it's only the photographs and paintings we have in here. We did have a gorgeous sculpture of the old and new bridges together, but that recently sold."

My heart sunk a bit.

"That's too bad, I would've loved to have seen that. How long did I miss it by?"

"Oh, at least three months back, I believe."

Good, I thought. That was clearly out of my time frame.

"You said, 'yes and no.' Is there something else?" Anna Beth said.

"There is," she said as she walked across to the middle of the room where there were several pieces of metal approximately four inches high and six inches long, each being rough cut on the edges. "Here."

She was holding one of the pieces up. I looked and saw that each had an image, a Charleston image, painted on it. However, none of them were of the bridge.

"These are done by a group out of Charleston. They salvaged actual parts from the old bridges and cut them into these pieces. Then did acrylic on each of them. We once had images of the bridge, but those went quite fast. All that's left are various Charleston scenes."

"These are actually, well, the bridge?"

"Yes."

"How fascinating," I said. "I'm sure one of these will have to come home with us, don't you think?"

"I certainly do."

"I'll leave you to look about," Virginia said as she disappeared once again.

We watched her walk out of the room and then immediately started looking under each of the pieces of the old bridge.

Of course, it was the last one.

FIFTY-TWO

We both stared at the small object taped to the bottom of the last of the painted bridge pieces. Plain paper stapled into a small envelope perhaps an inch and a half by two and a half. There were two handwritten letters:

"NP"

"I guess we're in the right place." We were still alone. I quickly grabbed the envelope and put it in my pocket.

We headed out of the bridge room. I noticed Anna Beth still had the painted bridge section in her hand.

"What? We should buy something?"

"I didn't say a word."

I took her hand and lead her back through the gallery to the front.

Virginia greeted us with a smile as we stopped at the front desk.

"Found something I see."

"That we did."

Virginia looked at the piece for a moment.

"Lovely scene from downtown Charleston."

"Isn't it though?" Anna Beth said. "We have an office just a bit further down the street, really just out of the frame. It's almost like it was made for us."

"Wonderful, you'll just have to come back again when you can stay longer."

"Our friend Rebecca told us about your place. Can't wait to tell her we stopped by."

I waited to see if there was any acknowledgement as I mentioned Rebecca's name, but got nothing.

"That is simply the best advertising, word of mouth."

Anna Beth paid and I waited for something more from Virginia, but there was nothing.

Virginia walked us to the door. I was anxious to get to the car and examine the envelope, but she was telling us about several upcoming presentations, stopping from piece to piece telling us about different artists. Finally, she opened the front door for us.

"Please do come back and visit again soon."

"We'll be back before you know it."

"I do hope so and I hope it's both of you. I'll be hoping everything you have going on works out for the best. Drive safely," she said as the door shut and she turned away, disappearing back into the store.

We stood in stunned silence for a moment.

"Looks like we were expected."

"She could have just told us."

#

I gave Anna Beth the keys and directions to my hometown of Loris guiding her by way of the back roads.

After we left Calabash and were comfortably on our way towards Loris. I took out the envelope.

I opened it, turned it upside down and dumped the contents into my hand. A single secure digital memory card fell into my hand.

"Shouldn't say I am surprised."

Anna Beth glanced over to me.

"Do you have anything with us to read it?"

"Nope, but I have an idea."

A short time later we entered my sleepy hometown.

"There. Turn in just past that row of trees," I said as I pointed.

Anna Beth turned the car into the parking lot of the Loris Memorial Library.

"A library?"

"Yes."

We parked and walked inside passing through the children's section as we made our way into the main area. Several of the library's patrons and the librarian stopped what they were doing to ever so briefly glance at us before returning to their respective tasks.

"There," I said as I took Anna Beth's hand and headed to a bank of computers.

A teenager was sitting at one. The others were unoccupied.

I sat at a vacant machine, moved the mouse and the dark monitor came to life.

"Okay, let's hope there's a universal drive for this card."

I searched the computer's tower and monitor to no avail.

"Can I help you?"

We turned to see the librarian behind us.

"I was just checking to see if the computer had a drive for this SD card."

"No, none of these do."

"Could you tell us anywhere around that may?" Anna Beth said.

"I'm just not sure. Is there anything else I could help you with?"

"No, thank you."

"If you do need something, I'll be at the desk."

The librarian turned and walked away.

"Now what?"

"I guess we head back to Charleston and deal with it there."

"Got an SD card?" a voice said.

I leaned to my left and, as I peered past the computer monitor, saw the voice belonged to the teenager from the other computer.

"Yes. I need to find out what's on this." I held up the SD card. "Any idea where I can find a computer to read it."

"Sure. Hold tight."

He rose and disappeared behind one of the stacks and then returned.

"Here," he said as he handed me a digital SLR camera. "Just put it in the card slot and plug the camera into the USB. May want to lock the card so whatever you have on there isn't erased."

He handed over the camera, a nice Nikon D7000, and a USB cable. I stared at them a moment.

"You need a hand?"

"No, I got it."

He watched as I dropped the card in the slot, closed the door, attached the USB to the camera and then the computer. I turned on the camera and moments later a dialogue box popped up on the screen. A few mouse clicks later we were looking at a single file on the screen.

It read, "Noah.doc."

"Moment of truth. I don't want to open it here so I'll just print it and we can read it in the car. Did you see a printer?"

"Over there," the friendly teenager said.

We looked in the direction he was pointing where a printer sat.

"Thanks," we said in unison.

I right clicked on the file and selected "Print." Anna Beth headed off to the printer.

"Thanks for your help."

I disconnected the camera and removed the SD card.

"No worries. Happy to help."

I looked up and saw Anna Beth was back. Quickly. Odd. I guess she needed money for copies.

"Need money?"

"No. Come on, let's go."

"What about the file?"

"I've got it," she said, holding up a single folded sheet of paper. "I'll drive."

FIFTY-THREE

She handed me the paper as we got in the car.

"Can you get home?"

"Yes. Read the letter."

"What? Why?"

"Just read the letter."

I unfolded the letter. There wasn't a lot of type on it. Certainly not enough to qualify as a journal:

"Noah.

I've thought about this a lot. I really wanted to give you the journal, but if I did that, you'd be back hoping for more, needing me to talk to more people and maybe even needing me to testify in court.

I won't do that.

I'm not playing games, I promise.

This will have to do. I know you'll want to look for me, but please don't.

Talk to Jack Nance. He used to be a Charleston police officer. I'm guessing Gabriel can find him. He knows everything and is more than happy to talk about it. Everything Andrew knew, he learned from Jack Nance.

Please don't look for me. I won't do anything more.

R."

"What now?"

I was angry. Pissed. Another dead end, just when it seemed like progress was just ahead.

"Take a deep breath. We have a new name. A name we've never heard before. Why not do exactly what Rebecca suggests? Let's call Gabriel and see if he knows this Jack Nance."

"Let's head straight to Gabriel's, I'll give him a call," I said. "No sense in putting off finding out about this Nance guy. That and I need to make sure things are smoothed over with him, us going out of town."

"We need gas. You call, I'll fill up."

She turned into a Shell station near the IOP Connector, the road that lead to the barrier islands of the Isle of Palms and Sullivan's Island. She pulled up beside a pump, started filling the Jeep and then appeared at the front of the Jeep where she motioned that she was going inside. I smiled and watched her. As she disappeared inside, I pulled my phone out and called Gabriel.

"Parks."

"I'm sorry for not telling you we were going out of town, but I knew you'd say no, and, well, I didn't want to tell you I wouldn't go, and then go."

"You're back?"

"We are. Getting gas near the IOP. Thought we would stop by and give you a rundown on what we found. You home?"

"I am. Come on over. Hopefully your trip wasn't a waste. The house and both dogs are fine."

The door on the white Volvo opened.

"Thanks for going by," I said. "We'll be over in a bit."

I ended the call and as I looked up towards the front door I watched as Tamara Michaels, the solicitor's wife, walked out of the gas station.

She stopped and pulled out her phone, looked around and then started to type on the screen. I looked back to the station door and saw Anna Beth walking out.

Tamara Michaels looked up and saw Anna Beth. She dropped her phone. Anna Beth reached down, picked it up and handed it back to Mrs. Michaels. They spoke briefly before Anna Beth walked away. Tamara turned and watched her walk all the way to the car. She was still standing in the parking lot staring at us as we drove away.

#

"No, she looked like she had seen a ghost. I was walking out of the station and I noticed her. I've only met her that once, but I knew exactly who she was. She looked up from her phone and when she saw me she dropped her phone as I said, 'Hello Mrs. Michaels."

"From my end, it looked like the two of you were having a really friendly chat."

"She really looked like she had seen a ghost. She thanked me and asked if we had been in Myrtle Beach."

"What did you say?" Gabriel said.

"I lied. She said I shouldn't let the reputation ruin it and that I should visit sometime. We stood in silence a moment and I said I had to go. She just watched me walk away."

"Did you notice if she was following you? From Myrtle?"

SEAN KEEFER

"I just don't know. I hope not. If she was, the solicitor will be the first to know."

"She was the last person I expected to run into," Anna Beth said.

"That's the thing, you shouldn't have just run into her. Makes me wonder what's up. What the solicitor is playing at? God Parks, you can work your way into some situations," said Gabriel.

"I've got nothing for you on that one, but I really hope it was just coincidence."

"If you believe in that," Anna Beth said as she disappeared inside.

"What did you get from Rebecca?"

"Not much. Read this. This is as close to a lead as we have."

I handed him the single page and waited as he read it. He raised his eyes and looked at me.

"Now you want me to help you find some guy that used to be a cop?"

"That's right. And probably come with me to talk to him."

"Remember the conversation about me still being a cop?"

"I do. But, well, I need your help. I'm short on people I can trust. This is all we have. But how hard can it be for you to dig up the address of a retired cop?"

"Probably not too hard at all, but Parks, this is getting a bit ridiculous. This Rebecca person is playing you, plain and simple. I'm getting worried what you have there may be the last note from Andrew's killer."

"Something is going on with her, but I don't see her killing Andrew. You would have had to have seen her when I told her he was dead."

We were sitting on the front porch of Gabriel's house, Rudy at our feet. The occasional car passing or neighbor out for a stroll was all that punctuated the otherwise quiet afternoon.

"You've got choices. Prepare for your defense. Get someone to give a hard look at this Rebecca person. You could even ..."

"Don't even suggest it."

"Suggest what?" Gabriel said.

"Suggest I think about a plea."

"All I am saying is the possibility."

"That's all it is. A possibility and not even a remote one."

I stood, walked across the porch and placed my hands on the rail, gripping the old wood tightly. I felt a hand on my shoulder.

"Remember you're not in this alone," Anna Beth said.

I stood upright.

"I know you're exactly right. And I've told more clients than I can remember the exact thing. It's funny. I hear what you're saying and I know it's the God's honest truth, but it doesn't make a bit of a difference. No offense."

"None taken. Just remember you're among friends," Gabriel said.

I took a deep breath.

"You'll help me find this former cop?"

"I will, but, at some point there's going to be a reality out there that needs to be faced."

"Fair enough."

"Come on, let's go home. We can decide what to do next when Gabriel finds this Jack Nance."

"She's right. Nothing you can do now but wait. I'll call as soon as I have something."

#

It took less than a day for Gabriel to dig up Jack Nance's address. Perhaps I'd watched too many police movies, but I half expected Gabriel to tell me he was in some generic retirement home attached to an oxygen tank. Needless to say, I chuckled to myself when Gabriel told me the retired detective lived just one county over, in a modest neighborhood in a house complete with a pool. I was even more surprised when Gabriel provided a phone number for me.

He answered on the first ring.

"Nance," a not entirely unpleasant voice said.

"Yes, Jack Nance please."

"You got him. Who's this?"

"My name's Noah Parks Mr. Nance and --."

"I've been waiting for you to call. We should have a little sit down, you and me. I've got some things I expect you'll want to hear."

"I, well, absolutely, I'd be quite interested in talking to you. I could come up to your place, if that's okay with you."

"That's fine. I'm not going anywhere."

"Would you mind if a friend came, a police officer?"

"Bring whoever you like. The more the merrier. How about tomorrow morning, say ten a.m.?"

"That would be excellent."

"Feel free to bring coffee, it might take a while. I'll guess you know where I live."

"I do and I'll see you then Mr. Nance."

"Call me Jack," he said as the phone went dead in my hand.

FIFTY-FOUR

The next morning couldn't come quick enough. Though I was soon to be headed back up the coast again, this time there was a purpose. Someone who was going to talk, someone who could answer questions. Someone who I hoped could turn the tide and put me on the path to innocence.

As I backed out of the drive, I looked up to see Anna Beth and Austin side-by-side on the porch. Seeing that made me happy and sad. Happy because they symbolized what was important to me: a home and a family. It made me sad because I realized that keeping all I loved was not entirely in my power. I smiled and waved, paused for a moment, then backed out of the drive. They were still standing there on the front porch when I glanced in the rearview as I turned the corner out of the neighborhood.

With the lack of early morning traffic the drive to Gabriel's was quick. Gabriel was waiting on his front porch when I drove up. He motioned to his car, meaning he was driving. He liked to drive.

Jack Nance lived in Pawleys Island, a community with a reputation as a friendly place where the locals were quick to let it be known that they "Liked people who liked Pawleys."

Nance lived in a modest neighborhood just off of Highway 17. It was an hour and a half drive from Charleston which meant Gabriel would have us there at just over the hour mark.

"What did you find out about Nance?"

"Not a lot, but I really didn't dig too deep."

"How deep did you dig?"

"Deep enough to find out he saw a lot in the department while he was there. He started in the fifties and retired in the mid-nineties."

"A lot changed for a lot of people in those forty years. Anything jump out at you?"

"Like I said, not really. He was a beat cop, a patrol officer, worked a desk for a while and was a detective for twenty plus years. Nothing special, positive or negative."

"I can only imagine what it was like for him. He almost has to be the stereotypical old school cop."

"You'd probably be right. I'm guessing he did his time with the department, stuck a little money away and with his retirement he could disappear into his own little world and no one would really care."

"Right about now that doesn't sound like a bad plan."

We were passing through Georgetown and were less than fifteen miles from Nance's house, well ahead of schedule.

"You and your driving."

"What's that supposed to mean?"

"It's easy to see why you're never late for anything."

"No sense wasting time, I always say."

#

Coastal South Carolina apart from Charleston, Myrtle Beach, and Hilton Head Island is largely a chain of small coastal communities.

Pawleys Island was one of those.

Pawleys itself is a barrier island that lived up to the tour guide image of a South Carolina coastal resort area--row after row of beach houses occupied for literally every moment of the vacation season.

"We're going to be early."

"Is that another comment about my driving?"

"No, we're just going to be early."

"Call him and let him know."

"Better idea, let's find his place first, then call him and let him know we're running early and we can pick up coffee. I'll offer him some to break the ice."

"Parks you're priceless. Coffee for a cop to break the ice. I'd bet you a week's pay he's on at least pot number two but then again you don't presently have a job as I recall."

"Low Gabriel, even for you."

"But funny. What did you say the name of his street was?"

"Rattan Circle off of Red Rose Boulevard."

"Then we're almost there. Give him a call."

I dug out my cell and dialed Nance's number and listened to it ring. I listened to Nance's voice instruct me to leave a message, then I heard the telltale tone of an actual answering machine.

"Mr. Nance. Noah Parks here. I'm actually running ahead of schedule and will be there about ten to fifteen minutes early. If you can, please pick up but if not, I'll see you in a bit."

"We'll be there a good bit earlier than ten or fifteen minutes."

"Maybe that will put him off guard for our questions."

"Or maybe just piss him off."

#

We pulled up in front of Nance's house.

"425 Rattan Circle. That's the place. And look," Gabriel said as he pointed to the dark sedan in the drive. "Once a cop, always a cop."

"Yeah, I guess."

"What? Cops like cop cars."

"I know, I know. It's just that car looks familiar."

"All cop car's look familiar, that's why we call them 'cop cars.' Come on."

We parked on the street and walked up the short walkway to the front door. Gabriel rang the bell. We waited for an answer, but none came. I looked at the door, reached out and gave it a push.

"Now that's unexpected," Gabriel said as the door swung open.

I stepped across the threshold and listened. Nothing.

"Mr. Nance. Mr. Nance, it's Noah Parks. Are you home?"

I heard a squeal of tires from just behind us.

"God dammit."

I turned to see Gabriel running to the street. The sedan from the drive shot out, turned, and disappeared around a bend in the road.

"Dammit. And who the hell was that? Nance?"

"I almost hope so. Do we have a look around inside?"

"I can't believe I'm saying this, but probably so. Let's at least have a look at the door."

We walked back to the front where Gabriel knelt to examine the door. I leaned over his shoulder and called for Nance again. I heard a faint sound in response.

"Did you hear that?"

"Hear what"?

The sound came again.

"That." I said as I rushed past him into the house. "Mr. Nance. Are you here?"

"Help," a low voice said.

"There, back that way," Gabriel said as he rushed by me.

The entry gave way to a small living room and beyond a kitchen that seemed to be the location of the voice. I was a step behind Gabriel as I saw a body on the floor in a growing pool of crimson. Gabriel rushed to his side.

"Hold on, hold on," Gabriel said. "Parks, call 911."

I pulled out my phone as Nance was struggling to speak. He was aspirating blood and the words he was trying to form wouldn't escape his mouth. His eyes grew wide with the realization he was dying. He lurched on the floor in what I first thought was his final throes before dying, but then he pulled at Gabriel's hand and raised his head of the floor.

"S. Bart. The evidence. Warden. Stephens. I told him," Nance said as he collapsed back to the floor.

FIFTY-FIVE

Gabriel and I watched a steady stream of police, EMS, and firefighters come and go from Nance's house for the better part of an hour. I'd never understood why the fire department always showed up for a body. Not a bit of smoke in sight but we had a battalion chief and two fire trucks on the scene. Add to this four marked, three unmarked police cars, the two EMS vans, and the otherwise serene neighborhood street was anything but. If ever there was a time to rob a bank in Pawleys, today was the day.

The first patrol officers who responded--police generally respond quickly when a frantic call comes in about someone being murdered--stormed into Nance's house with guns drawn minutes after my 911 call. They found Gabriel over Nance trying to resuscitate him while I knelt beside the body not really knowing what to do.

The only problem with this is apparently, to police responding to a murder call, resuscitation looks a lot like assault particularly when a black man and a lot of blood are involved. The younger of the two responding officers, without warning, launched himself across the room and tackled

301

Gabriel. He was in the process of cuffing him when he noticed the Glock on Gabriel's belt.

This prompted a cry of "Gun!"

Upon hearing this the other officer turned to face me, gun trained on my head. He then commanded me to, "Hit the Floor!"

Which I immediately did.

As I watched the officer covering me, he was dancing back and forth looking like a nervous quarterback staring down a defensive end.

The police officer trying to cuff Gabriel must have expected some degree of struggle after he noticed the gun. He jumped from his kneeling position beside Gabriel only to lose his footing in Nance's blood. Actually, the term "losing his footing" doesn't do it justice.

He went from kneeling on Gabriel's back, to almost standing, to being sprawled out on the floor. As I watched, it appeared as if he was momentarily suspended in midair. Momentarily being the operative word. Gravity quickly took over and he crashed to the floor thrashing about, unable to regain his footing on the bloody tile floor. He finally rolled to the side of Nance's body, rose to his hands and knees, then stood. Covered in blood.

Gabriel remained face down on the floor.

Silence blanketed the room.

"Officer?" Gabriel said.

"Shut up. Where are my cuffs?"

"Um, on his back," the second officer said nodding towards Gabriel with his head as he kept a shaking gun pointed at me.

"Cover me."

The officer, covered with blood, moved to Gabriel and retrieved his handcuffs. He then knelt on the blood-free portion of the floor, lifted Gabriel's jacket and pulled the Glock from its holster.

"Why you carrying a gun?"

"Most detectives do."

The two officers exchanged looks.

"You're a detective? A cop?"

"He even has a badge."

"Quiet, Parks. Officer, my ID's in the inside jacket pocket, badge is on my belt."

The officers looked at each other again.

"Roll over," the one with the gun on me said to Gabriel.

Gabriel kept his hands over his head and rolled away from Nance's body onto his back. He even managed to avoid any bloodstains. His jacket fell open revealing his badge.

"That's not one of ours," my officer said.

"That's because I work for Charleston and not your department."

"Ok, yeah, right, yeah. Stand up and show me your ID."

Gabriel slowly stood, careful to keep his hands in view. With his left hand, he pulled open his jacket, showed the officers his open right hand and slowly pulled out his ID. Just as it fell open, three more officers appeared, guns drawn. It had to be quite the scene. A body, one officer holding two guns, the other covered with blood, a large black man holding a police ID and, well, me.

"What the hell?" one said.

"Just get these two guys outside," the blood-covered officer said. "I've got it under control.

#

The officer, after I asked, let me go to the bathroom rather than rushing me straight outside. I likely looked as bad as I felt. I managed to hold it together until I shut the door. It wasn't every day I saw someone die in front of me. It brought back memories of the one other time it had happened.

Claire.

I didn't think of her too often. I understand it was a part of the mind's normal defense mechanisms to suppress traumatic events but seeing your fiancée lying in a pool of blood clearly qualifies as such an event. Suddenly I was worried about Anna Beth. I couldn't let anything happen to her.

My pulse started to race. I splashed cold water on my face and took a deep breath. Focus, I needed to focus. I concentrated on what Nance had said.

'*Warden.*' What the hell did he mean by that? I found myself looking around the bathroom checking to see if anything was out of place then it occurred to me I didn't know what was normal in Nance's house. I took another deep breath and turned to leave.

Gabriel was waiting with his hands in his pockets just outside the door. He'd washed up in the kitchen though he still had some blood on his jacket. He did a double take.

"You okay? You look like crap, pardon me if I say so."

"That was a little more than I had expected. I didn't realize I was freaked out till I got in the bathroom."

"That's never easy. Hang on, I suspect they'll want to escort us outside."

"Excuse me sir, Chief says you and your friend need to wait outside."

We followed the officer back to our car where he told us to wait. I was surprised no one questioned us and let us remain together. No one had even taken our names.

We waited and watched.

FIFTY-SIX

Crime scene tape had been placed around the entire front of Nance's house with Gabriel's car serving as a pivot point. We were just inside the police line watching as it continued to unfold before us. I'd lost track of time when a plainclothes officer approached us.

"You're the Charleston detective?"

"I am."

"What happened?"

Gabriel paused for a moment apparently waiting for more of a question. When none came, he answered.

"We came by to see Jack. He used to work for the department. We called just before we got here, running a little bit early. When we pulled up, just as we got to front door, I heard a car in a hurry to get out of the drive. Looked and saw the dark sedan that had been parked in the drive heading in that direction," Gabriel said as he pointed down the street.

"See who was driving?"

"No. I'd guess male, but that's as much as I'd feel good saying."

"That how it happened?" the detective said looking to me.

"Exactly," I said.

"Then what happened?"

I kept my mouth shut. This discussion was cop-to-cop.

"I ran out to the street just in time to see the car disappear around the curve. I came back to the door, saw it was opened and went inside when we heard a call for help. He called 911 and I was starting CPR just as you guys showed up. We've been out here ever since. Oh, one interesting thing. No license plate on the car."

"You sure? No license plate."

"That I'm sure of. When we pulled up, thought it was Nance's. Dark sedan. When I ran out into the street I saw there wasn't a plate."

"It might have been random, but a car with no license plate probably means whoever it was did a bit of planning."

"I'd say you're looking at it right," Gabriel paused. "Not that you wouldn't be."

"No, I know what you're saying. We heard your message, the one you left for the victim. Far as I'm concerned you guys were in the wrong place at the wrong time, but you probably kept whoever it was in there from doing anything else," the officer said. "Not that that helps Mr. Nance."

"Out of curiosity, you find anything in there?"

The officer laughed and shook his head.

"The first two guys in pretty much trashed the crime scene so probably won't get a lot. Any idea what happened to him?"

"Not a clue," Gabriel said. "But nothing good."

"Looks like he was stabbed a couple of times in the back. No forced entry so he probably knew whoever did this, or thought he did. With him a former cop the suspect list probably isn't small."

Silence.

"I'm sorry about how things went when the officers first responded. I wish that had gone down differently."

"Don't worry about it. From their side of the fence it couldn't have looked good when they walked in. They did a great job controlling the scene."

"You're being too kind. I'm Crook by the way."

"Pardon?" Gabriel and I both said.

"Crook. Jim Crook. Chief of Police."

"Oh," we said in unison.

"It's okay. I get my share of raised eyebrows. Hold tight for just a few minutes and I'll have an officer get your info if we need anything else. Sorry for your loss, but you're good to go whenever you want."

"Thanks," Gabriel said as he shook Crook's hand.

As Crook turned to go, I looked to Gabriel and started to speak. Gabriel gave me a, "Shut up" look. A bit later the non-bloody officer who'd found us in Nance's house came over and took our information.

He apologized as well. The Pawleys Island Police Department was definitely polite.

When he had our contact information, he extended his hand to each of us and told us we were free to go.

We wasted no time in getting on the road to Charleston.

#

"You didn't exactly give the chief one hundred percent."

"I answered his questions. Not my fault he didn't ask the right ones."

"We got lucky with those two cops."

"We did but it doesn't give us any help as to who was in the house."

"Or what Nance meant with what he said. Well, other than Stephens knew something."

"You've got me convinced someone's pulling some strings here and that you didn't kill anyone."

"You're just now figuring that out?"

"You know I never believed you killed Andrew, but you wouldn't be the first defendant to claim there's a big conspiracy going on. I don't know what's going on or who's behind it, but it's clear it's not just coincidence. Andrew, Melvin, now Nance. When you start to get that many bodies piling up around you, it makes me think there's something someone doesn't want us to find. You can't go to Brady or the solicitor with this. Last thing we need is either of them seeing three bodies around you. He'd probably make you his first serial killer."

"No, you're exactly right. That's how this whole case has gone. Things keep coming back around to me. We need to figure out what Nance was trying to tell us. What do you think he meant by 'Warden?'"

"No idea. But in his forty-plus years I'm sure he's sent a lot of people away and any one of them could have had a run in with a prison warden."

"I guess we find out what Nance was into as a cop."

"You're right. And there's only one way to do that. We go through his records and there'll be a lot of them. Fortunately, they're electronic and we can access them remotely. We start tomorrow."

"We? You not worried about what the department might think?"

"Let me worry about that. You said I was one of the few you trusted. I happen to agree that right now you shouldn't trust anyone else."

We didn't talk the rest of the way home.

As the forest, rivers, marshes and rural Charleston County passed by my window, I felt myself slipping back into that which was becoming all too familiar.

Wondering how all of this had happened. And I kept thinking back to the vision of Jack Nance lying in an expanding pool of blood.

Even the beautiful scenery of the South Carolina lowcountry couldn't trump that image. An image that was going to stick with me for a while. A long while.

With Gabriel driving, we made it back to Charleston faster than the trip up to Pawleys Island. I got in my car to head home and checked my phone for the first time all day.

It's never a good thing when you have more than thirty missed calls.

FIFTY-SEVEN

Thirty-one missed calls to be exact. And twenty texts. Most from Anna Beth, several from Brady. I called Anna Beth not expecting anything good. I only hoped the dogs hadn't caused a big problem or worse, given the past events. Anna Beth answered on the first ring.

"Hey, I'll be home in --"

"Oh Noah, thank God. Don't come home."

"Why, what's wrong? Are the dogs okay? What --"

"Listen. Don't come home. Go to where you took me the day I got arrested and I'll be there as soon as I can. Don't use your phone."

"Anna Beth. What's going on?"

"Just go. I'll be there soon."

And the phone went dead.

"Go to where you took me the day I got arrested."

That was Andrew's house. I looked at my phone again and saw I had a new text--from Anna Beth.

"The dogs are fine. Park in the garage."

I turned around and headed to Mount Pleasant. I'd ask questions later.

#

I stopped short of turning onto Andrew's street, first looking both directions. No one was out. I turned and quickly pulled into his drive stowing my car in the garage. I quietly got out of the car and waited, watching the yard through the windows.

No one there.

I still had the key to his house. I opened the door. With the high hedges, no one would see me at the house, but I'd have to keep the lights to a minimum. The last thing I needed was to be arrested for trespassing at the scene of the crime that had resulted in my arrest. I was pretty sure nothing good could come from that.

I wasn't sure why, but while the electricity was still on, the alarm still wasn't armed. There was literally no sound in the house. Finally, the air conditioner kicked in. It was too late in the season for the air conditioner, but I thought it best not to mess with anything. It started to get chilly.

I wandered into the kitchen and went to the pantry. I slowly opened the door, turned on the light and stood for a moment staring. No sign at all Andrew had been founding hanging here. There was not a single sign that the police had poured over every surface of the house. Finally, I took a seat at the kitchen table and waited.

I sat thinking of all the times I had been in this very room. I thought back to the night of the party. The longer I sat, the longer I waited, the more I felt the house almost closing in on me. A text appeared on my phone.

"Almost there."

I heard a car outside. I rushed to the entryway and peered carefully through the blinds, pulled back just enough to look out. Gabriel's personal truck was in the drive. He backed the truck up tight against the garage. Even if someone walked part way up the drive past the hedge row they wouldn't see it until they cleared the garage. The doors opened and Anna Beth and Gabriel appeared each with a dog in hand.

I opened the door.

"Alright. What's going on?"

"Inside," Gabriel said.

He, Anna Beth, Austin, and Gracie made their way into the house.

"Pull the blinds and curtains in all the windows and keep the lights low. Don't want anyone to know we're here." He moved down the steps and jogged around to the back of the house.

Anna Beth closed the door and Austin and Gracie took off to explore the house.

I stood at the door for a moment then headed off to check the curtains and blinds. I finished with the den first, then looked for Gabriel in the backyard. No sign of him. Anna Beth was in the kitchen. I walked up and before I was able to say a word she wrapped her arms around my neck and pulled me close to her.

We stood locked in that embrace until Gabriel came back inside.

"Okay, let's talk."

#

I looked at both of them as they looked back to me.

"Don't look at me, I've got no idea why we're here."

Austin had wandered back into the kitchen with Gracie in tow. He nudged at my hand. I scratched his head.

"I was halfway expecting a surprise party."

"Noah, this isn't funny."

"I was --"

"Parks, listen to her. We've got a bit of a problem here."

"Okay. Okay. What's going on?"

"The police were at the house today. They had a warrant," Anna Beth said.

"For what?"

Gabriel reached inside the breast pocket of his jacket and pulled out a document. He slid it across the table to me. I picked it up and scanned it. I skipped down to the portion of the affidavit that set out what I was alleged to have done.

I dropped the arrest warrant to the table.

"Witness tampering? Really?"

"I made some calls. Someone from the solicitor's office knows you've been talking to Rebecca. My guess is that investigator, Gaines, followed you. I checked around and word on the street is that the solicitor thinks you had something to do with Rebecca leaving town. Bottom line is this is serious."

"Did you call Brady?" Anna Beth said.

"I didn't."

"It's after hours, but he has a service."

I pulled out my phone and dialed his number. A cheery sounding receptionist answered.

"Noah Parks here. Is Mr. Brady available?"

"Hold please."

I covered the phone.

"I'll put him on speaker. You be quiet," I said pointing at Gabriel.

Moments later, Brady was on the line.

"Noah. Where are you? I've been calling all day. We have a rather serious problem. I'm not going to ask what you've been up to, don't want to know, but whatever it is, it's attracted the solicitor's attention. There's a warrant for your arrest."

"It's not a coincidence I called. His people were at the house today. Fortunately, I wasn't home."

"Do I want to know where you are?"

"No, and don't ask. I have no intention of turning myself in. Witness tampering? It's complete bullshit."

"Noah, you're talking like a guilty man. If you chose to, for lack of a better characterization, 'go on the lam,' it will be against my counsel."

"Counsel all you want. The charge's crap and it only convinces me S. Bart has no interest in catching the real killer. Tell the solicitor to come find me if he wants me that bad."

"Noah you're upset. Take some time and relax. We can talk tomorrow."

"You're wrong. If I was just upset it wouldn't be so bad. I hit upset days ago. Talking tomorrow won't change a thing."

"I can't and won't advise you to avoid this warrant."

"I know and I'll never say you did. But I'm not coming in. Tell the solicitor whatever you want. Tell him you told me to turn myself in and I wouldn't listen. Tell him you can't find me. I don't care."

"I'll convey it in a delicate manner. You do realize this will limit my ability to represent you? And I don't need to tell you it could put your bond in jeopardy. I can also promise more than a few police officers will be looking for you."

"You don't need to remind me. I'll make it work. I'll call in a few days."

"Noah, this is against my counsel and if you get arrested, you'll be in jail till trial. You may be innocent, but innocent people generally don't go into hiding. And Noah?"

"Yes?"

"It's not just you that they'll be looking for. Anyone that is helping you, well, be careful who you keep around."

"Understood."

#

"How did you guys get here? I figure the Sheriff's office would've been watching Anna Beth," I said.

"They forgot you have a back to the house."

"After we talked, I went out the back and took the dogs for a walk on the greenway. I met Gabriel. My car will be at the house if anyone looks. Thank God you called before you came home."

"Good thinking to come here. Pretty sure this is the last place they'd look," I said.

"I thought so. Course we'll have to go out and get some food."

"I'll take care of that in a few minutes, but we need a game plan," Gabriel said.

"I thought we had one. We need to see if we can decipher what Nance told us and find out who the Warden is. See where that takes us. We can do it from here. We'll have to be careful with the dogs and can only go out at night, probably shouldn't order pizza, but we can make it work. Only thing I'm worried about is you're getting deeper into this and I'm pretty sure you're probably breaking at least one law being that I'm now officially on the run."

"You're right, but we need to figure this out."

"Alright. But if it gets too close for you, you're done. The same goes for you," I said to Anna Beth.

We stared at each other in silence for a few moments knowing that we were all about to take a turn from which, no matter how we tried to spin it, there was no turning back.

PART SIX

FIFTY-EIGHT

I was in the kitchen of my dead friend's house. So were Anna Beth and the dogs. I'd basically transplanted my life to my dead friend's home. And I was being prosecuted for his murder. For some reason the thought made me laugh. Some things simply couldn't be planned.

Two dog heads appeared over the couch curious about the sounds from the kitchen. Anna Beth rose to look at me as well.

"What? Were you laughing?"

'How funny were dogs,' I thought to myself.

"Yes, the whole situation makes you want to laugh, no?"

I walked into the living room and joined her on the couch.

"It's okay to find humor in the situation, but you have to hold it together. We passed serious a long time back and, not that I'm worried, but I need you in the game. You're the best attorney I know and us getting through this is going to take you at one hundred percent."

I looked at her. She was serious.

"I know. And I'm all in, but I have to laugh or else I may not be. We're in this together and we'll get out of it together."

"Good. Then we're on the same page."

Gabriel had excused himself to go out for supplies. Our being at Andrew's did have an element of genius to it. His place was likely the last place anyone would look, but our staying here was a short-term fix to a long-term problem. The longer I was on the run, the more those around me--Anna Beth, Gabriel, even the dogs--were at risk. We'd be spending a lot of time inside and the dogs were just going to love that, but we could make it work for a while. But for a short while. Time was not a commodity we had available to us. Gabriel soon returned with a stock of food and other supplies to see us through a couple of days.

"I did some thinking while I was gone. I'm pretty sure no one'll expect I'll be helping. It's just crazy enough we maybe can pull it off for a little while. I'll stay away in the day and come by at night so we can work on this Nance thing. Stay inside and be careful. No going for runs, no credit cards, no phone calls. You're on lockdown. The three of us, we'll figure this out."

He stopped and looked back and forth between us. I think he expected questions, but neither Anna Beth nor I said a thing.

"Okay, I'm leaving and I'll see you tomorrow. Oh, one more thing. I picked these up. Clean throwaway cells for us. But only use it to call or text me."

He looked at us then turned to go.

"Gabriel," I said and he turned to look at me. "I, your helping, I…"

"You don't have to say anything. You'd do the same."

"I would."

We stood in silence for a few moments then watched him leave through the back door. We didn't hear his truck as he drove away. We put the groceries away, fed the dogs, then after taking them for a quick walk through the shadows of the backyard, we were back in our adopted sanctuary. I walked to the kitchen and put the dog's leashes on the counter.

Anna Beth walked over and kissed my cheek.

"I'm going to bed. You should come. It's been a long day."

She disappeared upstairs with Austin in tow. I sat at the kitchen table. Gracie came over and nudged my hand. She'd integrated into the mix in a very short time and was healing nicely from her wounds.

"Hey girl."

She looked back at me, the nub where her tail should have been moving slightly. I often found myself wondering what went on behind their eyes. Dog eyes. So peaceful. All that mattered to her at this moment was me rubbing her head.

"Poor girl, I show up, your master gets killed, you get shot, and just when you're getting better you end up a fugitive. Sorry about all of that."

She nudged at my hand again and I scratched her behind her ears. She gave a quiet "woof."

"It's all going to work out. Let's go to bed, what do you say, girl?"

I headed upstairs with Gracie following. Stopping at the door to Andrew's room, I looked in at his empty bed. Gracie continued down the hall disappearing into the guest room. I took my shirt off as I walked down the hall. Peering inside I saw two dogs curled up on the floor. Anna Beth was under the covers. I'd slept on Andrew's guest bed countless times before but never with company. I quietly slid under the covers.

#

Suddenly I was wide awake on the floor of the jail with Melvin staring at me, fire in his eyes as his hands closed around my throat. I tried to scream, but no sound escaped my lips.

It was my fault he was dead. I fought to escape from his grip and to get away from him but I couldn't move. I was paralyzed by fear. Completely disoriented it took me what seemed like a small eternity to realize I wasn't in a cell but in a bed.

But where?

It wasn't my house. The image of Melvin slowly faded to one of an unfamiliar room.

Andrew's house. Anna Beth was asleep beside me with her arm across my chest. A dog snored at my feet. Slowly sleep released me from its grasp and my head cleared.

Being as careful as possible I moved from under Anna Beth's arm and slid from the covers, pulled on my pants and shirt and headed downstairs. The clock read Three-thirty a.m.

I wandered from the house to the water. I probably shouldn't be outside, but who would see or be looking for me in the shadows of the harbor in the middle of the night?

The Charleston city skyline filled the horizon across the harbor. Lights dotted the outline of the peninsula, reflecting in the water. I let the view and the night take me away. Away to a place where Anna Beth and I weren't on the run. A place where Andrew was still alive. A place where I wasn't accused of his murder.

Quiet footsteps shocked me back to reality. I had no idea how long I'd been staring at the water. Instantly my heart rate jumped. Certainly, whoever was walking up behind me could hear the "thump-thump" from my chest.

I realized I was holding my breath. Run? Stay?

"Noah," Anna Beth said.

"Oh, thank God."

"What are you doing down here?"

"I couldn't sleep and didn't want to wake everyone. I thought I'd come sit by the water for a bit. Think about things."

She sat close to me on the bench.

"What have you figured out?"

"Barely anything at all."

"Barely is something."

I put my arm around her and kissed her on the cheek.

"But not much. Not so much. I probably need to call Brady and let him know that I'll turn myself in and then let him earn his fee. See how good of a deal he can work out. Just like you believed Andrew would get elected, I've got to believe that a jury will see the truth in all of this."

"We don't have to decide now."

She didn't say anything else but pulled her knees to her chest and moved closer still, resting her head on my shoulder.

We sat in silence until the dawn started to creep over the horizon.

FIFTY-NINE

We made our way back to the house just ahead of the sunrise. The dogs were yet to get up. We both dressed and I turned on the TV to check out the morning news, and not long after the canines came downstairs, stretching and yawning. I was telling Anna Beth more about the events in Pawleys Island.

Coffee was brewing and the dogs were pacing about the downstairs eager to go out. Suddenly they rushed to the front door, whining and jumping. That meant only one thing, a visitor. Anna Beth and I froze and looked at each other. The dogs went silent. Then they came running back through the house, barking then looking out to the back yard.

"Is someone out there?" Anna Beth said.

"I think so."

"What do we do?"

As I was about to answer, I saw Gabriel appear on the back porch with a brown paper bag.

Anna Beth and I breathed a collective sigh of relief. The dogs barked and moved up to greet him.

"You scared the crap out of us."

"Hey dogs and good morning."

"Why here so early? I thought we were going to work at night."

"Bagels," he said.

"You're in a really good mood this morning. Care to share?" Anna Beth said.

"I have news. Good enough I wanted to tell you in person and it couldn't wait."

"They've arrested the real killer?" Anna Beth said.

"I would've called with that."

"Okay, then what."

"I think I know what Nance meant when he said, 'Warden.' "

Anna Beth and I looked at each other.

"You're kidding?"

"No. I'm not one hundred percent sure, but I think I'm on the right track."

"Okay. Back up a bit. Last night we were stumped and now less than twelve hours later you think you've got something?"

"I do."

"Okay, we're all ears."

I poured Anna Beth and me each a cup of coffee and motioned for Gabriel to sit after he waved off my offer of a cup of his own.

"I spent some time with the bonsai last night. I kept going over what Nance said. 'S. Bart,' 'Stephens,' and 'Warden.' "

"Ok, I'm with you. I've been thinking the same thing."

"Two of the three are specific people, 'S. Bart' and 'Stephens.' Right?"

"Yes."

"What if 'Warden' was too?"

"Isn't he? A warden somewhere we were thinking?" Anna Beth said.

"Maybe, but not likely. If Nance was going to point us towards a specific warden, why not just say his name. These are his last words. He talks about two people and specifically uses their names. Then he uses a general word like 'Warden?' I don't think so."

"What are you thinking?" Anna Beth said.

"I think Warden's the guy's last name."

Anna Beth and I looked at each other and raised our eyebrows and then looked back to Gabriel with a smile on our faces.

"Okay. Go on."

"Nance's a cop for more than forty years, sure he would have had contact with prisons, but normal rank and file don't usually interact with correction higher ups, so I asked myself who do cops see the most of?"

Silence.

"That was a question," he said.

"I don't know, the public, attorneys, snitches, people from the court."

"No."

"Cops and criminals," Anna Beth said.

Gabriel looked towards her with a look of surprise on his face.

"Brains and beauty. That's exactly right."

"That would make sense. So how do we narrow it down?"

"We get to work tonight and look at the department's records of past officers and arrest records. I'm going to download a few databases for us to search. You guys try to relax today. I'm going to poke around a little to see if I can find what's going on with your warrant. I'll come over after dark. Keep a low profile till then."

A quick visit but encouraging nevertheless. We watched as Gabriel walked around the house and stepped through the neighbor's hedgerow.

#

I decided to hold off on calling Brady, After all, I could do that anytime.

What I realized was, I just wasn't good at waiting.

I was anxious to begin working, but night was hours away and there was nothing we could do till then except wait and be nervous.

We were both nervous about the police coming to the door.

We were worried the dogs might start barking and attract attention.

We were worried someone might see a light in the house.

Every noise, and Andrew's house was quite noisy given its age, had us on edge. This was going to be tough if we had to stay in hiding too long.

I found myself roaming a circuit through the house, peering out of the front blinds several times an hour. Whenever I checked the time it was if the clock had slowed down. A couple of times I was pretty sure it was moving backwards.

Probably best to focus somewhere else.

I was busying myself in the kitchen making a late lunch. A good meal always helped, or so my mother had always said. Gabriel had done a good job at the store. He wasn't your normal meat-and-potatoes kind of guy. Though I initially hesitated, I made use of Andrew's pantry.

For the first time all day, cooking, I felt almost normal, but it didn't last long.

SIXTY

I looked up to see that Anna Beth had wandered into the kitchen to watch. This was the norm at our house and I was glad to see her doing this, given all we had going on.

She'd taken a seat at the island in Andrew's kitchen. I was standing across from her. Considering wine with lunch. After all, I was on the run, so why not? I saw that Andrew had a bottle of Mira Pinot.

"What are you going to do if you find this person named Warden?"

"I guess it depends on who he is and where he may be. Talk with him I hope, and hope he can help."

"You can't go to jail."

I stopped and walked around the kitchen island and put my arms around her from behind.

"We're going to get through this. You, Gabriel and I, if we can't get this figured out, well, I don't have anything clever to say, but we are going to do this. I promise."

"I hope that's a promise you can keep."

"I intend to, and ..." I said as my voice trailed off.

I removed my arms from around Anna Beth and walked into the living room. The television was on one of the local stations, but the volume was muted. A local news anchor was on the screen, talking; however, that didn't bother me, what did was the photograph behind her.

My mug shot. I turned the volume up as the anchor broke to a reporter.

"This is News 2's Morgan York reporting live from the Charleston County Courthouse where we're awaiting a press conference. We're told there've been some breaking developments related to the murder of Andrew Stephens. As you will recall, Noah Parks, local attorney and a close friend of the victim, was arrested and charged in Stephens' murder. Stephens was initially declared the winner of the election, which ultimately saw S. Bart Michaels sworn in as solicitor. According to sources close to the case, given the overwhelming evidence in the possession of the solicitor, it's believed a speedy plea from Parks will be the likely result. As well, if you will also recall…, oh it appears the solicitor is coming out."

In a jerky motion, the camera pulled back from York then quickly focused in on S. Bart. The shot tracked him walking up to a podium situated in the square of the Charleston Courthouse. A sparse crowd of what appeared to be mostly, if not all, reporters ringed the front of the podium. The solicitor reached the podium and the space behind him was filled in with a group of others in suits. He turned to speak to one of them then turned back to the microphone. There was the slightest wind noise from a breeze at the courthouse as he adjusted the height of the microphone.

"I didn't know solicitors gave press conferences," Anna Beth said.

"Rarely. Talking to reporters is one thing, but press conferences are another. This should be good and I say that expecting the worst."

The camera zoomed in, tightening the view until the solicitor filled the screen.

"Thank you for coming today. As you know I've made the prosecution of Andrew Stephens' murder priority one. There are several assistants and investigators in my office working on nothing else. As you know, we arrested and charged Noah Parks for Mr. Stephens' murder. Today we received new information concerning statements Mr. Parks made to the victim in the hours before Mr. Stephens' death. The nature of these comments has been very telling as to Mr. Parks' frame of mind, motive and to the planning of his heinous crime. It has also led me to make the very difficult decision to seek the death penalty in this case."

Anna Beth and I stared at the television. Neither of us said a word.

We heard a voice off-camera but couldn't make out what was being said. We watched S. Bart slowly nod. Then he spoke again.

"Excellent question. As to a press conference to announce this. I felt it appropriate given the story that needs to be told in obtaining justice for this crime, particularly given the present circumstances. Mr. Parks has been out on bond since shortly after his crime, but recently he engaged in witness tampering, resulting in a warrant being issued for his arrest. It is my intent to have his bond revoked so he will remain incarcerated pending trial. However, we have just learned Mr. Parks has disappeared. As a result of this he is now considered a fugitive from justice."

There was another voice.

"We believe he may have been gone for as much as a week, perhaps more. A condition of his bond was not to leave the state. We can't say whether he has abided by this, only that he is not at his residence. We do know his girlfriend," he paused and turned to speak to one of the men standing behind him. "A Ms. Anna Beth Cross, recently inherited a sizable, quite sizable, amount of money. She posted Mr. Parks' bond and we believe she is also assisting him in his efforts to avoid prosecution. My office is being proactive to ensure that Mr. Parks has to answer for his crimes and we will not allow him to make a mockery of our system of justice. If we receive any information as to where he may be, even sightings, we will alert the property authority. I understand the local news stations will be posting his photo on-air and on their web sites. If anyone spots Mr. Parks or Ms. Cross, do not approach them, call law enforcement."

Several more voices.

"Another interesting question. He did kill a man many thought his close friend and he did it in cold blood. What do you think? Does that sound 'armed and dangerous?'"

The solicitor pointed then nodded.

"His avoiding prosecution did not factor into my decision to seek the death penalty, but it did make the decision easier for us. With additional information my staff brought to me just today I came to the final decision, but I won't get into the new evidence at this point."

The screen changed from the live view of the solicitor to my mug shot once again. The solicitor's voice continued.

"We haven't been able to obtain a photograph of Ms. Cross yet, but as soon as we do, we'll see it's released. I want to thank you for allowing me this time. Have a good day and a good evening."

As he walked away, the camera followed him. He stopped and spoke to two men.

One was Dave Litman, his newly anointed assistant and the other was Litman's father, Billy. The three nodded while they spoke, then Billy Litman laughed and placed his hand on the solicitor's shoulder. The solicitor did the same in return and then the two men shook hands. Billy Litman turned and walked away while the solicitor and Dave Litman walked back into the courthouse.

"What was that?" Anna Beth said.

"Damn Billy Litman."

"You heard what he said, right? Death penalty."

"He doesn't care about the death penalty. He's doing that to turn the screws on me. Billy Litman was at Andrew's party. Remember just before he left with his son and wife?"

"I remember that."

"Now Litman's working for the solicitor. I guarantee the Litmans are behind this new evidence and maybe made the whole thing up."

I dialed Gabriel at the police department.

"Hold on." A moment passed. "What's going on? Things just got crazy over here."

"You're not watching the news, are you?"

"No why?"

"Our timeline just got pushed way up."

"What happened?"

"The solicitor just gave a press conference about the case. The term 'death penalty' was the theme."

"Stay put, I'm on my way."

335

SIXTY-ONE

Plain and simple. I didn't do it.

Without lying no one would be able to say I did. I wasn't going to wake up one morning and suddenly admit to being a murderer. I wasn't going to be the guy that, after a trial and an acquittal walked from the courtroom and intimated I got away with murder. There was no tell-all book in my future.

And I certainly wasn't going to tell anyone a lie and say I did this heinous crime. Andrew had been my friend and I. Did. Not. Kill. Him.

But none of this mattered. And the result was a conundrum. The solicitor wanted me dead or in jail and I wasn't excited about either possibility. With the solicitor having free access to the press, with my attorney being limited to the 'No Comment' response, I could only imagine the reality of how my story would play out.

My story was more likely to be one where the accused (me) lived for years in a prison cell after being found guilty. One day there's a ripple in the news where DNA has been tested or someone makes a deathbed confession admitting to being the real murder. Much fanfare is given as an innocent man is released from prison, but into a world where everything he had before was lost.

The mere chance such a tale could become one's reality has an immediate and profound impact on one's character.

#

And my character was about to change.

Later I saw a figure emerge from the hedgerow. Gabriel. I rushed through the house to the back door.

"Where the hell have you been? You said you were on your way and--"

"Calm down, calm down. I had to do something and I think you'll like what I found."

"It's been six hours since the solicitor came on, and -_"

"Noah," Anna Beth said. "Shut up."

Gabriel looked at me. I held my hands up.

"Fine. Just call next time, I've been a little on edge here."

"Sit," he said and pointed to a chair.

I did as he said. Anna Beth sat beside me, taking my hand in hers.

"Relax," she softly said into my ear. "Gabriel. Can I get you anything?"

"Thanks, but no."

He fished out several flash drives.

"Hand me that laptop please."

Anna Beth retrieved a MacBook from the kitchen counter. It sprang to life as soon as Gabriel opened the cover.

"This may be the key. After you called I pulled up the press conference video. There were several different angles on YouTube. I saw this the first time though and was sure after watching it a couple of more times, but Billy Litman was there, talking to the solicitor and not looking at all shy about it. That got me thinking ..."

"That Litman told the solicitor I threatened him at the party?"

"Yes, that's exactly what I was going to say. Should I go on?"

He paused and held his hand out towards me as if offering me the floor. I raised my hands in defeat.

"Okay, okay, finish. I'll be quiet."

"Thank you. I made a few calls. I still know a couple of the investigators over at the solicitor's office, and no one in that office has ever been able to keep anything quiet. Turns out Billy Litman told his son over the weekend he'd witnessed you threatening Andrew at the party."

"Well of course he did. And that's complete crap. I never said anything to Andrew that anyone could think was a threat. I, I ..." I rose from the table after slamming my fists on its surface, startling everyone in the process.

"Parks, sit your ass down and shut the hell up till I'm finished."

I started to speak, but Gabriel silently pointed to the chair.

I sat.

"You're forgetting one thing. Litman won't hold up, he can't hold up as a witness."

"But it's Noah's word against Litman's and with Noah on the run, I mean who'll believe him?"

Apparently, she was allowed to talk.

"No one has to believe Noah, we have a witness."

"Who?" we said in unison.

"Well, two, actually. One, your lovely girlfriend, and two," he said and paused to look each of us in the eye. "Me."

The room was silent. I replayed that night in my head.

"That's right, you saw everything we did. You walked out just after the Litman. I hadn't even thought about that."

"Exactly. And I don't think the Litmans saw me there. Better yet, I'd called in I was going off duty at Andrew's location so HQ has a record I was there. Now," he said as he inserted a flash drive into the Mac and unleashed an unexpectedly quick series of keystrokes. "Look at this."

He turned the computer to face Anna Beth and me. We scrolled down and read the file he had pulled up.

"Oh, that's interesting," I said as I read the screen.

"Isn't it? Seems you have another theory of your case. I seem to remember an attorney once told me having an alternate theory of the crime was a good thing, so thank you very much."

SIXTY-TWO

I knew Billy Litman as a businessman and nothing more. Through the years, he'd had his fingers in real estate, restaurants, nightclubs, and even part of a car dealership or two. But from looking over the file Gabriel had—Litman's police record--it also looked like he'd learned a few skills not presently being put to use, namely, license plate making, learned courtesy of the South Carolina Department of Corrections.

He'd been incarcerated for what in South Carolina is known as Assault and Battery of a High and Aggravated Nature, about as close to a murder charge as one can get without someone dying. From there it was a short step to murder.

This was huge. Litman had a motive. He wanted his son on Andrews' staff. Andrew refused. Dave Litman now worked for the solicitor. He had opportunity. All he had to do was drop by Andrew's after the party.

New theory: Litman played both sides to get his son a job. Andrew said no job for junior. If the younger Litman wasn't going be working for Andrew, then Billy Litman wasn't going to let Andrew be solicitor. That left S. Bart as the only other option, but Andrew was still in the way, and Litman had to ensure he didn't win.

This is where opportunity came knocking.

Literally.

Litman left things poorly with Andrew on election night. Litman returns to Andrew's house after everyone, including me, had left. Maybe he wanted to just talk without the others around. Maybe he came to do Andrew harm. Either way would explain why the alarm was off. Andrew had known his killer. Regardless of what Litman's intent may have been, the result was the same.

Andrew ended up dead.

"That's great news. This means I actually have something. Something solid."

"If I'd been in charge of this investigation and I found out Litman's making up evidence, with his record, the motive, and with what happened at the party, I'd certainly worry about whether you could be convicted, much even arrested."

"Ok," Anna Beth said. "But how does Warden fit into all of this. Remember what the guy said when he was dying. Why wouldn't he have said 'Litman'?'"

We exchanged looks.

"I don't have any idea, but it has to tie together. Right now, I need to go see Brady. Print out that arrest report, this he can work with."

#

I was in Andrew's car in a playground parking lot just down the street from Brady's Sullivan's Island home. Litman's arrest record was on the seat beside me.

341

A visit to Brady's office was out of the question and I wasn't going to chance a call. But I needed to see him. Sure, I'd be pissed if a client ever dropped by my house, but unless I took care of things now, I might never have the opportunity to have clients again.

I saw a car pulling in and I followed into Brady's drive.

His home sat on a large back lot of Sullivan's Island facing a small cove off of Charleston Harbor. Two huge oaks provided a canopy of shade over the large front yard; palmettos lined the drive, which I followed until it opened onto a basketball court-sized area in the rear of his home. The stone drive transitioned into a surprisingly large, immaculately kept backyard that meandered down to a dock. The practice of law had been good for Brady. He was getting out of his car as I drove up. It was clear he didn't recognize the car, but I saw recognition on his face as I stepped out.

"Noah, my God. What are you doing at my house?"

"It's good to see you too. I needed to talk to you and didn't want to call or come by the office."

"For God sakes, you're a fugitive. I could be accused of aiding you."

"No one knows I'm here and I won't stay long, but I have information."

He looked at his watch and glanced towards the street. There wasn't a very clear view, but I saw a white sedan drive by.

"Be quick about it. I want to help, but you're not making it easy."

"Fine, look at this," I said as I handed him Litman's criminal record.

He studied it for a moment.

"Yes. And what does this show me? Billy Litman served time for ABHAN. How does that help us?"

"He was at the party the night Andrew died. He's the one that came forward to the solicitor with this new evidence supposedly proving I was planning to kill Andrew. But I never said anything. Anna Beth was there and before you say anything, I know there's a credibility problem, but Emmett Gabriel was there too and heard exactly what was said, or should I say, what *wasn't* said. He even followed the Litmans out of the party. He's my friend, but he's a cop with a solid record. They won't be able to make a dent in his testimony."

Brady looked at the sheet again.

"Anything else?"

"Do I have to spoon feed it to you? Litman has a history of aggression. He was upset Andrew wasn't going to give his son a job. He went back to talk to Andrew after the party and who knows what happened, but things got out of hand and Andrew ends up dead. Maybe he even pointed the solicitor in my direction, who knows. Clearly, he was playing both sides of the fence, I mean his son is working in the solicitor's office. Means, motive, and opportunity."

Brady crossed is arms and looked at me.

"I have to admit, on its own it's an alternate theory that could put us on the road to reasonable doubt at trial. But we can't use it."

"What do you mean? Litman is all but gift-wrapped for the solicitor. Hell, if Dave Litman is in on it at all he gets to convict two for the price of one. And still gets to pull a law license."

"There's something you don't know."

"Like?"

"Litman has an alibi."

"What are you talking about? Who? His son. His wife? Did he get arrested for killing bees?"

"Actually, yes to both, but in addition to the family members, he also has three Charleston police officers who will provide a rock solid alibi. After I saw the press conference today, I thought it might have been Litman who tipped off of S. Bart, so I did a little checking around. I can't say I thought of Litman as an alternate theory, but in looking into this, I found out there had been an altercation of the domestic variety at the Litman home the night of the election, so both of you have Charleston's finest on your side. Bottom line is that Litman couldn't have done it. But before you get down on things, I think this takes the death penalty off the table. If anything, it will likely make an offer similar to what we discussed earlier attractive to the solicitor. He shouldn't have listened to Litman and definitely shouldn't have used his word for the death penalty. And if it's any consolation you'll likely cause some problems for Dave Litman, but this won't end it for you, well, unless, well, that could be a problem."

"Brady, you're talking to yourself. Unless what?"

"No, there may be a way to use this to your advantage."

"Good God Brady, why do you think I'm here?"

Brady stared at the street again. I followed his gaze. I caught of glimpse of a white Volvo driving down the street. It looked to be the same car as before and oddly familiar. Hopefully I hadn't been followed. I turned back and Brady had moved over to lean against the BMW out of view of the street.

"This holds the potential of making the solicitor look bad. Very bad. Amateurish bad. He, by his own admission, quickly jumped to throw the death penalty at you. He all but said someone gave him a tip and then suddenly he's seeking the death penalty. He did no due diligence, he just decided and that's exactly how he explained it. It's a mistake we may be able to use to our advantage. The trouble is he needs to know what we have, to see our cards and if we all show up, he won't hear a word, he'll just arrest you and if you're locked up this won't make a bit of difference for months, if at all. I can't bring it up for a host of ethical reasons," he said as he waved Litman's arrest record. "The problem is how do we confront him? How do we show him you're innocent? How do we show him that it's not about convicting you, but about saving his career?"

I stared at Brady for a moment. He was right. For me to get any leverage, the solicitor needed to know we had something that leveled the playing field. Something that could be damaging to him.

"If it's a meeting with S. Bart that has to occur, I think I know how to make it happen."

"Noah, be careful what you do here. I'll have an obligation to report you, even if you're my client, if I think any harm may befall anyone. You know that."

We were dancing around a delicate subject. Brady was my attorney, but he couldn't become involved in a crime and while our meetings were attorney-client privileged, if he thought I was going to hurt the solicitor, he'd suffer no consequences from breaking the privilege and reporting me to authorities.

"Talking to him isn't a crime. Remember, I want him to decide to dismiss my charges all by himself. If it makes you feel any better, I'll start the meeting by telling him I'm turning myself in but first he has to listen to what I have to say."

"That would certainly be an acceptable way to approach him."

"Yes, it certainly would."

Brady chuckled and glanced to the street again. I looked over my shoulder.

"Paranoid or expecting someone?"

"Being careful. Just remember he'll probably still want your law license or something that will let him save face with the voters. Also, you should know this is the first time in my career I've even thought about encouraging a client to do this. But everything we have here, it's not your normal case. How are you going to make this happen?"

"I'm going to walk right up to his front door and invite myself in for a chat."

SIXTY-THREE

Gabriel and Anna Beth were waiting for me in the kitchen at Andrew's when I returned just after dark.

"Parks, I was starting to think you'd gotten yourself arrested again."

"You do have a way of getting a girl worried. I take it you saw Brady?"

"I did. Had a very productive discussion with him."

"You've been at Brady's all afternoon?"

"I have. Mainly waiting, but when he got home I drove right up. Worked like a charm."

We gathered around the island in the kitchen.

"I need a drink," I said as I retrieved a beer from Andrew's refrigerator. No one else seemed to want one.

"Okay. Brady was extremely encouraged about our discovery. And I say our discovery, but he doesn't know either of you are helping. We have one problem though. Litman didn't do it."

"How do you know that?" Anna Beth said.

"On election night, after the Litman clan left here, they took the festivities home and things got out of hand. The police showed up and were there for a good while smoothing things

347

over. Litman has his son and wife, as well as several police officers as alibis."

"But if Billy Litman didn't do it, we're back to square one. So why are you in such a good mood?" Anna Beth said.

"Hold on Parks. If you know Litman didn't do it you can't use that theory at trial. That's an ethical problem, isn't it?"

"That's right. And I am in a good mood. See, I can't suggest Litman killed Andrew, but if the solicitor uses him as a witness, which he plans to do, then I can use Anna Beth and you to impeach his testimony. The solicitor's hanging his case on Litman as the foundation for the death penalty. You and Anna Beth testify and that shoots Litman's testimony out of the water. He's already on shaky ground given his son draws a paycheck from the solicitor's office. If he's lying, which he is, the case loses credibility and we get the jury to ask the question that if the strongest witness is lying then what else is the prosecution concocting?"

"But it sounds like you're saying you'd still have to have a trial to make this happen. And if you don't win at trial then you go to jail," Anna Beth said.

"Not necessarily. Here's where we throw it back in the solicitor's face. This is his first big case. He'll want to be solicitor for a while and if it comes out in his first big trial, a trial he's personally handling, that one of his witnesses has lied and he didn't check on the witnesses' story, or worse, knew about it, and let it go forward, it's terrible for him. Worse than terrible. If the jury returns a 'not guilty' and it comes out they believed the whole case was fabricated, then his career as a solicitor is finished. The whole thing would ruin him."

"You know you can't just walk into his office and expect him to make it go away. If you show up, you'll be arrested before you get word one out."

"Exactly."

"I'm confused," Anna Beth said. "You have to get this information to him but you can't do that. What are you going to do?"

"I'm going to spoon feed it to him. Actually, you and I are going to. I hope," I said looking at Gabriel.

"Are we now? And how are we going to do that?"

"That's the second time today someone's asked me that and I'll tell you what I said the first time. I'm going to walk right up to his house and tell him."

"You and I are going to walk up to his house and he's just supposed to say, 'My mistake. Come on in, let me make a couple of calls and we can get this straightened out?'"

"More or less. Look, his new deputy solicitor brought him a lying witness. A witness who's going to commit perjury on the stand: the deputy's' own father. People don't want criminals walking the streets but they don't want to think their solicitor will make a death penalty case by creating evidence. I'll lay out what I learned about Litman and I need you there to explain exactly what you saw. Then I'll suggest we talk resolution. Telling him myself makes me look crazy. Having you there gets him to understand it's not crazy, but you're ready to put your job on the line rather than seeing an innocent man go to jail with false testimony."

"The part about me losing my job is certainly right. If this doesn't work, not much of a way to spin it. Suppose it goes south? What do we do?"

"I don't know."

"You don't know?"

"No. Or I guess I should say I do know and this has to work. S. Bart is a lot of things, but he certainly doesn't want his first case to ruin his career. I'm sure about that."

I looked to Anna Beth who was staring out the back window to the harbor beyond. "There's just one problem with everything," she said.

"What?"

"Let's say you get the solicitor to go along with this, to save his career. That creates a difficult spot for him."

"Meaning?" I said.

"You said he wouldn't ruin his career by offering false evidence to get a conviction, but if he goes along with this, he'd be letting a murderer go free, a murderer against whom he's said the evidence is overwhelming. How do you get him to do that?"

"He has to throw Dave Litman to the slaughter. He'll have to lay the blame at Litman's feet, say Litman tainted most of or even all of the evidence. It'll probably cost Dave Litman his law license, his job at a minimum, but I couldn't care less about that. I won't plead guilty, but I would essentially agree to an Alford plea, sorta like a 'nolo contrendre' or 'no contest' plea. I'd have to accept a long period of probation, but no jail and certainly no death penalty. That way he doesn't let me walk, I don't plead to murder, and no jail."

"It that all?"

"I'd probably have to surrender my law license."

\#

The loss of my law license didn't have Anna Beth jumping for joy, but she took it better than I'd anticipated. Actually, better than I did. I had no idea what I'd do with myself. I'd been a lawyer so long the thought of doing anything else was a void. I couldn't even imagine, but if that was what it took to put this behind me, I was ready.

"Maybe I'll take up private investigation, find the real killer."

"You've always wanted to be a cop," Gabriel said.

The two of us were heading downtown to S. Bart's house. I decided there was no time like the present and no better time to put this all to rest. The whole thing was just crazy enough that it might actually work. I probably should have been nervous, but I found myself quite calm.

We decided we would walk up to the door, knock, and walk in. Whether he wanted us to or not. I had what I needed to tell him down to less than ninety seconds, so it wouldn't take long.

We traveled down East Bay Street past the Market where throngs of tourists were making their way back to a cruise ship docked at the port terminal. We headed on towards the Battery and White Point Gardens, turning right onto South Battery. Some of the oldest and grandest homes in Charleston were on this street. Looking at the homes through the car window as Gabriel slowly drove down the street, each with a mask of history covering a grand exterior, I found myself wondering about all they'd witnessed through the years. Slavery, wars, depression, and all in between had been played out in and around these stately manses. The next hour would go a long way towards painting the picture of what my ultimate history would become.

We turned onto Council Street. The solicitor's street. I took a deep breath as I saw his house.

Gabriel slowed the car.

"You ready?"

"Actually, yes. For the first time in weeks, I feel like we're on the right path."

He pulled the car to the street's side and turned to face me.

We each opened our door and then quietly shut them. It was close to nine p.m. Fortunately, only a few houses were lit. That meant the foot traffic would be minimal. We ducked to the shadows on the inside of the sidewalk. The solicitor's home was a few houses up the street. We stayed in the shadows and moments later, I stood at the end of his drive and looked towards the house. I could see no one through the windows. His home was a traditional downtown Charleston residential structure, two stories high with porches on each level. I could see a garden in the back and a carriage house attached to the main structure.

Nice place, I thought.

I took a deep breath and headed up the drive with Gabriel right behind. It was less than twenty feet from the walk to the front door. As we worked our way into the shadows, my eyes adjusted to the dark. I noticed something and I stopped.

"You okay? What happened?"

"Wait here," I said to Gabriel.

In the carport, there was a white Volvo. In the evening dark, you couldn't see it from the street. I made my way around to the front of the car. I was probably being paranoid, but I'd seen a white Volvo drive by Brady's twice and needed to see something. When Brady and I were talking, the second time the car passed, I caught a brief view of a front vanity plate and I had to see if there was one on this car. A green plate with a white cross. I made my way around the front and couldn't see a thing. I pulled out my iPhone and held it close to the tag. As I light the screen a white cross appeared. I crouched again and quickly made my way around the car.

"Come on, we're going."

"But what about S. Bart?"

"Now, let's go," I said as is ran to the street.

He caught up and we both jumped in his car.

"What happened? Good lord, you look like you've seen a ghost."

"That would have probably been better. Drive."

SIXTY-FOUR

To Gabriel's credit he didn't say a word until we got back to Andrew's.

"Mind telling me what happened back there?"

"There was a car in the drive. I've seen it before. Several times. I saw it driving by Brady's house today. And I think I saw it the night Andrew was killed."

"And?"

"I, I think S. Bart may have killed Andrew."

"Okay. That's just crazy. After all we've just learned. Break it down, explain it to me. How do you go from seeing a car to S. Bart being a killer?"

"Let's go inside. Anna Beth needs to hear this."

It was clear we'd surprised her and the dogs as we came in.

"That was quick. A little too quick. What happened?"

I motioned to the table, "Nothing."

"Apparently, he was spooked by a car."

"Okay, I saw a car. It made me nervous. Listen. Today when I was talking to Brady I saw a white car pass by a couple of times. Then there's a white Volvo in the solicitor's drive. I remembered a dark plate on the front of the car with a symbol

354

on it. I checked the car at Brady's and there is a white cross on the front plate. And I know I've seen that car before, before Brady's. In our neighborhood. I'm almost sure it's the same car. And, I believe I passed it on the way out from Andrew's the night he died."

Gabriel was staring at me in silence.

"You're nervous. You don't see something till you're looking for a reason to see it. I think your mind's using that Volvo to fill in some empty spaces."

"I know that, but I'm positive I've seen it before. That and, it, well, it just seems like we're missing something."

Gabriel laughed out loud.

"Parks, hell, I'll guarantee we're missing something. Something like who the real killer is."

"You know me, I trust my gut and my gut told me something was off. I know it sounds crazy, S. Bart killing Andrew, but someone did and I know it's just an election, but people have been killed over less."

"Parks, get some rest, it's been a long day," Gabriel said. "I'll come back tomorrow and we can decide what we do."

We watched him walk through the side yard to the garage.

"Could S. Bart really have killed Andrew?" she said.

"I don't know. But Gabriel's right. I'm looking for white Volvos and my accusing him won't get me anywhere. Not without more."

"Then let's listen to Gabriel. How about we sleep on it. We can start fresh in the morning."

"You're right. Right now, sleep sounds wonderful."

#

Anna Beth and I, accompanied by two canines, went to bed. She was off to sleep not long after the lights went out.

Not so for me. My mind was racing. S. Bart the killer? Could it be? It was crazy for me to even be thinking it, but I was. I lay in bed listening to the rhythmic breathing around me in the room. It was like a wave washing over me then retreating to sea. Dog, dog, Anna Beth. Dog, dog, Anna Beth.

It was quite peaceful. Thoughts of Andrew's murder started to fade.

Dog, dog, Anna Beth. Dog, dog, Anna Beth. Dog, dog, Anna Beth.

As the cycle of breathing continued, with each pass I thankfully felt myself relaxing. My thoughts clearing.

Dog, dog, Anna Beth. Dog, dog, Anna Beth. Dog, dog, Anna Beth.

I was feeling myself beginning to relax.

Then suddenly I sat upright in bed.

How had we not thought to check that?

I slid from beneath the covers and pulled on a pair of boxers and a tee shirt.

I went downstairs to the table in Andrew's kitchen and found exactly what I was hoping for.

Gabriel had left all of his flash drives.

The databases from the police department.

#

"How long have you been up?"

I looked up and saw Anna Beth coming down the stairs wearing one of my tee shirts. She walked over to me, stretched, yawned then bent to kiss me and only then did I realize it was growing light outside. I'd been working all night.

"What are you working on?" she said.

"I've been answering questions."

"What questions?"

"I think almost all of them. I've been down here all night."

"All night?"

"Yep and I'm close. Give me a little more time. And call Gabriel. I know it's light out, but ask him to come over as soon as he can. Oh, good morning by the way."

She turned to the phone. Hopefully this wasn't going to cost him his job.

Back to work.

It took Gabriel several hours to arrive and I worked the entire time. It turned out for the best as I was only just reaching a stopping point when he came in.

"Parks, what's the emergency?"

"Sit down. I'm going to tell you a story. A story about our friend, Mr. Warden."

SIXTY-FIVE

"I started with Nance and worked backwards. At first there was nothing focused. There was too much information, but once I started looking in the right place, it jumped out. Anyway, Nance was a busy man, I mean he was a cop for over forty years, and sure Charleston was a smaller city, but the man was busy."

I waited for a response from Gabriel or Anna Beth, but getting nothing, I continued.

"I realized pretty quickly it would be too much for me to go through every arrest he ever made, so I started when he was a detective looking for something obvious. That made me realize I needed to look at it from a different angle. I was starting to get frustrated when it hit me."

"What?" they said in unison.

"Partners."

"We don't have partners. We might work with someone on a case, but we don't have the same partner. Well, wait, we don't have partners anymore."

"Exactly."

"Okay. That's interesting. What did that get you?"

"I found out he was probably hard to work with. Over twenty-eight years there were nineteen different ones."

"And you checked out all of them?"

"I looked at fourteen of them."

"Why just fourteen?"

"The first thirteen were dead ends. No idea about the last five."

"Something special about number fourteen, I take?"

"You could say that. His name was S. Bart."

"S. Bart? Is he related to the solicitor?"

"Nope. Not related, but one and the same."

"The solicitor?" Anna Beth said.

"The one and only."

"He was a cop? A detective?" Gabriel said.

"S. Bart worked as a cop for a few years in the late seventies. I'm guessing his father helped him get the job since he bounced up to detective pretty quick. Anyway, his one partner as a detective was Jack Nance and then all of the sudden he left and started law school."

"Sounds like there's a 'But' in there," Gabriel said.

"There is. Warden."

"Another partner?" Anna Beth said

"Actually, quite the opposite. Nance and S. Bart had been partners for several months and they catch a nothing case. Downtown liquor store's robbed. Somebody threw a hammer through a window, stole a half a case of bourbon and left the hammer behind. Nance and S. Bart ran the prints and they came back to a convicted felon. They arrest him. They have him dead to rights. The guy's looking at some long jail time from his record, but then it gets interesting."

"Interesting how?"

"Within a couple of weeks of the arrest S. Bart is no longer a cop, Nance is promoted and the charges are dismissed against Warden."

"Alright, alright, you've got me, what's the hook?"

"The guy they arrested. His name was Roger Warden."

"You're kidding?" Gabriel said as I turned the computer to face them, a black and white mug shot of Roger Warden looked back at them.

"Here's what I think happened. Nance and S. Bart arrest his guy. S. Bart is brand new and he screws something up with the arrest or the evidence. He's in hot water and his father comes to the rescue. He leaves the department for law school and a nothing case goes away. Nance gets a promotion so he keeps his mouth shut. This has to be it. This has to be the Warden Nance was talking about. Too much of a coincidence not to be."

"I agree. Okay, so we go talk to Warden and find out."

"That would be the next step, but Warden died a while back."

"Of course he's dead," Gabriel said.

"Don't get worked up over it, I don't think it matters that we won't be able to talk to him. Here's what we know: S. Bart was a cop and he hid it; A disgraced cop at that. No one knows he was a cop. Heck, Charleston's a small town and I've never heard about S. Bart being a former cop. Usually, solicitors market that for some credibility in knowing the criminal system from the ground up. The only reason S. Bart keeps this quiet is if there's something to hide," I looked at Anna Beth. "Think back to our visit to his office. Not a single photo on his wall from his police days. He's hiding it. He can't have anyone knowing he was connected to Warden. If he does, then the house of cards starts to fall. I'm thinking Nance reached out to his old partner, wanted cash to keep silent. S. Bart probably says no. Nance probably threatened going to Andrew, maybe he did, or maybe Nance just tells S. Bart he did. S. Bart goes to confront Andrew and Andrew ends up dead. I don't think S. Bart would plan to kill him, but we saw his temper the day we were there for the plea offer, and he can get fired up."

"Our new solicitor murdered his way into office and then turned into a serial killer since?" Gabriel said.

"What do you mean?"

"Andrew. Melvin. Nance. In the murder department, three gets you into the serial killer dance."

"It had to be him that killed Andrew. Nance too. With them, it's too close. Melvin, maybe, but there's no clear tie, least not that I can see. Well, other than me. But otherwise, yes, I think the solicitor may have murdered his way to office. After all, with them gone, who knows he was a cop?"

"We do," Anna Beth said.

"Wow," Gabriel said.

"That's all you can say?"

"No. It's not that. And I can't believe I'm saying this, but it could fit. I think it's weak on any proof he actually did it, but you've got the thing with the Litman's and I've got to wonder why he didn't mention he was a cop. That astounds me. If you're running for solicitor you don't open your mouth without saying you used to be a cop. Unless you've got something to hide."

"My point exactly. And it covers everything Nance told us. Andrew, S. Bart, Warden. They all knew he was a cop."

"But where does that leave us?" Anna Beth said. "I don't know him, but no way S. Bart admits to murder. No way that's going to happen. He's trying to get you to do that, remember."

"No, you're right."

"If you accuse him of murder with what you have, it just makes you look crazy."

"She's right, he'll never confess or admit it. So, what's the play?"

"We do today what we started to do yesterday. Only today we know about Warden and we have Litman. I think we get more telling him what we have and letting him fill in the dots. We want him to realize he needs us to be quiet. He needs us to go away."

"Leave a murderer as solicitor?" Gabriel said.

"It keeps me out of jail, who knows, maybe I get to keep my law license."

"Dangerous game, but I'm in," Gabriel said.

"Me too," Anna Beth said.

I thought about protesting. I looked to Gabriel, then to Anna Beth. Neither said a word. I thought about telling them to stay put, that I could handle it myself that they had come far enough, but, no, they were in the game and I liked the idea of strength in numbers.

"Alright, let's go."

SIXTY-SIX

Once again twilight found me in downtown Charleston looking at S. Bart's house. One plainclothes detective, a suspended attorney, and his girlfriend all stared through the twilight.

"This plan always seems a lot better from across the harbor."

"We don't have to go in you know," Gabriel said.

"You're right, 'We' don't, but I do. I'm fresh out of options."

"We're going with you," Anna Beth said. "You need witnesses."

"She's right. If you go in alone and he's done what you think, then I don't want to think about the outcome. I'm your friend, but I'm also a cop. It'll be harder for him to do anything with three of us there." Gabriel said. "If things go south, I'm here. If things go your way, I'm here."

"I like that. If it does go south, arrest me and save yourself. But let's hope we stay away from south."

We looked at each other in silence for a moment.

"Ok, let's go."

We checked up and down the street, moved to the shadows and quickly made our way to S. Bart's house. With a final glance to the street, we moved across the yard, past the white Volvo and up the steps to the front door. Anna Beth and Gabriel stood to the side of the door and I stood in front of it.

I took a deep breath then raised and lowered the brass door knocker three times. The knocks reverberated then faded.

Nothing.

Three more knocks.

The porch light came on. The door opened to frame S. Bart. It didn't take long for the shock of seeing me to set on his face.

"Mr. Parks. What the hell are you doing at my house? I'm calling the police."

"Not necessary, Mr. Michaels," Gabriel said as he stepped into view. "Mr. Parks came to me and turned himself in on the condition he could talk to you first."

"Is that so? And you can refer to me as 'Solicitor,' and what is she doing here?" S. Bart said as he looked to Anna Beth.

"My apology," Gabriel said. "If we could come in it won't take but a moment of your time."

S. Bart reached to pull the door shut. Gabriel put his hand on the door stopping it from closing.

"Really, just a moment." So much for being low-key, I thought to myself.

"Bart? Bart? Who is it? You know we'll be late if we don't leave now," a familiar voice from inside the house said.

S. Bart stepped to the side and let us in.

"You just ended your career, Captain," S. Bart said. "You're done."

Anna Beth closed the door behind us.

" .... Bart, damn it, just tell them to go away, we have to go, and--" Tamara Michaels said as she walked into the foyer fidgeting with an earring. She paused. "Well, Noah Parks and his little lady, Anna Beth Cross I believe. Yes, that's right. But I don't believe I know your friend."

She walked up to Gabriel and looked him up and down.

"Pay no mind to them, dear, they'll just be a moment. In fact, finish getting ready, I'll take our guests into the den."

"Now Bart, don't be rude. Introduce me."

"I, I'm sorry, introduce you?"

"Yes, please do."

"I, well this is Captain Emmett Gabriel. This is his last night with the Charleston Police Department."

"Oh yes, Captain. It's a pleasure to meet you. I wasn't aware you were retiring."

This was rather odd behavior. Interesting.

"Pardon me, Mrs. Michaels, why don't you join us, I think you'll want to hear this," I said.

"You believe you have something to tell us?" she said.

S. Bart started to protest.

We moved into a den off the front entrance. The room had the look of a small study about it: mostly books, photos, and small antiques, along with two couches.

"You sure you know what you're doing," Gabriel said in a low voice as we all entered the den.

I didn't answer him.

"Alright, Parks, what the hell do you want?" S. Bart said. "My patience is wearing thin."

"I've learned a few things about Andrew's murder you need to know. Things I think will give you a little perspective on your prosecution."

"Perspective? What the hell are you talking about? There's only one perspective and that's the story I'll tell: the story I'll tell to the jury. And that story ends with you on death row. That's the only perspective there is."

"Now Bart, don't be rude to our guests."

"Don't be what? Dear, these aren't guests, they're criminals," he said as he looked to Gabriel and Anna Beth. "All of them."

She laughed. Not at all what I expected. This woman never ceased in the bizarre behavior, every time I saw her.

"Mr. Parks, you came to see us, you came to see us to tell us something. Don't let Bart's blustering bother you. You go right ahead and get it off your chest."

This was not at all going how I expected.

"I came to talk about Jack Nance and Roger Warden."

I stared at S. Bart's face as I let the word's hang in the air, waiting for him to break. Only problem was he didn't break. He started to turn red. Really red.

"What the fuck did you say?"

"Bart. Such language. Please Mr. Parks, I've been looking forward to this. Since the cemetery."

I paused.

"You heard me, Warden and Nance. We know what you did. We know what happened," I said.

"What the hell are you talking about?"

"What I'm talking about, and Mrs. Michaels, this is where you should listen carefully."

Mrs. Michaels was staring at me with that same blank stare she had at Andrew's funeral.

"It's simple. It took some digging around but we found out about your old partner and about Roger Warden."

"God, I haven't heard that name in years. Nance's anyway. Warden you say. Who's that? Please tell me you don't think they have anything to do with your case."

I looked to Gabriel and Anna Beth. That had to mean we had him. Didn't it? I took a deep breath.

"We know about your screwing up Warden's arrest. How your screw up put a criminal back on the street. We know it cost you your job at the PD. Don't deny it, it doesn't suit you."

"Deny what? I haven't the slightest idea what you're talking about. Captain, he's crazy. I'll tell you what, onetime offer: cuff him now and your job's safe. Get him out of here."

Gabriel stood his ground.

"Not just yet. Still a few questions we need answered. A botched investigation, you leaving the department, the business with Warden. We know Andrew knew about it," I said as I looked slowly around the room. All eyes were on me. "And we know what happened on election night when you went to Andrew's house."

Silence hung in the room.

"Parks, you really are crazy. I suspected it when you rejected the plea, but now I know," S. Bart said. "If you think --"

"Bart. Really?"

He turned to look at his wife.

She walked over, stood before him, met his eyes then slid her hand gently to his face. He took her other hand in his as she smiled. Suddenly the smile faded away and she slapped his face. She slapped him once again, turned and walked out of the room.

We stood in silence.

"Parks," Gabriel said. "Do you have any idea what's going on here?"

I looked to Anna Beth.

"Go bring her back. And make sure she doesn't call the police."

SIXTY-SEVEN

As Anna Beth stepped out to retrieve Mrs. Michaels, S. Bart stepped to me and poked me in the chest with his finger rhythmically as he spoke.

"I don't know what the hell you're playing at here, but I've got no idea what you're talking about. I haven't seen Jack Nance since just after law school. The only cover-up was he was a dirty cop that ruined everything he ever touched. I'm almost surprised he didn't try to shake me down during the election. And I guess you're still not familiar with the term 'alibi?'"

"Let me guess. Your wife? The one who just slapped your face. I'm thinking that's probably not your best bet when it comes to an alibi."

S. Bart looked at me and smirked. He handed me his cell phone.

"I suggest you call the Planter's Inn. I'm guessing this may be news, but I rented the third-floor ballroom and the adjoining suites for election night. I was there from seven-thirty on, even stayed the night. Be sure to check with the valet. They had my car all night."

I looked at Gabriel.

"Really?"

S. Bart chuckled.

"A murderer storms into my home. Accuses me of killing the person I'm prosecuting him for, and when you realize I have an alibi, not that I'd need one, but the best you can say is 'Really?' But yes, really. And," S. Bart said as he held his hand out for his cell phone. "I think I'll call the police now."

I turned to see Anna Beth walk back in the room with Mrs. Michaels, who, for some reason was holding a revolver. She motioned for Anna Beth to join Gabriel and me. S. Bart stared, his mouth open but no words came out.

"Why don't you give me that dear," she said as she took S. Bart's phone. "I think all of you should have a seat. Captain, I'm betting you have a gun or two. If you'd be so kind as to take them out, you can just toss them over on the other couch across from you. Slowly please. Very good."

I watched Gabriel's Glock arc across the room and land silently on the opposite couch. It bounced a single time then came to rest in the middle of the cushion. He kept his eyes on Tamara Michaels and lifted his pants legs, one at a time to show there were no other guns.

"Very well. Please. Sit."

"What's going on here?" S. Bart said in my direction.

"I'm probably not the one you need to be asking," I said.

"All in good time, we'll have a short wait," Mrs. Michaels said.

We all four awkwardly crowded together on the couch in silence. Anna Beth hadn't reached her in time and she had been on the phone. But if she'd called the police, why was S. Bart sitting beside me on the couch?

"Just what are we waiting for?" S. Bart said.

Mrs. Michaels stared at him and without breaking her gaze spoke to me.

"Mr. Parks, you deserve some credit."

"Please, call me Noah. If you're comfortable enough pointing a gun at me, please feel free to use my first name."

"Oh, Mr. Parks, ever the charmer. Nevertheless, that was impressive work running down Mr. Nance and finding out about Roger. Oh, that brings back memories," she said as she fanned her face.

"Dear, please be quiet. We can let Mr. Parks explain himself to the authorities," S. Bart said.

"Both of you listen. I've got no idea what's going on here. I don't know what I've stepped in, but you two clearly have some things to work out," I said.

"Noah," Anna Beth said softly to my left.

I kept my eyes on Mrs. Michaels and didn't answer. I loved Anna Beth dearly, but she didn't have the gun.

"Noah. Look."

I kept my gaze on the gun in Mrs. Michaels' hand.

"Mr. Parks, I think your lady friend has something she wants to show you."

"Yes?"

"Look."

I turned to look at Anna Beth who had risen from the couch and was looking at a picture on the mantel just beyond the couch. She was staring at a single small framed photograph among the many on the mantel. From the looks of them there was a pictorial history of the S. Bart clan. I stood and stepped closer.

I looked at Mrs. Michaels and her gun. She smiled and pointed with the gun as if to say, "Go ahead." She had an almost cartoonish look on her face. She gestured with the gun again. My gaze returned to the small framed photo.

I knew that face.

Then it hit me.

SIXTY-EIGHT

The black and white photo was of a man kneeling beside a girl of perhaps five or six who was seated on a bicycle. The two were at the base of a palmetto tree and there appeared to be a party going on in the background. In the distance a lone bridge stood, the Grace Memorial Bridge. That put the photo pre-1966.

I didn't recognize the little girl, but the man was Roger Warden. It was a near perfect match to the mug shot we'd been looking at just a short time earlier.

But why was there a picture of Roger Warden on the mantel in S. Bart's home?

This didn't make any sense.

"S. Bart. Why is there a photo of Roger Warden on your mantel?

"Who?" S. Bart said.

"Here, this old photo, that's Roger Warden." I reached out and picked it up from its place on the mantel.

S. Bart stepped to the fireplace. Gabriel stood.

Mrs. Michaels took a step closer and nudged her husband with the pistol.

"You boys behave," Tamara Michaels said.

"Who," he said as he grabbed the photo from my hand.

"Bart, you be careful with that."

He looked to his wife, dismissed her with a glance and then returned his gaze to the photograph, studying it for a moment.

"What do you mean? That's my Tamara and, that's, I don't know who that man is. And who is this Warden you keep talking about."

I pointed at the man in the photo. That's Roger Warden. You and Nance arrested him. He broke into a liquor store."

"Who?" S. Bart said.

I started to speak but Mrs. Michaels stepped slightly to her left and when she did, I did a double take. I looked back at the photograph, then back to her. It was the eyes; the eyes were the same.

"I'll be damn," I said. "It is you. You knew Roger Warden? How? Who was he?"

"You really didn't know? Are you really just figuring it out?" Mrs. Michaels said. "Surprising."

"What's surprising?" S. Bart said.

"Apparently, Mr. Parks isn't quite the detective he thought he was. He's good, but he missed the most important part. He actually thought you did it. He really thought you killed Andrew."

"He's telling the truth? He didn't kill Andrew?" I said pointing at S. Bart.

"Him? No, he didn't do a thing." Mrs. Michaels said. "Neither of you did, but of course you knew the part about you already."

"For Christ's sake, Tamara, what the hell is going on? What are you talking about? Of course he killed Andrew."

"Oh Bart, the man in the photo. Dear."

"What about him? Who is he?"

"That much Mr. Parks got right. It's Roger Warden."

"Who the fuck is Roger Warden?" S. Bart said.

"Bart, you're a miserable bastard. All the time we've been married. All the times you've looked at that photo. The first time you ask who that is, the first time you want to know who is in the picture with me and it's when I'm pointing a gun at you. You're pathetic. You could've asked, but you never ask me anything," she said as she looked to us and made a waving motion with the gun. "He really doesn't. He just tells everyone what to do. And Bart, of course he didn't kill anyone."

"He didn't? Wait, why do you have a picture, a picture with this Roger Warden?"

"Oh, Bart, he was my father."

"Your father," S. Bart and I said in unison.

S. Bart stood in silence. His wife took the photo from his hand and placed it on a coffee table beside the couch letting her finger linger a moment on the frame. S. Bart collapsed back onto the couch. He was starting to look a bit pale, a bit too pale. I hoped he wasn't about to have a heart attack. I moved to check on him just as Gabriel did the same, but Mrs. Michaels leveled the gun at us.

"Not so fast, let her help him."

We stopped and Anna Beth slid in beside him and helped him loosen his collar.

"I'm fine, I'm fine. I just don't have the slightest idea what's going on."

"That makes two of us," I said. "Mrs. Michaels, perhaps you could enlighten us."

"Certainly. It's simple. There is about to be a suicide and a triple murder at my house."

SIXTY-NINE

This was definitely not going as I had planned. I was also pretty sure that she hadn't called the police.

"Dear, we've been married close to thirty years and you've never wondered a single time about that photograph. You've never wondered about my family. Did you realize that? Never asked about them. Not once."

"I thought you --"

"You thought what? You didn't think a thing except what people could give you. My family had nothing, so they were of no use to you. You've never done a thing on your own. Nothing. Ever. You're the most selfish, the most self-centered person I've ever met. If your family didn't have it to give, you weren't ever going to have it. You even had the election given to you."

I had absolutely no idea what she was talking about. And from the look on S. Bart' face neither did he.

"Roger Warden was my family, my only living relative. For God's sake Bart, you arrested him and you never realized it, he ended your career and brought us together. You don't even remember him. Do you know how insulting that is?"

"Tamara, you need to, whatever are you talking about. Why don't you sit down and, well, just sit down. I'm sure you father helped you quite a bit. I'm sure he was a great man."

"Bart, even now you don't understand. Daddy was a moron. He was a small-time crook and not a very good one at that. He broke into a liquor store. Threw a hammer through the window. Poor fool didn't even think about fingerprints. You arrested him, put handcuffs on him yourself and for all of our marriage you never even recognized his picture on your own mantel. Never even asked who it was in the photo with me."

"I --"

"Just shut up. Do you realize why your police career ended? Of course not. That bastard Jack Nance took the hammer Daddy used to break the liquor store window and put it in your car. He 'miraculously' found it there and took it to your father. Suddenly you're on the way to law school. Everything hush-hush. That never seemed odd to you?"

"Jack did what? Why would he do that?"

"Because he was greedy. You never knew about the money your father gave him, did you? You just went on up to law school like your daddy wanted, like a good little boy."

"But Jack, he liked me."

"Nance loathed you dear. You waltzed into the detective squad with your Daddy holding the door and Nance hated you for it. He saw you as his meal ticket. Why do you think he took you under his wing? When it looked like you screwed up Daddy's case, your father paid off Nance and got him a promotion. You're off the force, Nance's got a nice payoff and Daddy got out of jail."

Anna Beth and I stared at Mrs. Michaels as she spoke. She spoke with a polished and refined Charleston accent with the pleasant drawl that was such the mark of our fair city, that is until she said the word, 'daddy.' It came out as, 'deddy' dripping with the most country of country accents.

"And how was this man your father? He doesn't even have the same name."

"Oh, you poor fool, Roger Warden? Tammy Ward? I dropped the last two letters and "Tamara' just sounds better than 'Tammy.' Do you remember the first time we met dear?"

"Of course. It was the last time I saw Nance."

"Wrong. It was the day after you arrested Daddy, I tried to talk to you to get you to help but you wouldn't have a thing to do with me. You didn't even look me in the eye. Nance though, that was a different story," she said as she switched the gun from one hand to the other. "He was a problem solver. He'd been looking to cash in off you and, well, it worked for him. He stopped me on the way out of the station that day. You know, he always called me his bonus. After he came to me, of course I was happy to have Daddy out of jail. It cost me though."

"How do you know all of this? Wait? What? Did you pay Nance off?"

"Every Thursday afternoon for more than three years."

"You, you slept with him?"

A smile crept across her face.

"That's one way to look at it."

"You, you, whore."

"I'm not sure? Can you be a whore if you enjoy it? Actually, sometimes I'd go over on the weekends too. It kept him happy and kept him from asking for more."

"How could you?"

"Bart dear, I was young and I couldn't let my Daddy go to jail."

"So, you're saying S. Bart didn't kill Andrew?" I said.

"Oh, of course not. Poor Andrew, he just did too well in the election. It really was an accident. But Bart kill him? Really now, that would take initiative. During the election, I got a call from Jack Nance. I'd had to pay up from time to time through the years to keep him quiet. Sometimes he even asked for money. He didn't come that often but before the election he turned greedy and threatened to, well, he did go to Andrew Stephens but that boy scout didn't care when he heard about Bart's past. When I found out Nance had told Andrew, I had to do damage control. I couldn't have Bart's past out there. If Bart had just won, Andrew would have left things alone, I'm sure about it, but with it so close... With a chance, Andrew could win. Well he couldn't win and then be able to go after Bart. So other measures had to be taken. I couldn't have people knowing our little secret."

"You killed Andrew?" I said.

"Of course not, you did. Everyone already thinks that and after tonight, there'll be no doubt."

"Then if not you, then who?" Anna Beth said.

She walked over to where I was standing and ran the back of her hand along the side of my face then to the back of my neck. She pushed the gun into my stomach just hard enough to make it uncomfortable. She looked at Anna Beth.

"I can certainly see why you like him. He's a self-starter, a real go-getter. I get so turned on by a man with initiative. His coming over here tonight to confront that," she pointed to S. Bart then looked to Anna Beth. "God that turns me on. Does it you?"

She pulled my lips to hers and kissed me. I immediately pulled back and yelped. She'd bitten my lip.

"That's easy to do when your pointing a gun at someone, isn't it," Anna Beth said.

"Little lady, mind your business you might..."

Out of the corner of my eye I saw a movement. Tamara Michaels turned her head towards it. I saw a blur pass inches from my face and heard a slap.

"I'll say it again, you're a miserable whore," S. Bart said.

He'd jumped from the couch, quite deftly moved across the room and slapped his wife. He did it again. Hard. The gun flew from her hand and slid across the floor stopping near the door to the hallway. Gabriel quickly crossed the room and retrieved it. He opened the cylinder, emptied the bullets and bounced them in his hand.

"Parks, you do keep it interesting "

"Detective, if you would be so kind as to place the gun on the table to your right. You can put the bullets down as well. Then join your friends across the room," a new but familiar voice said.

A large revolver appeared from the hallway and came to rest at the base of Gabriel's neck. Gabriel put the gun and bullets on the table and walked across the room. A hand appeared, and then an arm with the rest of the body attached to it.

Unfortunately, the face was one I knew all too well.

SEVENTY

"Brady? What the hell are you doing here?" S. Bart said.

"Move away from Tamara please," Brady said. "Tamara, are you okay, my dear?"

Brady moved to where Tamara Michaels was kneeling on the floor.

"Not a move from anyone," he said moving the gun back and forth to each of us.

He kept an eye on us, but lifted Mrs. Michaels' head. There was a red welt swelling on the side of her face from where S. Bart had slapped her, a trickle of blood ran from her lip. Brady dropped his head for a moment then stood, the gun dropping to his side. He smoothed his suit with one hand, then moved to us. He stopped and looked S. Bart in the eye. Then he backhanded him across the face with the barrel of the revolver. S. Bart crumbled to the floor where he lay motionless.

"Seriously, where did you come from?" I said.

He turned his eyes to me.

"Tamara called me a short time ago. Fortunately, I was at my office and was able to get here rather quickly."

"Fuck, of course," I said. The white Volvo outside, that isn't S. Bart's car, it's your car isn't it."

"That's right," Mrs. Michaels said. "It's mine. Warren picked it out for me."

"It was you I saw at Sullivan's yesterday."

"You're right again. Tamara was on her way over to see me. I had the house to myself for the evening. Smart girl, she didn't drive up. That would have been awkward to say the least," Brady said.

"And last week, we saw you near the connector. And I thought you had followed me to Myrtle Beach."

"I have the house to myself at least a day or two each week. Tamara has plenty of free time to come by. And Noah, you shouldn't be traveling so much, but then again you are on the run."

Tamara stood and giggled.

"Now what are we going to do with the three of you? Oh yes. We have a murder/suicide about to occur. What a shame. Crazed murderer barges in on the solicitor. Your dear friend the police detective and your devoted girlfriend fail in a valiant effort to stop you. Of course, from your recent meetings with me, I should have known, I simply should have seen it."

"You'll forgive me, but how in the hell did you end up in all of this?" Anna Beth said.

Tamara moved over to Brady and put her arms around his neck.

"My Daddy may have been a man without anything, but he taught me well. That," she said as she pointed towards S. Bart on the floor. "That wasn't going anywhere. Do you realize he hadn't touched me in years? Then all I heard was 'Solicitor this and Solicitor that.' You would have thought he was going to be president. He should've known being solicitor meant nothing for me. He couldn't even win without my helping. But Warren, oh my: ambition, power, and so much more," she looked at Anna Beth. "I told you I liked a man with initiative."

She was literally draped around him now, almost gyrating on him.

"Isn't she just a delight. I do have to admit, this will make it incredibly easy for me to move things along. My insane client kills my friend and colleague, as well as his girlfriend, and a decorated police officer. I'll step in and sweep the next special election, and the governor's office is but a step away. It would be fulfilling S. Bart's legacy. I think people will understand it when the grieving widow and I happen to hit it off. It'll be almost like honoring her murdered husband's memory."

"You really meant it when you said I was innocent. I just realized that, when we first met, you didn't say not guilty, you said innocent. No defense attorney would've ever said that. You even said it again just the other day."

"Of course they wouldn't, but you wanted to hear it. I needed you to get proactive on your end. I needed you to screw your case up. It didn't take you long to start acting exactly like I wanted you too. Your coming by my house though, that was unexpected. But then I knew I had you, all it took was a little push and look where we are. Things are coming together so nicely. You did everything I needed you to do and now, well now, it's almost over."

I'd been played. He had owned me completely. At every turn, he dangled just enough in front of me to get me to dig the hole even deeper: Rebecca, the notes, even coming to S. Bart's home.

"I'm curious, how did you end up with S. Bart in the first place, Tammy? You don't mind if I call you Tammy, do you," Anna Beth said. "You're not smart enough to have had this planned for thirty years."

"Careful there Ms. Cross. No need to be disrespectful," Brady said.

Mrs. Michaels glared at Anna Beth.

"She does have a mouth on her doesn't she. No wonder he likes her," Mrs. Michaels said.

She was hanging on Brady as she spoke, one hand clinging to his shoulder, the other rubbing his chest, one leg raised up against his as if she were climbing him. She continued.

"Bart started out as my knight in shining armor. He didn't know it at the time, but he was the reason I was able to stop seeing Nance every week. Bart came by Nance's one day after he graduated from law school. Well, Jack and I could get loud and from the outside it probably sounded like an old cop beating on a sexy young girl. Maybe that's what it was? I don't know, I didn't mind it, but Bart just didn't like it. He went off on Jack and told him if he ever saw him hitting a woman again, he'd kill him. Oh, how that turned me on. He didn't even know me and was defending me. I was a little hurt he didn't remember me from when he arrested Daddy, but he was a lawyer. I started seeing him and we got married about a year later, but Bart's only ever cared about Bart. Turns out I was just a check in the wife box. One day I realized I just hated him. Warren though, he loves me and wants to take care of me."

Brady chuckled.

"When you retained me after you'd been arrested, it was like Christmas had come early. We already had you set up for the murder, but with you as a client, you did all the heavy lifting. Once you called, it just took a little planning, a few suggestions and, what can I say, I've always had a head for strategy. But Noah, you did make it easy to pull all of this together. So eager to get to the bottom of things," he said as he looked to Mrs. Michaels. "My dear, I think this about does it. You should head out to the Gailliard. That is unless you want to watch. He'll be here in a short while."

Who was coming over? I decided not to ask.

Brady glanced at us, then turned his head and kissed her. As he did I glanced at Gabriel then reached over and grabbed the picture of Tamara and her father from the mantel.

"Where do you think you're going?" Brady said.

"Nowhere. I just have a question about this."

I picked up the picture and moved back to lean against the fireplace leaving Anna Beth and Gabriel standing a few feet away.

"What? Buying time won't help."

"I'm just curious how the two of you ended up together. Though as I think about it, I guess I can see it. You're both crazy as hell."

"What did you say?" Mrs. Michaels said.

"You're both bat shit crazy. You're like two lovestruck stupid teenagers. Who murders a candidate for solicitor?"

Mrs. Michaels stopped gyrating on Brady.

"That's the second time in the last five minutes I've been called stupid. Do you know how mad that makes me?"

"Don't know, don't care, you stupid bitch," I said. "Here, look at this."

As I spoke, I tossed the photo in a soft arc just out of her reach.

Just as I thought, that photo was important to Tamara Michaels. She pushed off of Brady and tripped as she lunged for the photo, also getting tangled in his outstretched arm holding the gun. I heard a metallic snap, saw another blur then heard the sickening snap of bone breaking followed by a piercing scream. I couldn't tell which one it came from, but they were both on the floor. Brady's revolver fell and Gabriel pounced on it. I took a step to the couch and picked up Gabriel's Glock just as I heard the crunching sound of more bone breaking. I turned to see the solicitor follow through with a well-placed kick to Brady's rib cage. Brady, who was now on the floor cradling his arm and likely beginning to feel the pain of several broken ribs.

Our eyes met and we held each other's gaze.

There was silence.

"Could I interest you in a drink? I think we could both use one," the solicitor said.

Turns out Gabriel had his Asp, his collapsible baton with him. When I tossed the photo, it distracted Brady and Mrs. Michaels just long enough for him to grab it from his belt. He pulled it out, extended it with a snap of his wrist and brought it down hard on Brady's arm. When he hit him, his aim was spot-on. Turns out when police are trained on the Asp one of the things they learn about is the median nerve located in the arm. If you hit this nerve at the correct place, the person automatically drops whatever they may be holding, in this case a gun. Turns out Gabriel had really great aim. He hit the nerve and Brady dropped his gun, though given the blow also shattered Brady's arm, the aim for the nerve may not have been all that critical.

Anna Beth had wasted no time in calling 911.

It doesn't take long for the police to arrive, en masse, when a call comes in from a home invasion, assault, and kidnapping at the solicitor's house. Soon near a dozen police cars rolled up followed by the SWAT team close on their heels.

The first thing everyone did when they saw me was pull their weapons and level them in my general direction. They quickly raised them when S. Bart and Gabriel stepped in front of me, arms waving.

#

Gabriel had Anna Beth and me wait in the solicitor's kitchen while even more police, crime scene technicians, EMS, and all kinds of other folks arrived and started pouring into the house.

There was even a fire truck.

"You certainly know how to show a girl an exciting time," Anna Beth said. "Two times in just over a year we've had guns pointed at us. And how did you pick that attorney?"

"He was the only one I even considered, but I made it easy for him. I wasn't looking for it at all and he's right. All I needed was a little encouragement and he steered me just as he wanted."

Gabriel walked into the room.

"That played out a little differently than I'd imagined. Brady apparently doesn't like the idea of going to jail. He started singing as soon as he saw cuffs. Not that anything he said will help."

"What did he say?"

"Seems he and Tamara Michaels, Ward, Warden, whatever you want to call her, had been having an affair for several years, both planning on leaving their significant others. I'm no shrink, but from the sound of it Tamara's a bit off her rocker and I guess Brady likes crazy because he bought it hook, line, and sinker. When Nance showed up after S. Bart announced his candidacy and tried to shake down Tamara again, I'm guessing he would've been fine with a roll in the hay, but Tamara ran him off. Thing was, Nance told Mrs. Michaels he went to Andrew. She went to Andrew the night of the election and offered to pay him off to drop out of the election. He refused."

"She killed Andrew?" Anna Beth said.

"Well, those two in there are going to get charged for it, but looks like the actual killer was Norton Gaines."

"Gaines? From the solicitor's office?"

"That's the one. He's Mrs. Michaels' cousin. He's worked for S. Bart for years and told Mrs. Michaels everything that went on. S. Bart never knew his wife had a spy in his office. She wasn't kidding when she said Michaels' never asked about her family, he apparently had no idea. On election night Gaines was even at Andrew's party. I'd say he was good for drugging Anna Beth's wine. After the party, Mrs. Michaels and Gaines went to see Andrew to offer him the payoff. Andrew was a little drunk and apparently got a little vocal with Mrs. Michaels, that, and he mentioned a computer file. Gaines stepped in, they struggled, and Gaines hit him with a wine bottle. Then staged a suicide."

"You're kidding?" Anna Beth said.

"Nope. And with Andrew dead, they had to find the file he was talking about."

"They went to Rebecca," Anna Beth said.

"That's why Gaines told Rebecca not to talk to you just in case you didn't know about it. Didn't want you two figuring anything out. Not sure what was on it, but looks like Rebecca knew enough to get you in the right direction. Looks like Gaines was the one who broke into your house looking for your computers. I'm glad you guys didn't run into Gaines. He's got three bodies on him."

"And Nance and Melvin?"

"Pretty sure. I'm guessing he followed you to Melvin's and wanted to know what Melvin told you. Safe bet he poisoned Austin too. He was on his way over here tonight to do the actual trigger pulling."

"Damn. It makes you wonder where the gene pool in that family got so polluted. Where is he? Gaines. Did you get him?"

"No. I'm guessing he will be in the wind once he sees what's over here, but we'll be out looking for him."

We stood in silence for a long moment.

"Do you need anything else? I think we might head back to Mount Pleasant and then head back home tomorrow."

"No, take my car. I'll get a ride home and we can catch up tomorrow. One more thing," he looked back at the mass of officers in the front of the house. "I made one of these for you while everyone was running around in here. If it's what I think it is, you'll probably find it interesting."

He handed me a flash drive.

"I'm pretty sure this is the journal you've been looking for. It was on Tamara Michaels' laptop."

I didn't say a word, but took the drive and put it in my pocket.

Anna Beth gave him a big hug. I didn't think they were going to ever let go. Then Gabriel turned and gave me a hug, too. First time ever. Kinda made me smile.

"I think we'll sneak out the back."

"Good idea."

We turned to go when I heard my name.

"Mr. Parks. I mean Noah. A moment if I may."

I turned to see the solicitor walking down the hall. He stopped in front of me and looked to his feet for a moment. He was sporting a bandage on his temple from Brady's gun barrel. After a moment, he took a step forward and looked me in the eye.

"I'm sorry. It seems there was a lot going on in front of me I didn't know about and it all landed on your doorstep. I want you to know I realize I was quick to rush to judgment and listened to the counsel of some who had other motives."

This was unexpected.

"Thank you," was all I could say.

"Seems Andrew Stephens made a wise choice when he asked you to be his deputy. Had things worked out differently, I would have been fortunate to have had you in my office," he said as he extended his hand to me. I stared at it a moment then shook it.

"Thank you, Mr. Solicitor."

"Thank you, and call me Bart. Oh, and watch the local news in the morning. Ms. Cross, good night. And I want a rain check on that drink."

He stood for a moment and then turned to walk from the kitchen.

Anna Beth and I drove back to Andrew's house and were greeted by two very excited dogs. We turned on all the lights in the house and then we took them for a walk through the neighborhood. Then we ordered pizza.

EPILOGUE

S. Bart held a press conference the next morning and explained everything that had   happened. He announced Dave Litman no longer worked in his office and that he, along with his father, Billy Litman, were to be charged with providing false information as part of the investigation into Andrew's murder. He informed the viewers that his wife along with an investigator from his office, were to be charged for Andrew's murder; both of them having conspired to kill him. He also read off a list of charges that would be filed against Warren Brady. He talked about his past as a police officer and how his career ended. He formally dropped all of the charges against me and gave a heartfelt apology for his rush to judgment in my case.

He ended by announcing his intent to resign from office. Though immediately afterwards it seemed the whole of Charleston County was burning up the phone lines calling for him to remain in office saying the way he handled taking responsibility for the entire situation was an excellent show of character. Who knows? Maybe he does have a future in politics.

#

More interesting was what was on the flash drive.

After the press conference, I took the Mac to the bench by the water at Andrew's as the dogs played in the yard. They played, I read. There was a rambling letter written in cop speak from Nance to Andrew. It was an outline to a conviction against Tamara Michaels for a variety of crimes. It set out, in sometimes lurid and graphic detail, their past. The relationship started as mutual blackmail. He blackmailing her about her father's charges, and her blackmailing him not to tell S. Bart about their decades-long relationship. I'm not sure it was blackmail, rather just two maladjusted people having sex and trying to justify it. But along with that, it seemed like Mrs. Michaels had quite the history of drug use, even after she and S. Bart were married. She also took to providing information about Michaels' clients so Nance could extort them; sometimes Mrs. Michaels did it herself. She also had a habit of befriending her husband's drug dealing clients and becoming their customers. It was clear S. Bart knew nothing about his wife's involvement with Nance. Turns out S. Bart never even knew why he left the police force. His father said it was time and he obeyed.

The more I read, the more I realized Andrew would have walked into office if he'd released or even leaked the information I was reading, but that wasn't Andrew. He never wanted something the easy way, he wanted to work for it and this just showed he was even more of a man and a friend than I realized. I wasn't the least bit self-conscious about the tear I felt roll down my cheek.

I was surprised to see a copy of Andrew's will on the flash drive. He left everything he had to me. That was unexpected.

Seems Tamara Michaels had found that too and was waiting to leak it to help tie things up with my case.

My inheriting everything Andrew had would have been quite the motive for murder.

Andrew's journal was also on the disk. I went to the first date in the journal and read forward. A lot of it was just a note or two on what he did that day, but on virtually every day one thing stood out. He had been in a relationship. A serious one. Each day there was a note about something they had done, something that stood out, something memorable to him, something he had told her.

Rebecca clearly was much more than an employee, much more.

But the most surprising thing on the drive was a note, short, but to the point. It was written by Rebecca in an email to Andrew. Reading it I understood the real reason she didn't want to be involved.

Calling it a note probably took away from it, it was more of an announcement. The email was dated the evening of the election, the day Andrew died. I'll never know if Andrew saw it, but I'm going to believe he did. I'm also going to believe once he saw it he would have changed his will. Since he couldn't change it, I'd have to take care of making sure things ended up how he would have wanted. After all, I'm sure Andrew would have wanted his and Rebecca's child to start life with a good future in place.

There was one thing Andrew left me I decided to keep. Attached to Andrew's will he had left a note for me. It directed me to his closet where there was a small box. Inside I found a beautiful engagement ring. It had belonged to his mother and he wanted me to have it. Or should I say he wanted Anna Beth to have it.

#

Anna Beth had come out and was playing with the dogs by the harbor's edge.

My phone rang.

Gabriel.

"How are you today?"

"Doing well. Just wanted to call and let you know you were the talk of the PD today, that, and wanted to see how you guys were doing."

"We're doing good and thanks for asking. And thanks for helping me out yet again."

"You know I'm here for you, my friend."

"Good to hear. That makes me think, I do have a favor of sorts to ask you."

I could hear Gabriel chuckle.

"What's that?" he said.

"Interested in being my best man?"

THE END

CPSIA information can be obtained
at www.ICGtesting.com
Printed in the USA
FFOW03n2016190817
38886FF